only for my daughter

emma robinson

bookouture

Published by Bookouture in 2022

An imprint of Storyfire Ltd.
Carmelite House
50 Victoria Embankment
London EC4Y 0DZ

www.bookouture.com

ISBN: 978-1-80314-196-1
eBook ISBN: 978-1-80314-197-8

For my Ali

Who has always believed in me

PROLOGUE

Please, baby, where are you?

I've searched every inch of this terrible place and I have no idea where else you could be. What kind of mother doesn't know where her daughter would go when she's in pain? If I could just *think* where you might be, I'd come and find you. I'd keep you safe.

Where *are* you?

Last time I lost you, you were only six years old. At a petting zoo, I watched you and Keira wander into a barn to find the rabbits. It wasn't until Samantha and I picked up your discarded coats and followed you in that we saw both the hutches and the barn were empty – and so was a second doorway at the back. I ran through it as fast as the blood pumping in my veins, yelling your name at the top of my voice. People were staring at me, but I didn't care; icy fear made them surreal and distant. After what seemed like forever, a man waved at me. *I think they're over here.* You were on the swings in a small playground. I grabbed you and squeezed you tight, determined to never let you out of my sight again.

At fifteen, though, I can't follow your every move any

longer. Or know where you are each minute of the day. Even double-checking that you are taking a coat on a cold day makes you roll your eyes at me. I have to trust that you will do the right thing, be sensible, keep yourself safe.

But what if you don't *want* to keep yourself safe? What if your biggest danger *is* yourself? How can I keep you safe then?

Oh, Grace, my precious, precious girl. Where *are* you?

ONE

JULIA

Good friends understand that life can be hectic. Which was why Julia was grateful for Nina, who hadn't whispered a complaint about the fact that she could only meet for a strictly thirty-five-minute coffee. Or that it had to be at Bentleigh Garden Centre in the middle of a Saturday afternoon. Or that they had to spend fifteen of those available minutes trawling the shelves for the soft, double pink flowers of Rosa Bonica.

While Julia peered at the shelves, Nina picked up a small terracotta pot. 'I might get this for my kitchen window. I'm going to grow some herbs.'

That made Julia smile. 'And by grow, I'm assuming you mean plant and then watch slowly die?'

Nina laughed as she put the pot back on the shelf. 'That's fair. Maybe I'll stick to the dried parsley in jars. Anyway, my point is that you have to come out on Friday night. I'm not taking no for an answer.' Since Nina's youngest had started university, she had stepped up her campaign to get Julia out of the house more often.

Nina might not want to take no for an answer, but she was

unfortunately going to have to. 'I can't. Grace isn't great at the moment.'

Nina tilted her head to one side, a sure sign that she was about to give a lecture. 'I'm sorry that Grace isn't happy again, but you can't turn into a hermit, Jules. You're working every hour God sends, too. I have to meet you here for a coffee rather than at an actual café, like normal people or, heaven forbid, we actually get to go to a bar in the evening. You need to get out more. Meet up with people.'

Even the thought of getting dressed up to go to a busy bar made Julia weary. 'Yes. Because I'm terribly good at that, as we both know. Complete social butterfly, me. Anyway, it's not just Grace. Money's a bit tight at the moment. I've had a lot to pay out for with her starting at St Anne's. Their uniform costs a fortune. And you have to buy all this sports kit, which she is probably never going to wear.'

Though St Anne's was a state school, the calibre of student from its very small, very wealthy, catchment area gave it delusions of grandeur. Looking at the uniform list she'd been sent at the beginning of the summer had made her feel sick. Hockey kit and leotards and blazers that cost more than she'd spent on her wedding dress. John had contributed towards the school uniform at least, but it had stretched her budget to the absolute limit.

Nina nodded agreement. 'Yeah, kids are expensive. Try having two at university. Sometimes I think I might as well get our wages paid directly into their account. Then Rob and I could live on Pot Noodles instead.'

Julia didn't even want to think about Grace going to university or anywhere else that wasn't their flat on Westley Road. And not only because Grace was so vulnerable right now. Whether it was healthy or not, Grace was her whole world. When she left, she would take half of Julia with her.

It was different for Nina, though. 'Are you and Rob enjoying the time to yourselves?'

Nina wrinkled her nose. 'Actually, we are. I mean, I do miss them both, but it's nice only having ourselves to please. When they're away, I don't have to worry about what time they are getting home or what they are up to. It's weird, but I don't.'

Was it possible that Julia would ever get to the point where she didn't worry about Grace? 'That's great.'

'It would be even better if I could persuade my friend to come out with me.' Nina took some of the plants Julia was balancing. 'Don't get me wrong, if I have to visit a garden centre, there's no one else I'd rather be with, but I'd much prefer somewhere that sold grapes *after* they'd been harvested and decanted into bottles. Anyway, you don't normally come here for plants, do you? I thought you had some sort of wholesale supplier.'

She was right. The plants there were much more expensive than Julia would normally pay. But she needed to get something specific. 'I have to put together some pots and displays for Samantha. That's who these pink roses are for. She's got something going on with the mums from school next month, and she wants her garden to look good.'

Nina rolled her eyes. 'Something you're not invited to, obviously?'

Nina didn't have much time for Samantha. They'd only met a couple of times and Nina couldn't understand why Julia spent any time with her. 'More like something I don't *want* to go to. Honestly, Nina, you should see them all. I think they spend more on eyelashes and nails than I do on shoes.'

Nina leaned her head to look at Julia's grubby boots. 'To be fair, that's not difficult.'

'If I didn't have my hands full of flowers, I'd give you a shove for that. You know what I mean. I don't fit in with that lot. Anyway, if you want a coffee, we need to get these plants to the van first. I've got about twenty minutes before I need to leave for my next job and then after that I need to be at Samantha's by six. As well as arranging this lot into pots, I need to clear all the leaves from the lawn and the borders. It's a couple of hours' work, at least.' She didn't add that she was grateful for the extra two hours' money, in addition to her regular Tuesday appointment at Samantha's. On top of paying for the St Anne's uniform, she was hoping to save up enough to take Grace away for the weekend to cheer her up.

Nina raised an eyebrow. 'Miss Perfect can't wield a leaf blower?'

'Stop it. You know that she pays me to do the garden. It's kind of my job.' She pointed at the embroidered 'Julia's Landscaping and Gardening' logo on her shirt: a Christmas gift from Grace. 'Come on, let's get through the tills and then venture to the cafe. I'll cheer you up with a slice of carrot cake.'

The queue for the cashier was surprisingly long for a late Saturday afternoon in October, although more people seemed to buying early Christmas decorations than plants. That was something else she'd need to think about. Would John want Grace at his for Christmas this year, or would he prefer it to be just him, Angie and the new baby? That would suit Julia; she hated it when Grace wasn't there.

Nina nodded at the display of fairy lights on the counter and sighed. 'That comes around quicker every year, doesn't it? The months are skidding by. Are things really no better for Grace?'

'No. Not really. It's obviously difficult starting a new school, but I'd kind of hoped that having Keira there would help. It doesn't seem to have panned out that way, though.'

Nina frowned. 'Samantha's daughter? I thought they were friends?'

So had Julia. That was one of the reasons she'd chosen St Anne's. 'I don't know what's going on, to be honest. After everything that happened at The Grange, she really seemed quite positive about making a fresh start at St Anne's. But she hasn't mentioned Keira or any new friends, and I can hardly get her to go out of the house in the evenings or at weekends.'

Nina's face was kind and full of sympathy. 'Has she tried any of the clubs at school? She might make some friends if she finds other people who are interested in the same things as her.'

Julia couldn't imagine what those things might be. Dressing in dark, baggy clothes? Reading books? Listening to depressing music? 'I've suggested that. There was a whole extra-curricular booklet in the welcome pack when she started in September. But she doesn't seem to be much of a joiner. Sadly, I think she gets that from me. Maybe I should send her to you for lessons on how to make friends?'

Nina shook her head. 'Nonsense. You are a lovely friend. Why do you think I'm always nagging you to spend more time with me?'

Julia was so grateful for Nina. Her optimism and kind ear had been a life saver this last year. 'I'm really worried about her. I just don't know what I can do to make her life easier. She's the sweetest girl and I just want her to be happy.'

'Oh, honey, she will be. Just give her some time. It's not easy starting a new school at fifteen. She'll find her way.'

Julia wiped at her eyes with the back of her hand. 'I know, you're right. I just can't help feeling that I've let her down. Everything that she was going through at The Grange, and I had no idea.'

'You need to stop that. Blaming yourself isn't going to get you anywhere. I'm sure that my boys were getting up to things that would make my hair curl. It's not like when they were little. We can't know everything. You're such a good mum. You're always there for her.'

Of course, Nina was going to tell her that. She was her friend. Julia knew it wasn't true, though.

They were finally at the front of the queue, so she paid for the plants and the two of them carried them to the car park and loaded them into the back of her van. The transfers on the side, 'Julia's Landscaping and Gardening', were starting to peel away. It was a pretty good analogy for how she felt, right then.

Once she'd slammed the doors shut, Nina reached out and pulled her into a hug. 'Come here, you. Stop worrying about everyone else but yourself. I know that Grace needs you, but you're not going to be any good to her if you work and worry yourself into the ground.' She held her out at arm's length. 'I'll let you off Friday night, but let me know when you're free and I'll chuck Rob out for the evening. You can come to me for a takeaway.'

Julia smiled. 'That would be great.' She looked at her watch. After her next client, she wanted to get to Samantha's with enough time to chat once she finished in the garden, because she was hoping to find out whether Keira had said anything about Grace at school. This time, she wanted to make sure she knew everything before it got out of hand.

TWO

SAMANTHA

Samantha had spent a lot of time and money making her house look good, but it felt like a pale imitation of the show home that was Constance Fielding's beachfront property: heavy, dark furniture that had been handed down from grandparents, with modern art pieces in sharp, effective relief made the place reek with superiority.

Once a month, there were eight of them – all St Anne's mothers – who met up for afternoon tea. Next time it would be her turn to host and she was already worrying about anything being less than perfect. Nick always laughed at her when she said anything like that. 'For goodness' sake, you make it sound like we live in a hovel rather than a five-bedroomed house.'

When the other mums had left for appointments or to get ready for an evening out, she'd stayed behind to help Constance carry the cake plates from the sitting room back to the kitchen. Keira was out with her friends and Nick was away until Sunday, so she was in no rush to go back to an empty home.

The kitchen was vast: acres of granite worktops and dozens of glossy cupboard doors. Samantha wasn't sure what

Constance's husband did for a living, but it was certainly lucrative.

Constance opened the cavernous dishwasher and took the plates from her hands. 'Your gardening lady is working out brilliantly, by the way. Thanks for the recommendation.'

Samantha felt strangely uncomfortable referring to Julia as her 'gardening lady'. 'Oh, that's good. She's coming over to do mine later.'

Constance stacked the plates and dropped the tiny silver forks they'd used into the mesh cutlery tray. 'Pippa mentioned that she'd seen you having coffee with her last week. I hadn't realised that the two of you were *friends*.'

There was an edge to her tone which made Samantha's cheeks warm. 'Well, it's the girls who are friends, really. You know what it's like. It's easier to get to know your daughter's friends' mothers.'

Constance smiled as if she had no clue what it was like. 'How do the girls know each other?'

'They were at the same nursery. The Montessori one on Prince's Street.' She almost winced at how eager she was to impress Constance by name-dropping the private nursery. She could almost hear Nick mocking her.

'Oh, yes. I know the one. I think we looked at that before we decided on the St Anne's nursery. So much easier to have their education continue in one place.'

Even though it was connected to the school, the St Anne's nursery was actually privately owned and had cost twice as much as the one Keira had gone to. They even wore a uniform with little peaked caps. Samantha had tried to persuade Nick that they send Keira there, but he had suggested that she'd need to go back to work to pay for it and that had been the end of that.

'Isn't the daughter at St Anne's now, too?'

'Grace? Yes. She started this term.'

'What's the story behind that, then? Why has she changed schools?'

Samantha was torn between not feeling comfortable gossiping about poor Grace and wanting to keep in with Constance. It had taken a long time for her to be accepted into this group. The first few times they'd met, she'd had to reintroduce herself because Constance hadn't seemed to remember Samantha from the time before. Therefore, the latter won out. 'There were issues with some of the other children at the school. Bullying.'

Constance raised an interested eyebrow. 'Her or them?' She laughed. 'I'm only joking – she looks like a stiff breeze would blow her over. Cleo told me she doesn't say a word at school. Said she's a bit of a loner.'

To be honest, Samantha didn't know many of the details about what had gone on at Grace's previous school. Julia had just said that there was a group of girls making Grace's life a misery and she wanted to start again somewhere new. Grace was a sweet girl, but she *was* quite odd. In many ways, she couldn't blame Keira for keeping a bit of a distance between them, now they were at the same school.

When she got back home, Julia's van was on the driveway so Samantha had to park on the road, which was irritating. Although it was late enough to be dark, lights flooded the back garden and, from the French doors at the back of the kitchen, she could see Julia on her knees in front of the raised beds. She knocked on the window and held up a coffee mug. Julia gave her a thumbs up.

Having a drink together after Julia had done the garden had become a routine. Samantha got the cups ready but didn't make Julia's black coffee yet. She'd known her long enough to know she liked it scalding hot. She still felt a little guilty for denying their friendship to Constance. They really had been friends when the girls were younger and inseparable. But situations changed. They weren't as close as they once had been and that was just the way things were. No one's fault.

The kitchen door opened. Julia slipped her feet out of her gardening shoes and stepped inside. 'It's getting cold out there now.'

Samantha filled the cup from the hot water tap. 'This will warm you up. It's only instant, is that okay?'

Julia grinned. 'As long as it is hot and wet. That's what my dad used to say.'

Samantha was going to suggest that they take their drinks to the sitting room, but Julia's trousers looked particularly grubby, so she placed the mugs on the kitchen island and took a stool. 'Constance Fielding has just been singing your praises. Said you've done a great job on her garden.'

Julia sipped her coffee and pulled a face. 'I'm surprised she knows what I've done. Aside from the initial consultation for the landscaping, she barely spoke to me. I'm not sure what you see in those women. That one PTA meeting I went to, all they did was talk about other parents as if they were something nasty on the bottom of their shoe. They're terrifying.'

Samantha stiffened. 'I don't remember that. They are very nice when you get to know them, and Keira is very close with their daughters.' She wasn't sure how much she believed the first part, but the second was definitely true. The other children had all grown up together, but they had included Keira in the group when she'd started secondary school and that was when one of the mothers had invited Samantha along to their monthly get-together.

Julia raised an eyebrow and sipped at her coffee. 'Where is Keira tonight?'

Samantha felt a twinge of guilt, though it wasn't her fault that their daughters were no longer close. 'She's with the St

Anne's girls. They were going to the Adventure City theme park this afternoon and then back to one of their houses.' She glanced at her watch. 'She should be home soon.'

She'd half expected Keira to be home for dinner, but there'd been a text to say they were going to get pizza. She'd been pushing her boundaries a lot lately. When Nick got back from his trip tomorrow, the two of them were planning on sitting her down and telling her that she needed to focus more on her school work and less on her social life.

Still, she was glad that she *was* so sociable. Sending her to St Anne's had been a good decision. It was a shame that Julia's Grace hadn't settled as well as she'd hoped. 'How's Grace doing now? Is she happier?'

She could tell the answer to that by the look on Julia's face, but Julia just shrugged. 'She's okay. Changing schools is a big deal. She just needs some time.'

What she needed was a bit of backbone, but Samantha wasn't about to say that. Keira had started secondary school knowing no one there and she'd been fine. Now, she was part of the most popular group at school. Had Grace just expected Keira to let her join in? She needed to make her own friends. 'I'm sure she'll get there. Where is she now?'

'At home.' Julia glanced at her watch. 'I should get back soon. I've had so much going on today that I haven't seen her since this morning.'

Samantha couldn't help feeling that this was part of the problem. Julia was so busy that Grace was left to her own devices. Much as Samantha missed working in the city, she'd never regretted giving it up once she'd had the children. Both Adam and Keira were doing so well. 'I've got baking to do tonight. Keira FaceTimed Adam at university yesterday and she was taunting him with a slice of lemon drizzle. I promised I'd put together a little hamper of goodies to send up to Durham for him.'

'Lucky him. Your lemon drizzle is legendary.'

Julia's smile made Samantha soften. 'Well, I could always put another one in the oven for you and–'

She was interrupted by the loud chime of the doorbell. Keira must have forgotten her key again. It didn't matter how many times Samantha reminded her, she had a habit of leaving her belongings everywhere she went, like a Hansel and Gretel trail of crumbs. 'Hang on, I'll be right back.'

But as soon as she entered the hallway, she could see from the dark shapes on the other side of the frosted glass that it wasn't Keira on the front step. When she opened the door, a female officer held out her identification. 'Mrs Fitzgerald? Can we come in?'

THREE

JULIA

The kitchen was at the end of a long hallway, so Julia couldn't see who was at the door, or who followed Samantha into her sitting room at the front of the house, but she could hear snatches of the conversation.

The first voice was deep. 'I'm afraid there's been a... Eight p.m.... We can take you...'

Oh, no. Something must have happened to Nick. He often drove home late at night after a business trip rather than staying another night in a hotel. Samantha was always worried that he was going to fall asleep at the wheel. Or Keira's older brother, Adam? Something could have happened on a university night out. She'd been sitting here worrying about Grace, while poor Samantha's son might be in a hospital 300 miles away.

The conversation in the sitting room stopped and Samantha appeared at the entrance to the kitchen, her face ashen. 'I have to go. Keira is hurt.'

Keira? Julia hadn't even considered it might be her; she was indestructible. Her heart thudded in her chest as she slid down from her stool. What kind of accident? A car? 'Oh, no. What's happened? What can I do?'

Samantha's face was devoid of any expression. Her eyes round as cake plates. 'She's been stabbed.'

Surely, she must have misheard. Stabbed? Keira? There had been a lot of trouble on the seafront these last few weeks, but not with the kind of kids Keira spent time with. St Anne's girls with their designer coats and shoes. Had it been a random attack? This didn't make sense.

Samantha was picking things up and putting them down again. 'I have to go. The police are taking me to the hospital now. Can you...?' She looked left and right, waved a distracted hand.

Julia shook herself into action. 'You just go. I know where the spare keys are, so I can lock up here. Shall I call Nick?'

Samantha looked at her as if she didn't know the name of her own husband. 'No, the police are...'

She was clearly in shock. Julia put an arm around her shoulders and led her gently into the hall where the two officers were waiting. She took a long navy coat from the rack on the wall and helped her friend into it. Beneath the thin fabric, she could feel her tremble. 'If you need anything brought to the hospital, or anything else doing, just text me.'

Samantha nodded and followed the police out to their car.

As soon as the front door was closed, Julia sank down onto the bottom step of the staircase. She needed a minute to take this in. How could Keira have been stabbed?

On the long white console table in the hall, Samantha had arranged framed photographs of all their family and friends. The kind of display you could indulge in when someone else was dusting and cleaning. Julia stood and picked up one of Keira and Grace on the beach in Southwold, surprised that it was still there. Samantha had hired a beach hut – goodness only knows how much it had cost – and had invited Julia and Grace to join them. Julia had tried to give Samantha half the cost, but Samantha, with her usual generosity, had refused. *Let Nick pay.*

He's the one jetting off to New York instead of coming to the beach with us. You can get the ice creams.

How old had the girls been then? They must have been at primary school. Five? Six? In the photo, they both had the soft features of their babyhood, not yet sharpened by age and puberty. From the moment they'd first met, they'd become best buddies; even here, they had an arm around each other. It had been a lovely friendship, more like sisters than friends. Was it their instant bond that had brought her and Samantha closer together?

Grace looked so happy in this photo, her grin wide and toothy. Keira was a fraction taller – over the years they had taken it in turns to have height-bragging rights – but her pigtails made her look so young. Julia stroked her hair in the photograph. 'Oh, Keira, honey. Please be okay.'

She replaced the frame behind a newer picture. Even though it was a school photo, and she was in the purple V-neck they all hated, Keira looked at least three years older than her actual age of fifteen. Salon hair, flawless make-up, possibly even false eyelashes. She couldn't look more different from Grace, who was always in dark jeans and long-sleeved T-shirts with her hair flopping over one eye and her glasses slipping down her nose. A couple of weeks ago, an older gentleman had tried to get past her in the supermarket with an, 'Excuse me, young man.' Not that Grace had cared.

Grace. She needed to get locked up here and get home to see her.

Now her legs had stopped shaking, Julia moved quickly around the kitchen. She checked the bi-fold doors that ran across the back of the sitting room were locked, indulging herself in a glance around the raised beds she'd planted. Lit up in the evening, they looked beautiful in a completely different way than they did in the daytime. The next best thing to having a garden you could work on for yourself was having one you could visit regularly.

It only took a couple of minutes to wash up the coffee cups, collect her tools from the garden and lock up, before throwing her bag in the back of the van. She loved her bright green Citroën Berlingo almost as much as Grace was mortified by it. At least it made her keener to walk than beg for a lift. Although, she couldn't help thinking, if only Keira had called her mum for a lift home, maybe she wouldn't be in the hospital right now.

Julia shuddered and turned the key in the ignition. The engine turned over. She closed her eyes. *Not now. Please start.* She tried a second time and, thankfully, it spluttered into life.

It took no time to drive the couple of miles from Samantha's house to Julia's flat on Westley Road. The two neighbourhoods couldn't be more different, though. After she and John had sold their house, there hadn't been enough in her share to get another one. At least with a ground-floor flat there was a small square of garden she had been able to claim for a few pots and a tall, narrow greenhouse for growing seedlings.

Traffic lined both sides of the one-way street and she had to park so far down the road, she may as well have walked from Samantha's. Before getting out of the van, she checked her mobile and then sent Samantha a message.

Hope she's okay. Please call if you need anything.

There was a cold edge to the evening air so, after grabbing her tools from the back of the van, she picked up her pace. Now that she was nearly home, she was desperate to see Grace and give her a hug. She spent so much time trying to persuade her daughter to leave the house, see Safa and Jasmine (the only two girls she'd even mentioned from St. Anne's) or go the cinema – anything that wasn't sitting in her room with her headphones on – but tonight she was glad that Grace was at home. Safe.

It took her a minute to realise that her keys weren't fitting in the lock because they were actually Samantha's spares. Hers were in her other pocket. She pushed the door open on a darkened hall and reached to snap on the light. 'Hi! Grace! I'm home! Where are you?'

There was no answer. Probably plugged into something loud and unable to hear anything short of a bomb going off. Julia hung up her bag and slipped out of her coat. She frowned at Grace's trainers below the coat rack; they hadn't been there when she'd left. She remembered because she'd picked up her school shoes and slotted them into the small shoe cupboard they'd bought from IKEA when they first moved in. The trainers looked wet and muddy, too. Had Grace been out?

Unlike Samantha's lengthy hallway, Julia could get from the front door to Grace's bedroom in about four steps. She knocked on the door and pushed it open. She wasn't there.

This time, she called a little louder. 'Grace? It's Mum. I'm home. Where are you?'

The bathroom was at the back of the flat. As she got closer, she could hear the shower running. That was strange. Grace had just got out of the shower when Julia had left for work that morning. Why was she in there again?

She knocked gently on the door. 'Grace, honey? Is everything okay?'

'Yes. I'll be out in minute.' Her voice was breathless and higher pitched than usual. Concern prickled in Julia's chest. What was going on? Had she heard about Keira already? She knew how quickly these girls posted online after something happened. Had Keira's friends been with her when...? Julia didn't want to think about that.

Her kitchen was about a quarter of the size of Samantha's, but that bothered her a lot less than the garden. Cooking was not her forte. When Grace was young, she had tried really hard to make sure she ate healthily. Now she was fifteen and it was just the two of them, they had takeaway food a lot more often than they should. Grace had decided to become vegetarian a year before and that had been even more difficult, especially as she wasn't keen on vegetables.

The bathroom door opened and Grace came out swaddled in a towel, her hair wrapped in another. When she was small, she had always wanted Julia to help her to twist her hair up in a towel like that, just the same as Julia would. Back then she wanted to dress the same, too. *Mummy, let's be twins.* Nowadays, she'd rather cut a hand off than look like her mother. Still, when Julia saw her with her hair wrapped up in a towel, she couldn't help but think fondly of those days.

'Hi, love. Everything okay?'

Grace wasn't meeting her eye. 'Yes. I'm fine.'

She knew better than to push and ask why she was taking a shower when she'd been home all day. 'Have you eaten? Do you want me to make you some pasta?'

Grace was already at her bedroom door. 'No, I'm fine.'

Julia needed to talk to her about Keira. But where to start? 'I'm going to make a drink. Do you want one?'

'No, thanks.'

Grace's bedroom door clicked shut. She'd give her a minute or so to get dressed, and then talk to her. It wasn't as if Grace and Keira were as close these days, but it was going to upset her. Without knowing the extent of Keira's injuries, it was hard to work out what to say.

She'd made a tea and was sitting at the round table in the kitchen where they ate most of their meals when Grace's door clicked open. She was back in her uniform of dark jeans and an anime T-shirt, her wet hair in thick strands down her back.

'Grace, can you sit down a minute? I need to talk to you.'

'I'm really tired, Mum. I just want to grab some crisps and chill in my room. Can we talk tomorrow?'

In some ways, that was a good idea – she would know more

tomorrow about the extent of Keira's injuries – but what if one of her friends sent Grace a text tonight? Bad news was better coming from Julia.

'Not really. It's about Keira. She's been hurt.'

Grace didn't turn around; her hand was frozen on the cupboard door. She didn't speak for a few moments, then, when she did, there was a tremor in her voice. 'What do you mean?'

If Julia had been waiting for divine inspiration, it still hadn't arrived. 'I don't know all the details yet. But when I was at Samantha's, the police came. They said that Keira... Well, they said that she'd been... attacked. Actually, they said she'd been stabbed.'

Still Grace didn't turn around. Why hadn't she moved? Was it shock?

'What did the police say? Do they know who did it?'

Julia's heart sank. This would be yet another reason for Grace not to leave the house – the fear of a random attacker on the loose. 'Grace, honey. Sit down here with me for a minute.'

Grace turned and her face was deathly pale. It must be shock, after all. 'What do they know, Mum? The police? What did they say?'

Julia frowned. 'They didn't say anything. They took Samantha to the hospital. I don't know anything else yet. I just thought you should know.'

Grace's face flushed, and her tone was sarcastic. 'Why? Because Keira and I are such great friends?'

Julia stood up and held out her arms. She wanted to pull Grace into a tight embrace. Hold her close. As she reached for her, Grace stepped back and it tore a piece from her heart. 'Love, I know this must be a shock.'

In seconds, Grace had darted away and was back in her bedroom, the door slammed behind her. She should let her alone, give her some time to process what she'd told her. But a closed bedroom door frightened Julia; she couldn't just leave her with something this big.

She knocked gently on the door. 'Grace?' There was no answer. 'Grace, can I come in?' Still no answer. There was nothing else for it. 'Grace, I'm coming in.'

When she pushed open the door, Julia steeled herself to see her daughter doing something awful. Would that feeling ever go away? The fear of her hurting herself again?

But she could never have expected to see what was in front of her.

Grace, sitting on her bed, staring at her school uniform. Which was covered in blood.

FOUR

WHEN THEY WERE FOUR

'Mummy. I hurt my finger.' Four-year-old Grace thrust out a forefinger wrapped in a bright yellow plaster. Her other hand held firmly to the hand of a slightly taller girl with perfectly even blonde pigtails.

'And I have been looking after her.' The girl's voice was breathy but confident. 'I'm Keira. I'm four and a half.'

Grace gazed at the girl with something approaching adoration. 'Keira is my best friend.'

Aside from a young boy with scabs on his knees hunting for his lunch box, they were the last two children at the nursery. Beside them, a tall slim woman with the same colour hair as Keira seemed to be waiting. She was poised, well-dressed and on time: everything that Julia wasn't. 'Hi, I'm Samantha. Keira's mother. She insisted we wait for you to come before she relinquished her patient.'

She smiled, but her large sunglasses made it impossible to see if it was genuine. What was she thinking about Julia's last-minute dash into the building? 'I'm sorry that I'm so late. There was an issue with something at the bank and I had to get it solved before I left.'

Why was she apologising to this woman? It wasn't as if she'd asked her to stay. It irritated John when she did that. *You sound like such a doormat.*

Still, it was nice to see Grace with a friend. The first couple of weeks of nursery had been so difficult. Whoever was on welcoming duty had had to peel Grace from her like a limpet, sobbing as if the world was going to end. Julia would walk the twenty minutes to the train station in pieces and feel wretched for the rest of the day until pick up. She only worked three days a week at the bank now, but she hated it.

Samantha reached for her daughter's hand. 'Let's go, Keira. Grace's mummy is here now, she'll look after her.'

The girls looked at each other as if one of them was about to emigrate. Keira threw her arms around Grace and gave her a big hug. It was very sweet.

'Thank you for helping Grace, Keira.'

'That's okay. I like helping. And Grace is my best friend.'

Oh, how easy it is to make friends when you're four. Since they'd moved to Southcliff, Julia hadn't really got to know many people. Their neighbours were elderly and she wasn't about to grab someone's hand in the supermarket and ask them to be her best friend.

Samantha was clearly keen to get going because she brought out the big guns. 'If we hurry up, Keira, we can get an ice cream from the cafe on the corner before we go home.'

Keira's face lit up. 'Can Grace come for an ice cream, too?'

That was awkward. Julia tried to form a sentence which got Samantha off the hook by saying they had to get home or that it was too close to dinner, but then Samantha surprised her by shrugging. 'If that's okay with her mummy, she can.'

How could she say no to Grace's desperately eager face? John wouldn't be home for an hour yet, anyway. 'I have heard that ice cream is the best medicine for a poorly finger. Would you like that, Grace?'

She didn't need an answer; the girls were jumping around as if it was Christmas.

The cafe in question turned out to be very near to Samantha's home so, when they got there just as it was closing, Samantha staved off the girls' disappointment by inviting Julia and Grace to have ice cream at their house. Julia tried not to gawp at the size of the houses they passed, but as Samantha let them in their double front door into a wide, tiled hallway, it was impossible not to comment. 'You have a beautiful home.'

'Thank you.' Samantha took off her sunglasses and dropped them with her keys into a bowl on a console table. She clearly wasn't the kind of woman who would be dashing around in the morning, lifting piles of paper trying to locate her purse. 'Come through to the kitchen and I'll find that ice cream.'

By now, the girls had kicked off their shoes and were halfway up the stairs. 'I'm just showing Grace my new bedroom. We'll be back in a mimmit.'

The two women smiled at one another. At four, most of Grace's baby language had disappeared, so any last remnants of misspoken words were like precious artefacts. Samantha obviously felt the same.

Samantha's kitchen opened out at the end of the hall. It was a large airy space; beyond the kitchen was a conservatory and – beyond that – a huge garden. Julia was drawn to it. 'Your garden is amazing.'

Samantha was filling the kettle and she looked over her shoulder. 'It would be if my son didn't use it as a football pitch. At some point I'd like to get it landscaped, but there doesn't seem much point while the children are little.'

Whoever got that job would be a lucky person. 'That's my dream job. Garden design.'

'Really? Why don't you do it?'

If only it were that easy. She watched every garden show on TV and was proud of how beautiful she'd made their own small back garden, but there was no way she could afford to leave the bank. John was working his way up the police force, but his pay level wasn't enough to support all three of them. 'Maybe one day.'

'You should do a course. There's an adult education college near to the hospital, I'm sure they do courses like that in the evenings.'

She'd thought about doing a night class, but John's hours were so erratic. 'My husband is in the police. He can't always guarantee what time he'll be home.'

'Well, you are welcome to practise on mine any time you like. And it's probably worth contacting the college. Who knows, they might have a course at a time you can make.'

Just the thought of studying landscaping – and getting her hands on the garden beyond those windows – made Julia's stomach fizz a little. 'You're really kind. Thank you.'

The kettle clicked off and Samantha held out a mug. 'Tea or coffee?'

'Coffee, please. Black, no sugar. Where's your son now?'

'My husband has taken him to football practice. He's mad about it. Nick works away a lot, so when he's home, he likes to do as much with the kids as he can.'

Julia tried not to be jealous. John was at work so much that she was the one who did everything for, and with, Grace. Would it have been different if Grace had been a boy and interested in going to rugby matches or fishing with him? 'What does your husband do?'

'He's in telecommunications. A different world to me – I used to work in fashion in London.'

Julia blushed. She hadn't even thought to ask her what she did. It explained why she was so glamorous, though. 'That sounds like an exciting job.'

'Sometimes. Although, to be honest, I mainly did a lot of admin. Got to go to some fun parties, though, and wear some great dresses. And it looks as if I'm not the only one.'

As she was speaking, the door had opened to reveal the two girls dressed in Disney costumes with enough plastic jewellery around their necks to sink a small boat. Keira held her hands aloft. 'Ta dah! Are we beautiful?'

Grace stood a little way behind her new best friend, her face pink with a mixture of pleasure and embarrassment. Julia reached into the bag she'd hooked onto the kitchen stool for her mobile. 'You look amazing! Can I take your picture to send to Daddy, Grace?'

The two girls posed with their glittery arms wrapped around one another. As soon as she tried to take the picture, though, Julia's phone died. 'Dammit. I'm not sure if it took the picture or not.'

Samantha had taken one, too. 'Give me your number and I'll send you this one. And then' – she was talking to Keira now – 'you'd better have that ice cream before Grace has to go home. Daddy and Adam will be back soon.'

The girls ran back out of the room, holding hands. Julia dictated her number to Samantha for the picture. After she'd sent it, she held up the picture for Julia and the look of joy on their daughters' faces made her smile. She decided to be brave. 'We won't hang around after the ice cream if your husband is coming back, but maybe we could meet up with the girls again sometime? At the park, maybe?'

It was a huge relief when Samantha didn't make an excuse or put her off. 'Good idea. How's this Saturday?'

FIVE

SAMANTHA

Samantha had thought she would be rushed to Keira's side, so that she could hold her hand, look her in the face, reassure her that everything was going to be okay. But when they got to the hospital, Keira was in surgery. Samantha was ushered into a small room where she was offered tea, which she didn't take, and a chair, which she did.

'When can I see her? Is she going to be okay?'

The police officers who had brought her there had only been able to give her minimal information. The attack had happened in Recreation Park. There had been no one else there when the paramedics had attended her at the scene, and then she had been brought to Southcliff Hospital. The whole way there, Samantha had turned that information around and around in her head, trying to understand how this could have happened. What was she doing in the park? Why was she alone? The police car had been too hot and she'd found it hard to breathe. When they pulled up at the traffic lights on Station Street, she could see people staring at the police car. It reminded her of Nick's father's funeral. People stopping in their tracks to stare at the hearse going by. Then, like now, she wondered if they were thinking, *Thank God it's not me in there.*

The nurse who had offered the tea smiled kindly. 'She's in the best possible hands. We'll get a doctor in to speak to you as soon as we can.'

The police officers stayed with her. One – the woman, blonde, younger than she'd looked with her hat on – sat on the chair nearest to her. 'My colleagues have picked up your husband. He'll be here in a couple of hours.'

It all sounded so much like an episode of a television drama that Samantha nearly laughed. Nick was in Birmingham. Had been in Birmingham. A telecoms conference. Had he been having dinner? In the middle of a meeting? It struck her that her mobile phone was still sitting on charge in the sitting room. Nick was probably going frantic trying to call her.

'Can I call him? I mean, I don't have my phone with me. Is there a phone I can use?'

'Of course.' The other policeman – he was taller and older, grey at the temples – handed her a telephone. Thank goodness Nick had kept the same telephone number for years. She didn't know anyone else's number by heart these days. Even Keira's. A sob pushed its way out of her. Her poor baby girl. What was happening to her right now?

Nick answered his phone before she'd even heard the first ring. 'Samantha. Thank God. I've been trying to call you non-stop.'

It was so good to hear his voice, even though it made her all the more desperate to see him. If only they could get him here faster. 'Sorry, I left my phone at home.'

Normally, he would have made a joke at that. Asked her if she'd finally had it surgically removed from her palm, but not tonight. 'Are you at the hospital? How is she? What happened?'

Samantha felt as if her whole face was twitching with the effort it was taking not to cry. 'I don't know. She's in surgery. I don't know anything. Oh, Nick, you need to get here. Please come quickly.'

His voice was so steady, so strong. 'I'm coming as fast as I can. Can you call someone to be with you? One of your friends?'

Who would she call? Her mind threw up a picture of the women she'd spent the afternoon with. For some reason, she couldn't see herself sitting there with one of them. It didn't matter. She didn't want anyone else there. Just him. 'Julia was with me when the police came, but she has Grace to look after. Do you think we should call Adam?'

There was a pause on the other end. 'I've been thinking about that. I guess it depends how... how serious it is. I don't want him tearing down from Durham in a panic.'

Samantha shuddered. Nick was right. If they called Adam, they wouldn't be able to stop him from jumping in his car and joining them. She didn't want another child in an ambulance tonight. 'Okay. Let's wait until we've spoken to the doctor.'

As if she'd summoned her with those words, a woman in a white coat and scrubs opened the door to the small room. The police officers stood up and stepped outside.

Samantha tried to stand, but her legs weren't taking instructions from her brain. The doctor motioned with her hands for her to stay seated. 'I've just come to update you on Keira.'

Samantha waved the phone in her hand like a talisman. 'My husband is on the phone. Shall I put it on speakerphone so he can hear?'

The doctor nodded. 'If you wish.' She waited for Samantha to press the screen. 'Keira is stable, but she's in a critical condition. She has sustained a great deal of blood loss. Our first priority was to stop that bleeding and to investigate for any further internal damage. She's still in surgery right now because we want to be fully confident that we haven't missed anything. At this stage, any further bleeding could be very serious indeed.'

The doctor paused as if to give Samantha a chance to take everything in. Critical, but stable. Was that good or bad? Samantha's hand fluttered to her mouth to stop her lips from trembling. 'Is she going to be okay?'

The doctor was cautious. 'We are doing everything we can and we're hopeful we stopped the bleeding before the blood loss caused further damage. I'll have more news for you in another hour.'

An hour? She may as well have said a year, it felt so long. 'And will I be able to see her then?'

The doctor was already standing; maybe she had other parents to speak to, other lives to save. 'As soon as she's on ICU, we'll get you in to see her.'

The clock in that room went backwards for the next hour and a half. The doctor had returned an hour later as promised, but Keira had still been in surgery. At the third time of asking, Samantha had accepted a cup of tea, but had let it go cold in her hands. When the door opened to admit Nick, she nearly dropped it on the floor.

It wasn't until she was wrapped into his thick, warm arms that she let herself cry. Huge sobs that shook her whole body. So intense they were almost painful. Nick rested his cheek on the top of her head. 'I'm here, it's okay. It's okay.'

She'd called Nick after the doctor had spoken to her the second time, so he knew that Keira was still in surgery. She had also told him everything she knew about the attack. Keira had been found unconscious in Recreation Park. No knife had been found at the scene. She had been alone. The 999 call had been from another girl who had not left a name.

Once she'd finished crying, Nick led her back to her seat. The police officers had respectfully stepped outside the room again. He brushed her hair away from her face where the tears had glued it to her skin. 'Have the police said anything else? Have they spoken to her friends yet?

Samantha had given the police a list of Keira's friends. Due to the absence of her phone, she couldn't give them numbers for the girls' parents, but they'd said they could find them. 'I haven't heard yet. I just can't understand why she was there on her own. Or why she was in the park at all.'

Nick frowned. 'Me, neither. She knows better than to come home on her own. We've told her enough times.'

Samantha couldn't work that out, either. She'd drilled it into Keira – into both her children – to stay with their friends if they were out in the evening. 'I just can't stop thinking about her lying there, on her own, hurt. My poor baby.'

Nick pulled her close and held her. While she had waited for him, she had thought about the last time she'd been there at the hospital with Keira. She'd been about five and she'd had a high temperature that they couldn't bring down with Calpol and ibuprofen. When she'd started to become sleepy and listless, they'd been really worried and had brought her straight to the emergency department. Within half an hour of being there, her temperature had returned to normal and she'd been running around in the waiting room, the picture of health. Samantha had felt such a fool, but the doctor who saw them had been understanding. 'You did the right thing. Kids are like that sometimes. They just bounce back.'

With her face in Nick's chest, she uttered the mantra she'd been repeating to herself since she'd got into the police car. 'Please let her be okay. Please let her be okay.'

There was a knock on the door and the same doctor came in. 'Keira is out of surgery. Would you like to come and see her now?'

SIX

JULIA

'Oh, no. No. Are you hurt? Grace, are you hurt?'

The shock of seeing her daughter, holding blood-stained clothes, had frozen Julia to the spot. Memories of last year came flooding back; her first thought: *Please God, not again.*

Grace just stared at her; her own terror mirrored back in her daughter's eyes. She shook her head.

Then Julia's instincts caught up with her and she reached for her daughter. Although she'd given Grace the bigger bedroom when they'd moved into the flat, it was still small enough for Julia to be at her side before taking another breath. She reached for her arms, felt relief that there were no fresh marks on them. In fact, there was no blood on her anywhere. 'What's happened? Where has the blood come from?'

Again, Grace shook her head, but didn't speak.

Julia sat down beside her on the bed. 'Grace, baby, you need to talk to me.' Another thought crept into her head, but it seemed too ludicrous to be true. 'Does this have anything to do with Keira?'

Grace started to shake her head and then stopped, nodded, slumped onto Julia's shoulder and started to sob.

With her arms around her daughter, Julia's mind was racing. Had Grace been there? Had she been hurt? What had she seen? She pulled away from her daughter and ducked her head so that she could look into her eyes. 'You need to talk, Grace. What happened?'

Her voice was a staccato of sobs. 'I don't know. I just found her. She was lying there. In the park. She was moaning, crying. Oh, Mum, it was so awful.' She clutched onto Julia like a life raft, burying her head into her collarbone so hard it hurt.

It had been a while since Grace had let her hold her close like this, and Julia wanted to squeeze her tight, keep her safe, tell her that she would make everything better. But she didn't have that luxury. Again, she pushed her gently away, keeping hold of her arms. 'My poor girl, it must have been so frightening. But you need to tell me what you saw. And we need to tell the police.'

Grace's head jerked upwards. 'No. Not the police. Please, Mum, please. Don't call the police. I just found her. I don't have anything to tell them. I don't know anything. There was no one else there.'

The words fell from her mouth so quickly; she was working herself up into near hysteria. Julia put a hand on her back and started to rub, like she'd done for hours when she was a young baby, refusing to give in to sleep. 'Shh, shh. Calm down, baby. I'm right here with you. Nothing is going to happen. But we need to do anything we can to help poor Keira.'

This time Grace stood, so abruptly that she knocked Julia's chin with the top of her head. 'I did help her. I called the ambulance. I told them where she was. I stayed with her, I held her until I heard the ambulance siren really close.'

That explained the blood on her clothes. 'So, why did you leave? Why not stay until they got there?'

Grace was pacing backwards and forward across her carpet. Wringing her hands, one then the other. 'I couldn't stay. I couldn't. Oh, Mum, it was so scary. Her breathing was wrong. It was bubbly and she kept looking as if she was about to go to sleep. So I kept her awake. I kept talking to her and making her talk to me. I said all this stupid stuff. I was gabbling on about the beach we went to when we got soaked and you had to buy us those clothes from the charity shop and Keira decided to dress up like a grandma and she had that hat and... and...' She stopped pacing and looked at Julia. 'Do you remember?'

Of course she remembered. They had been about ten. Grace was so quiet, but she'd fed off Keira's confidence like a baby lamb. Keira had scoured the charity shop for the most old-fashioned dresses and hats and scarves that she could find and had insisted they spend the rest of the afternoon calling each other Beryl and Gladys. 'I remember. You were so brave and clever to keep her talking. Well done, sweetheart.'

It was possible that Grace had actually saved Keira's life. But it still didn't explain why she hadn't stayed when the paramedics came.

Grace was pacing again. 'I thought she was wet. The ground was wet. I was holding her and she felt wet and cold. But it was blood. I didn't realise until I got home. There was so much of it. So much blood.'

Fear gripped Julia. She still had no idea how seriously hurt Keira was. But if there had been that much blood, it couldn't be good. 'And you didn't see anything? No one running away? Nothing left behind?'

'No!' Grace roared so loudly that Julia jumped. 'I didn't see anything! But they won't believe me. None of them will believe me. No one ever believes me.'

This was awful. Grace was running her hands through her hair and pulling it up from the roots. She was in such a state – Julia had to calm her down. 'I won't call anyone. Not until we've talked it through. Sit down, baby. You need to calm down.'

Every part of Grace was trembling. It was awful. The last year had been horrendous for her. Changing schools. Starting again. They had just been coming out the other side, and now this.

At least she did come back over to the bed and sit down, although she left a space between them. 'No one will believe me, Mum. You know it's true. They will think I saw something or someone. They might even think I was involved. The police won't believe me and nor will anyone else.'

Julia wasn't sure who she meant by 'anyone else'. 'Your dad is a police officer, Grace. You can tell him.'

'No!' Her eyes were wild. 'You cannot call Dad. I mean it, Mum. If you call him – if you call anyone – I won't be here to talk to them. I mean it.'

Did she mean she would run away? Or something worse? Either way, the look on her face was not that of an empty threat. 'You need to help me out here, Grace. I don't understand. I don't get why you won't speak to anyone. It's not as if you've done anything wrong.'

'You said that last time. You said last time that I hadn't done anything wrong and look what happened. It doesn't matter, Mum. It doesn't matter what is true. It matters what people say and what they believe about you. You think that the truth is important, but it isn't. It isn't.' She crumpled again into Julia's arms and sobbed into her chest.

Julia cradled her like a baby, rocking her gently, her own tears falling into Grace's hair. She had failed her daughter. A year ago, she had failed her so badly that she'd almost lost her. That wasn't going to happen again.

If Grace said that she'd seen nothing, then she would believe her. If she had nothing to tell the police, then there was no urgency to call them right then, was there? Julia would wait until she was calm, over the initial shock of finding her childhood friend in a pool of blood. And then she would try – gently, slowly, calmly – to persuade her to speak to the police. John would help. Even though he worked in London now, he would know people in the local force.

It must be terrifying to be in Samantha's shoes, but sacrificing Grace's mental health was not going to help Keira right now. She prayed that Keira was going to be okay, tried not to look at Grace's screwed-up uniform covered in blood.

Grace's sobs had subsided, but she kept her face on Julia's chest. Still rocking, Julia pressed her lips onto the top of her head, smelled the coconut shampoo she liked so much. 'I'm here for you. I'm here for you. It's going to be okay.'

Another hour or so would make no difference to anything. She would try again then.

But why was Grace so adamant that she didn't want to speak to her dad?

SEVEN

WHEN THEY WERE FIVE

The entrance to the private room at Sussex Hall was framed with an arch of pearlised pink balloons. Beyond was a haze of glitter and excitement. Grace gripped Julia's hand tightly and Julia squeezed back. 'Are you ready?'

Grace nodded and they stepped inside the room.

Everywhere they looked, there was something happening. To their left were two women dressed as Disney princesses, surrounded by adoring five-year-old girls. To their right, a white, decorated sweet cart jostled for room with a chocolate fountain and an ice cream dispenser. In front – on a small chequered dance floor – a children's entertainer held court, teaching another group dance moves to the music which was filling the room with a loud, electronic twang. This wasn't a children's party, it was a full-on festival.

Grace pressed tighter to Julia's side, her arm wrapped around the gift she had made for Keira. Julia had wanted to buy a gift, but Grace had been determined that she wanted to make something 'special' for her new friend. They had compromised on a wooden jewellery box from Hobbycraft, which Grace had spent the week decorating with paint and glitter and shells she had collected from the beach. Their kitchen table now resembled the dressing table of a pantomime dame.

'Grace! You're here!' From nowhere, a sparkly tiara-wearing Keira burst out on them. She grabbed Grace's hand and pulled her out of Julia's grip. 'Come and meet the princesses.'

Grace took two steps and then turned back to Julia, passing her the clumsily wrapped gift. 'Don't go, Mummy.'

'I won't, baby. I'll be here.' With that reassurance, Grace allowed herself to be dragged away. Which left Julia standing in the middle of a children's party with absolutely no clue what to do or where to put herself.

A tall man in an open-necked shirt came to her rescue. She and Grace had been to Samantha's house twice more since their original meeting, and she recognised Nick from the photographs in their hall. He leaned in conspiratorially. 'You look about as lost as I feel. You must be Julia? Keira hasn't stopped talking about Grace coming today.'

She smiled at him gratefully. 'Yes. That's us.' She waved the gift in her hand. 'Where should I put this?'

'I'll show you. Then I'll try and track down my wife so that she can say hello.'

The table of gifts was heaving with large boxes extravagantly wrapped in foil and ribbon. Julia tucked Grace's offering behind them. When she turned back to the room, she could see Nick steering Samantha in her direction.

'Hi, Julia. So glad you made it.' Samantha wore an electric blue dress and silver heels. She looked amazing. Was Julia imagining her eyes flicking up and down her 'good' jeans and T-shirt? Surely the instruction to wear 'party clothes' had been for the children, not the parents?

'Sorry that we're a little late. I had to wait for John to get back so that I could have the car.' And also, for them to have a hissed argument about how selfish it was for him to take a detour to the fishing tackle shop on his way home from the station when he knew she needed the car to make the twenty-minute journey to this place.

'That's no problem. You're here now. Come and meet some of the other parents.'

Julia's palms started to sweat at the sight of the women sitting around an oval table, glasses of Prosecco in hand. Behind them, Nick and the husbands stood at the small bar area. Julia hadn't even thought of inviting John, but she knew what he would have said, anyway.

'Hi, girls. This is Julia. She's Keira's friend Grace's mum.'

Politely, all the women nodded hello, but no one moved to make space for her. She didn't recognise any of them from the school pick-up. She smiled, but her toes were curling in her trainers. 'Hi. Nice to meet you. Can I get anyone a drink from the bar?'

'No need.' Nick appeared at her elbow and pressed a glass of Prosecco into her hand. She'd meant to get herself a soft drink. She didn't even like Prosecco. Still, she smiled and took it as he disappeared back to the dads' corner.

Samantha had gone, too, and Julia was left hovering near the table of mothers. One of them – blonde, poker-straight hair, amazingly white teeth – smiled at her. 'Your daughter is at school with Keira, is she?'

Her hands were so sweaty, the glass of untouched Prosecco nearly slipped out of them. 'Yes. They're in the same class.'

'Ours' – the woman circled her wrist to encompass everyone sitting at the table – 'are all at St Pierre's.'

St Pierre's was a private school out near the airport. These people were obviously not married to policemen or working part-time in a bank. 'That's nice. How do you know Samantha?'

'From the gym. Well, from the cafe at the gym, actually.' They all laughed together and Julia felt like a gawky fourteen-year-old who had accidentally stumbled into the cool girls' area. When they'd discussed swimming lessons last week, Samantha had mentioned that she took Keira swimming at the Santoria gym she belonged to. Julia had googled the membership prices when she'd got home and nearly choked on her sandwich.

'Do you live near to Samantha, then?' Another mother – dark hair, very red lips – asked.

'Quite near.' This was literally, if not metaphorically, true. Their houses weren't in the same league.

The dark-haired woman narrowed her eyes. 'And you're a gardener. Is that right?'

So, Samantha had spoken to them about her. Julia didn't want to think about what she might have said. 'Not yet. I work in a bank. But it's something I'd like to do someday.'

'Well, please let me know when you do. It's impossible to keep up with mine. I could definitely do with some help.'

The woman smiled as she spoke, but there was something about the way she said 'help' that made Julia blush. 'Will do. Actually, will you excuse me? I just want to check on my daughter.'

She left her glass on the bar where it was out of the reach of young hands and scanned the room for Grace. She was on the dance floor with Keira; they were holding hands and giggling with one another. Though she hated herself for it, Julia couldn't help but notice the difference between Grace's party dress and the sequin-covered dresses of the other girls. Grateful that Grace didn't seem aware of it, she turned to find the bathroom, and bumped straight into Samantha.

'Everything okay?' Samantha's smile was tight.

'Yes, I'm good. This is some party.'

Samantha looked around the room. 'I hope so. Nick thinks it's ridiculous to do all this for a five-year-old, but I just wanted it to be magical for her.'

Julia was most definitely in Nick's camp, but she'd never say that. 'You've done a great job.' She nodded towards the girls. 'Those two are having a great time together.'

'Yes. They are very sweet. Keira was desperate for Grace to come. I have to go and talk to the caterers about bringing out the food, but let's arrange a play date for the girls next week. Keira has been begging me to invite Grace to the pool at the gym, if you think she'd like that?'

The last place on earth that Julia wanted to be was in a pool full of women like those she'd just left, while wearing a swimming costume. But Grace would absolutely love it. 'Great. Yes. Let's do that.'

EIGHT

SAMANTHA

When Adam was first born, Samantha had lain awake watching him in his crib. Checking his blanket wasn't loose, that he was lying on his back, that the temperature in the room was just right. Keira was her second born. She was a different mother second time around. More relaxed, more calm. It wasn't that she cared any less, just that she no longer saw danger in every possible cough or murmur.

She was making up for it now.

On the bed, where Keira lay hooked up to machines that monitored heart rate and oxygen levels and goodness knows what else, Samantha was too scared to take her attention away from her for a minute. It had been a long time since she'd held her daughter's hand even to cross the street, but now she encased it in hers and wouldn't let go.

She and Nick spoke in whispers to each other. 'I still don't understand what happened.'

On the other side of the bed, holding Keira's right hand, Nick shook his head. 'Nor me. Why was she on her own?'

Samantha had given the young policewoman her house keys and told her where the mobile phone was on charge. They'd retrieved it from the house so that she could scroll through her address book for the names of anyone she'd forgotten; they were now calling the parents of Keira's closest friends. Samantha had wondered whether she should ring them first to warn them. Spare the parents the panic of getting an unexpected call from a police officer. But she couldn't bear to be away from her daughter for more than a second.

Plus, she couldn't trust herself not to get angry when she asked them what had happened. Why had they abandoned Keira? And was it one of them who had made the emergency call to the police?

Nick was talking to Keira again. He had tried every ten minutes or so for the two hours they had been sitting beside her. 'Hi, sweetheart. We're still here. Mum and Dad. If you can hear us, we love you very much and we can't wait for you to wake up and talk to us. Mum has got one hand and I've got the other. It's just like when you were little and you used to make us swing you between us. Do you remember that? We used to go: one, two, three.' His voice cracked on the final word and the hand that wasn't holding Keira's covered his eyes.

Samantha had only seen him cry once before, at his father's funeral. If her heart wasn't already in agony, this would have done it. She tried to reach over to him, but it was too far across the bed.

They sat in silence for a while. Listening to the beeps and hisses that were keeping their daughter alive. The surgeon had explained that the amount of blood she'd lost had been life-threatening, but that they'd managed to stop the internal bleeding. 'Her body has been through a big shock; we hope that she'll regain consciousness soon.' Samantha was trying hard to not over-analyse his use of the word 'hope'.

Nick sat back in his chair. 'I might pop out and speak to the police officers. See if they've found anything out. Shall I get you a coffee or something? Do you want a muffin? Or a sandwich?'

The offer of food and drink was his way of looking after her, of doing something. She wasn't hungry, but even if she had been, how could she sit outside the ward eating a sandwich or a cake while Keira was lying here like this? 'A coffee would be good. Thanks.'

She didn't want that either, but Nick needed something to do. Just sitting there, feeling useless, was killing him. He was a fixer: a mender of toys, a reader of stories, a chauffeur on nights out. Even when they went on a family holiday, he was the one making the sandcastles or splashing them in the pool. Their children were both too old for that now, and she knew Nick missed the days when he was Keira's hero rather than the man she rolled her eyes at because he didn't know what TikTok was.

He closed the door to the room with a quiet click and then she was alone with her girl.

Every mother thinks that their child is beautiful. Part of it must be genetic: the child looks like you or your husband, and you respond to the familiarity. Keira was properly beautiful, though. Her hair was thick and blonde, her skin glowed with youth and health. Like most of her friends, she layered on contoured make-up like a stage artist, but she didn't need any of it.

Samantha brushed Keira's cheek with her forefinger. It was so soft. 'Oh, my darling, what happened? Why were you there on your own? Why didn't you call me? I would have come and got you. Wherever you were.'

She laid her cheek down on the back of Keira's hand and closed her eyes. For the first time, it occurred to her that no one had mentioned Keira's phone. Did the police have it? Was it still in the park? Did someone else have it?

She tried to remember what the police had said. Everything until Nick arrived was still a blur. They'd said that they'd received an emergency call from a young woman. Had they mentioned Keira's phone at all? She would definitely have had it with her – teenage girls are inseparable from their mobiles – so where was it?

She took her own phone from her bag. Years ago, you weren't allowed to use your phone in a hospital. When she was young, her grandmother had been in hospital and her uncle had been told to turn off the huge brick of a phone he'd carried with him in those days. Somehow this had triggered another huge argument between her parents – this had only been weeks before they had finally separated; they had seemed to actually welcome an excuse to take chunks out of one another back then.

In between talking to Keira and trying to work out what had happened in the park, she and Nick had turned it over and over about whether to call Adam at university and let him know about his sister. In the end, they'd decided to wait until the morning and then tell him to get the train into London and out again, rather than drive down. He was a sensible lad, but shock could do funny things to you. She would much rather tell him in person, but that would mean one of them leaving Keira's side, and that was unthinkable right now. Not for the first time, she wished she had the kind of family you could call in a crisis.

Once she had her phone back, she'd seen a message from Julia, offering help. It was strange to think about how long they'd known each other: over a decade, in fact. At times, they had shared some of their most private thoughts, but it had been the two girls who were the great friends. Maybe they would have still been close if Grace hadn't started at the same school as Keira. Julia had thought it was a good idea as Grace had had such a tough time. A fresh start at a new school would be just what she needed.

Except it hadn't been. Obviously, Samantha had not mentioned anything to Julia, but Keira had said that Grace was 'just weird' at school. She didn't seem to be like the girls in Keira's group, or even try to be. It was okay, though, because she'd made a couple of other friends 'like her', according to

Keira. People just grew apart. It was a shame, but it was life. As long as they were both happy, it didn't matter.

Ironically, she and Julia still met at least once a month when Julia came to do the garden. Often, Julia would stay for a coffee and sometimes even a glass of wine. Samantha had a pretty good social life these days with the group of mums from the school, but sometimes a quiet night in chatting to Julia was nice. Especially as Nick's job took him away so often.

The door opened and Nick appeared with two paper cups of coffee. He passed her one, then retook his seat on the other side of their daughter. She thought he was going to speak to Keira again, but he was looking at her.

'I had a chat with the police officer outside. Apparently, they've called Katie, Phoebe, Mia, Tilly and Cleo and none of them were out with her tonight.'

Samantha frowned. 'They must have made a mistake. Did they speak to the girls, or just their parents? They were all going to Adventure City together. She told me.' She glanced at Keira. It didn't feel right referring to her as if she wasn't there. Could she hear them? Did she even know that they were there?

Nick shrugged. 'He checked the names with me and they were all the usual friends that she's with. According to every girl they spoke to, they did go to Adventure City today, but Keira cried off. She said she was going to stay home. That she was doing something with you.'

Samantha looked again at Keira. Why would she have told them that? In fact, the opposite was true. Samantha had asked her whether she should stay home and get her homework done, and Keira had invented some tale about it being vital that she go with the girls because otherwise there would be an odd number for the fairground rides. *No one wants to sit on their own, Mum.* 'I don't understand why she would do that.'

Nick shifted in his chair. Something told her there was more to come. 'Apparently, one of the girls also told the police that she'd been suspicious at the time that Keira wasn't telling the truth. She thought that Keira was letting them down so that she could do something else. With her boyfriend.'

Boyfriend? Now Samantha was completely confused. Had the police spoken to the wrong people? 'But Keira doesn't have a boyfriend. Did you tell the police that?'

Nick glanced at Keira. Was he also uncomfortable having this conversation in front of her closed eyes? 'It seems that she did, love. The girl told the police that she'd been seeing this boy for about three weeks.'

Three weeks? As relationships went, that hardly made it the romance of the century. But Keira had never had a boyfriend before, and that was a long time to keep something like this a secret. Why hadn't she told them?

Something else occurred to her almost immediately. 'Oh, Nick. Do you think he was there?'

NINE

JULIA

Julia had taken the blood-soaked clothes out of Grace's bedroom, but now she didn't know what to do with them. When they told the police what had happened, would they want these clothes as evidence?

She pulled a plastic bag from the cupboard under the sink, shoved them in and then stowed them inside the washing machine, slamming the door on them. But the bright orange of the bag showed through the glass window like a warning light, so she took them out and slipped them into the cupboard beneath the sink instead.

Grace wandered out from the bathroom, where she had gone to wash her face. The face that still looked so young. At fifteen – with make-up and the right clothes – some girls could easily be mistaken for women, but Grace still had a lot of the girl about her.

'I made you hot chocolate.'

There was the ghost of a smile on Grace's lips as she slipped onto the kitchen chair and wrapped her hands around the mug, shoulders hunched, head down.

Julia needed to take it slowly. But the clothes in the bag

wouldn't wait. They had to call the police soon. A couple of hours could be explained away by shock, but any longer and Grace's behaviour would look suspicious.

'Is it good?' Julia nodded at the mug.

Grace took the smallest of sips, then nodded. 'Yes. Thanks, Mum.'

For a few moments, they sat in silence: Grace staring into her mug, Julia watching the top of her head. Before she'd had a child, she'd known that she would love her, but she hadn't prepared herself for how strong, how deep, how all-encompassing that love would be. Maybe it was because Grace was her only child. Maybe it was because they had lived alone for the last few years since she and John had split up. Whatever it was or wasn't, Grace was the sun she orbited.

That sun hadn't been bright for quite some time, though. 'How are you feeling now?'

Grace brought the mug to her mouth, still not looking at Julia. Was she just buying time? Again, the tiniest of sips before she spoke. 'A bit better. Less shaky.'

That'd be the sugar; it was good for shock. That's what Julia's mum used to say. Although it was usually when she was about to read Julia's school report, and would be accompanied by a wink. *Make us a brew before I read this, Julia, love. An extra sugar for the shock.*

She always knew what to do. How to broach a difficult subject. Julia could remember the weight of her mum lowering herself onto the side of her teenage bed, the warmth of her hand on the small of Julia's back. *Come on, love, it can't be all that bad.* She would last out as long as she could, determined not to let go of whatever anger or fear or pain she was holding inside herself. Somehow, her mum would tease it out of her. Then it would come out all in a rush, followed by lumpy sobs of released emotion. Even now, she yearned for the softness of her mother's lap as she lay her head down on it and let her hair be stroked.

But Julia couldn't go to her mum for help this time. Her parents had emigrated to Spain years ago and, recently, her dad hadn't been in the best of health. She didn't want to give them something else to worry about. If only she could give Grace the same support that her mum had given her. Respite from whatever fear she was struggling with right now. She knew it was fear: she'd seen it before.

'Look, love—'

'No.' Grace was still not looking up, but her jaw was set in a stiff line: she looked just like her father. 'I know what you are going to say and the answer is no. I'm not speaking to Dad, or anyone else at the police.'

For a moment, Julia was speechless. This wasn't the way Grace spoke to her. In fact, when other mothers were consoling one another that 'all teenagers are like that', Julia had always been grateful that Grace, even when she was a little moody, was never outright rude.

Still, to be fair to her, she had never been through the experience of seeing an old friend covered in blood before. It was bound to make her react strangely. 'I just don't understand, love. I don't understand why you won't speak to the police. This had nothing to do with you. All they will want to know is whether or not you have information that might help them, and once they know that you don't, that will be that.'

Grace chewed on her lip, a sure sign that tears were coming and she was fighting them every step of the way. 'You don't understand. You never understand.'

That wasn't fair. 'Then help me. Tell me. How can I possibly understand if you won't explain what is going on inside your head?'

Now the tears came. 'They won't let me forget it. That I was there. They'll blame me somehow. It'll all get worse. And Keira will be so angry that I was even there.'

Julia reached out and took Grace's hand. 'Baby, you're not

making any sense. Who are "they"? Why would Keira be angry? You were the one who called the ambulance. You might have saved her life.'

'But *they* won't see it like that!' Grace was in danger of whipping herself back to hysteria. She squeezed her hands into fists and banged them on the table to punctuate her words. 'They will make my life hell!'

It was like they were in a cruel time warp. Back to all those months ago, when they'd sat at this same table and she'd had to listen to her precious girl recount all the awful things that had happened to her at school that year. The name calling, the graffiti on her books, the ostracising, the tripping, each story worse than the last. In all her life, Julia had never felt as devastated, as angry, as guilty. Surely this couldn't be happening again? Grace had started at this school so that she didn't have to put up with that every day.

It was all that Julia could do to push the words up from her throat. 'Who, sweetheart? Who is making your life hell? You need to tell me. I want to help. Please let me help.'

Now, finally, Grace did look up, but her eyes were so full of pain that Julia almost had to look away. 'Keira, Mum. It is Keira and her friends who are making my life hell.'

Julia's lounge was only marginally bigger than her kitchen, but it was a warm nest of a room. With only the two of them to please, she and Grace had indulged their love of throws and cushions to their hearts' content. Julia had built bookshelves into the recesses either side of the antique fireplace that she had rubbed down, tiled and filled with pillar candles. The floorboards were bare and covered with a rug, the curtains heavy and thick enough to shut out the rest of the world when they needed to.

Julia had carried both drinks through from the kitchen.

Now, sitting on the dark blue sofa, she kept silent as she listened to Grace's story of the last couple of months. 'When I started at St Anne's, I really thought it was going to be better. I was stupidly excited that Keira was there. I expected her to be popular, obviously, but I had no idea just how popular. The girls she goes around with control *everybody*.

'In the beginning, they just pulled faces at one another whenever I came over to speak to Keira. She was all awkward with me, saying that she couldn't stay and talk because she had to be somewhere. Then I'd see them whispering to her as they strolled away to the bench by the pond, where they hold court like a bunch of princesses. Glancing back at me. She would be shaking her head. I knew that she was denying that we were friends. And it hurt, Mum. It really did hurt.'

Julia could feel the anger boiling inside her. Of course it hurt. The two of them had been so close, even like sisters at one point. How could Keira treat Grace like this?

'So, I stopped talking to her when they were around. I kept away. But if I saw her alone, I would try and speak to her. Sometimes she'd be okay, other times she would try and brush me off as quickly as she could. She wasn't actually horrible to me herself. It was more that she didn't stop her friends from being horrible to me.'

Julia could just imagine those superior little witches. Of course Grace wouldn't be good enough for them, with their designer clothes and huge houses. But she was worth ten of them, if only she could see it. 'Why didn't you tell me any of this?'

Grace shrugged. 'Because you like Keira. Because you wanted me to go to St Anne's. Because I couldn't bear telling you that I'd failed again at being a basic human being with friends.' Tears were streaming down her face. 'It's me, isn't it? It doesn't matter where I go or what I do, this is going to keep happening. It's just not worth carrying on. It's always going to be like this.'

Fear clutched at Julia's heart. 'It's not always going to be like this. School is a cesspit of vipers. Those girls are not worth a hair on your head. It's not you, my darling girl. You have done absolutely nothing wrong.'

'But don't you see? This is why they can't know I was there. They will tell everyone their own version of the story, where I have done something terrible. They'll make it my fault.'

'But we'll make sure that they can't do that. The police will know the truth.'

'It doesn't matter what the police say. They will make it up and people will believe them. It'll be just like before.'

She lay her head down onto her arms and Julia reached around her.

Before.

That word held a saga of its own. When a boy had told the whole year group that he'd slept with Grace. When everyone had believed his lie, and all the others that followed about her body and her behaviour. *Before.* When Julia had had no idea why her sunny, clever, happy daughter had started to stay behind a closed bedroom door and beg to be allowed to stay home because of period pain or a headache or an upset stomach or any one of a number of minor ailments that would prevent her from having to go to school. *Before.* When she had discovered marks on her daughter's body that had made the blood run cold in her veins.

What the hell was she going to do? It was morally wrong to keep it from the police that Grace had been at the scene. But how could she put her back into that dark place when she had only just begun to emerge from it? 'Are you absolutely sure that you didn't see anything? Nothing at all that could help the police to find out who hurt Keira?'

Grace looked at her as if she was drowning and Julia was

holding a rope. 'Nothing at all, Mum. I absolutely promise. She was just there on her own and... and...' She started to cry and buried her head into Julia's shoulder.

Julia stroked the back of her head. 'Shush, now. It's going to be okay, baby. It's going to be okay.'

She closed her eyes. *And please let Keira be okay, too.*

TEN

WHEN THEY WERE SIX

Schools have a distinctive smell; a strange mix of gravy and plimsolls. As an adult, walking into a school hall can bring back memories of your own time as a student: good or bad. The lower school hall was lined with grey plastic chairs. The keener parents – and those who hadn't had to dash there after booking a half day from work – had already filled the rows. As Julia scanned the room for a space, her stomach was a knot of anxiety. Was Grace going to be okay? *Please let her not get upset.*

At the aisle end of the fifth row, Samantha waved to her and pointed to the seat she'd saved with her bag.

'Thanks.' Julia flopped down onto the chair and stowed her own bag underneath. 'I was worried that I might not make it in time. Work was horrendous this morning; everyone seemed to need an answer to their question right that minute.'

'I don't know how you do it. And that journey up to London every day. Can't you be transferred somewhere more local?'

Even if that were possible, it would mean a big drop in money. 'To be honest, I wish I didn't have to go at all. I still hate it.'

All the seats were filled now and parents were having to

stand at the back. Thank goodness for Samantha. After dashing there from the station, Julia was very grateful for the chair, however hard it was.

Samantha passed her a copy of the programme. 'What about that gardening course I sent you? It's online. You could do it whenever you had spare time. Can you imagine doing a job you loved? Have you even looked at it?'

Julia had imagined that, many times. Lying in bed at night, trying to work out the childcare for Grace for school holidays or if she was sick. Because – of course – it was her who had to work that out, and not John. 'I have looked at it and it seems great. But I've spoken to John and he said we can't afford for me to give up work and start a gardening business. In fact, he wants me to go back full-time now that Grace is at school.'

Even the thought of it made her feel sick. She couldn't argue with the fact that he had to work full time, so why shouldn't she? But he loved his job, whereas she hated hers. Plus, she would miss out on ever doing the school run, waving Grace through the gate in the morning, being the first person to scoop her up as she ran out of school, covered in splotches of paint and jabbering about the funny things that she and Keira had done that day. Julia knew that she was fortunate to be able to do it twice a week, but she didn't want to give it up completely. Especially as she wasn't bothered about the new car or foreign holidays that John said they'd be able to afford if she did go back to work.

'He's being very short-sighted. If you started a gardening business you could end up making more money. Why don't you do the course anyway?'

'Maybe.' There was no point, though. It would actually be more depressing to do the course and not be able to do anything with it. 'How was Keira this morning?'

Samantha laughed. 'Unstoppable. She beat the alarm clock by forty minutes singing "Away in a Manger" in my ear. It's pretty scary waking up to a pale-faced child singing like an out-of-tune angel at 6 a.m., I can tell you. How was Grace?'

It was hard to say. When Grace was worried about something, she would disappear inside herself. 'A bit quiet. She didn't want her breakfast this morning because she said her tummy was hurting.'

Samantha tilted her head to one side. 'Poor thing. She's so brave to do a speaking part. Keira says her lines differently every time, so she will be in good company if she forgets.'

It was kind of Samantha to try and make her feel better, but Keira would be able to shrug off any mistakes, whereas Grace would be mortified to her very soul.

The rumble of chatter gradually quietened as the head teacher walked onto the stage. As if they were a class of unruly Year 4s, she waited for absolute silence before booming out into the room, 'Good afternoon, everybody.'

Slightly embarrassed, half the room mumbled, 'Good afternoon.'

This was the second school play she'd been to, so Julia knew what was coming next. Sure enough, Mrs Radcliffe cupped her ear with her hand and boomed again. 'I can't hear you! Good afternoon, everybody.'

If only to stop this pantomime, the parents replied with more gusto. Except Samantha, who hissed under her breath, 'Why does she do this? It's excruciating. It's like being at a Butlin's holiday camp.'

Julia agreed, but she couldn't help but smile at the thought of Samantha at Butlin's.

After the usual preamble about not putting any photographs of other people's children on social media, and thanking the teachers for their hard work, Mrs Radcliffe exited stage left and the children filed in to a recording of Christmas carols.

Julia gripped the sides of her seat as the children arrived, so different in height and confidence. Some of them grinned out at the audience – a couple even waved at their parents, who stood up and snapped a picture of them – and then there she was. Little Grace in her Mrs Innkeeper costume, keeping her eyes straight ahead as if to block out the whole room.

A couple of nights ago, Julia had offered to speak to Grace's teacher and say that she was worried about her part. It wasn't just the lines. She was going to have to sing the opening verse to one of the songs as a solo. She did have a beautiful singing voice, but her fear of starting at the wrong time or forgetting her words was playing in her little mind on a loop.

'It'll be good for her,' John had insisted. 'She needs to come out of her shell.'

All of the children were now in their places. Grace stood next to a cardboard inn with a boy in a similar costume – Mr Innkeeper, presumably – and she finally raised her face, looking in the audience for her mother.

Julia stretched her neck as high as she could without actually standing up, waving a hand at shoulder height, willing Grace to see her. Eventually, they locked eyes and Julia beamed at her daughter, trying to transmit every ounce of confidence and belief and love that she could. She was rewarded with a little smile and a finger wave at hip-height. Then, after a stage-whispered, 'One, two, three,' from their teacher, they all broke into the opening song.

Samantha leaned sideways towards her and whispered out of the corner of her mouth, 'I feel as if I could perform this myself; I think Keira knows every line.'

Julia could imagine Keira putting on a one-woman show in their large sitting room. Grace, on the other hand, had been focused only on her one line – 'I'll take you to the stable' – and the opening verse of the song that she would sing solo.

When Julia had first heard from Grace's teacher that she was going to sing alone, she'd been proud but concerned.

'I think she can do it,' Miss Summers had said. 'And she has such a beautiful voice.'

Julia wasn't disputing that – had even enjoyed hearing Grace praised – but it was such a big thing for Grace to do, she couldn't help but worry.

Grace had impressed her, though: 'I will do my best. Miss Summers says that's all she can ask.'

After a tear-inducing version of 'Little Donkey', Mary and Joseph arrived at the makeshift stable to be told by a very dominant Mr Innkeeper that, no, there was no room at the inn. Possibly his clenched fist punched into his other hand was a bit much, but the audience laughed appreciatively.

Then it was Grace's turn. She held out her hand – as Julia held her breath – and pointed towards the middle of the stage. 'I'll take you to the stable.'

She had done it. Now there was just the song to go.

It took some organisational assistance to get Mary and Joseph to give up their hobby horse 'donkey' and to sit down behind the manger, Mary picking up a baby Jesus doll from the straw. Julia had to smile at the comment of the woman behind her: 'If only childbirth were that easy.'

And then it was Grace's big moment. She turned around to face the audience and the teacher on the piano started the opening to 'Away in a Manger'.

Maybe it was looking out at all the expectant faces, maybe it was the cameras pointed her way, but Grace froze on stage. The other children looked at her; they knew it was up to her to go first. Everyone must have heard Miss Summers whisper, 'It's okay, Grace. Just take a big breath.'

The piano started again, but still Grace didn't move. Julia wanted to run up onto the stage and pick her up. Take her away from the sea of faces watching her.

But she didn't need to. A shepherd with a tea towel on her head and a large stuffed sheep under her arm came striding towards her best friend. Nodding to mark every beat in the line, she grabbed hold of Grace's hand and started to sing: 'Away in a manger, no crib for a bed...'

Grace seemed to thaw in front of their eyes. Looking at her friend, she began to sing too: 'The little Lord Jesus lay down his sweet head'.

Keira nodded at her, then turned to the audience and belted out the next line, 'The stars in the bright sky...'

They made it through the entire first verse. What Keira lacked in tune, she more than made up for in volume. Grace's voice was sweet, but she directed the whole thing at her best friend, not taking her eyes from her for a minute. Across the hall, parents were fumbling into bags and pockets for tissues to wipe their tears. By the time that the rest of the stage joined in with the chorus, there wasn't a dry eye in the place.

Samantha was blowing her nose. 'Oh, Julia, they are so sweet.'

They really were. But Keira was more than sweet. She gave Grace confidence. She helped her. She was there for her. She was a good friend. And, for the rest of her life, Julia would love her for that.

ELEVEN

SAMANTHA

The hospital had a couple of rooms which were used for relatives to stay overnight. They were self-contained one-room apartments: a sofa bed, two kitchen cabinets, a small table, a kettle. Samantha had wanted to stay next to Keira all night, but the ward sister had all but insisted she leave. *You need to get some sleep. You'll be no good to her when she wakes up if you make yourself ill.* Grateful for the sliver of hope in that statement, in the early hours of the morning Samantha had allowed Nick to put an arm around her and the two of them followed the directions they had been given.

Making the bed up was the first time she'd had something tangible to do in the last few hours and it felt good to move, folding the sheets under the thin mattress, pushing firm hospital pillows into cases. She had waved away Nick's offer to help and he had busied himself with the kettle. He turned to face her now, with his back against the kitchen cupboard. 'I don't like leaving her up there on her own.'

One of the many things she loved about her husband was his openness about his feelings. Almost always, like tonight, they echoed her own. 'Me, neither. But they wanted us off the ward for the night. And we're not far if they... if they need to call us back.'

He looked at her intently, as if to project his words onto her state of mind. 'When she wakes up, you mean?'

She nodded. It was important to stay positive. 'When she wakes up, yes.'

As a baby, Keira had been an absolute devil to get to sleep. Every night, Samantha and Nick would have to take it in turns to walk her up and down the hallway. When she stopped wriggling, Samantha would turn her back to Nick so that he could see Keira's tiny face, to verify whether she was asleep. There would always be several shakes of the head before she got the thumbs up that it was safe to lay her down in her cot.

Nick must have been thinking the same thing. 'Do you remember trying to put her to bed when she was a baby? The minute her back made contact with the mattress, her eyes would open.'

Samantha nodded. 'The amount of time I would sit with my hand on her tummy through the bars of the cot, begging her to go to sleep.'

Samantha looked away from the pain in Nick's eyes; the contrast of that memory with this evening wasn't lost on either of them.

Quite early in their relationship, Samantha had confessed that she preferred to have space on her side of the bed rather than trying to sleep entwined. Nick had laughed in relief and agreed. Tonight, though, they clung to one another as if they were adrift in an endless sea.

Samantha was exhausted, but she couldn't sleep. Sometimes she would tell the children they were 'overtired'. Was that a real thing? If so, that's what she was. Nick had fallen asleep and – though he wasn't actually snoring – his breath was loud and heavy. The weight of his arm around her was a comfort, but maybe it wasn't helping her body to sleep. Gently, she lifted it and shuffled out from underneath, turning over to face him. In his sleep, Nick also turned over and she was able to nestle close to his broad, warm back.

Fifteen minutes later, she still wasn't asleep. It was impossible to empty her mind when her daughter was two floors away, fighting to regain consciousness. She reached onto the floor where she'd plugged in her phone. It was 3 a.m. – far too early to get dressed and return to the ward. On autopilot, she opened up her Facebook account.

She wished she hadn't.

There had already been plenty of text messages from local friends who had heard about Keira. Plenty of: *Are you ok? How's Keira? Let me know if you need anything. Thinking of you.* All of it well-meaning and kind, but she hadn't had the energy to reply. Apart from Julia, who had been at the house when the police arrived, she'd contacted no one to tell them what had happened. Julia wouldn't tell anyone; she wasn't even friendly with anyone at the school.

But someone had.

She scrolled through Facebook, and post after post was about Keira.

Devastated that this beautiful girl has been hurt.

Our gorgeous friend. Please keep her in your thoughts.

Charlotte went to nursery with this girl. Her poor parents.

Then it became increasingly depersonalised. A post from a local Facebook group being shared with exclamatory sentences:

This is a girl from Hayley's school!

OMG This park is ten minutes from us!

What is happening round here?!

And it wasn't just the posts themselves. Already there were hundreds and hundreds of comments. People she didn't know, who didn't know Keira, commenting on what had happened, speaking about her as if they knew her, knew their family.

She hadn't managed more than a few bites of a cereal bar in the last few hours, but felt as if she might throw it up. They were public property. People were claiming to know them, aligning themselves to increase their connection to the hot story of the moment. How dare they speak about Keira as if they knew her?

Her anger grew fast and hot. Now she had started down this rabbit hole, she opened up her Messenger app. Who had all these messages come from? Did she even *know* this many people? Many of the names she had never heard before. Where there were profile pictures, she vaguely recognised parents from Keira's school, and she must've accepted them as Facebook friends, but they were people to whom she'd never spoken.

She scrolled to a name that she did recognise. Pippa. The mother of Keira's friend, Tilly.

Oh, Samantha. I'm so sorry to hear about Keira. How is she doing? How are you doing? I didn't know anything about it until Karen added me to the WhatsApp group. We're all here for you. Anything you need, please just ask. Take care. Sending you love.

Added to what WhatsApp group?

Pippa was in the small WhatsApp group that Constance

had started, just the eight of them who met regularly. It was part 'do they need a packed lunch for the trip tomorrow?' and part 'who is free for drinks on Friday?' Sometimes it was a blessing, a source of amusement. Other times, it felt like a competition.

When Samantha checked it, though, the only messages on there were from the previous afternoon, thanking Constance for her hospitality. No mention of what had happened to Keira. This wasn't surprising; they had all messaged her separately. But that didn't explain Pippa's comment about being *added* to a group.

She didn't care that it was the early hours of the morning. If Pippa hadn't turned off notifications, it was down to her. She punched a reply to the message into the screen of her phone.

What WhatsApp group?

And then, in a heartbeat, the fire of her anger turned to ice.

What if Adam saw these?

'Oh, no. Oh, no.' She kept repeating this to herself as she looked back at the Facebook posts. Had anyone actually tagged her in them? Would they appear in her newsfeed?

She wanted to wake Nick. Ask him to check. But he wouldn't have a clue about Facebook. He had zero interest in any kind of social media.

Her hands trembled as she checked. In the early hours of a Sunday morning. Adam could be coming home from a night out with his friends. He had told her several times that 'no one uses Facebook these days, you dinosaur' but she knew his account was still active. What if he looked at it? What if one of his friends from home saw it and told him?

They had been so stupid, thinking it was the best thing to wait until the morning to tell him. How awful would it be if someone else – a near-stranger even – was the one to tell him about Keira's attack?

Nick moaned and turned over in bed. Should she wake him up? Send him to Adam now? No. That was ridiculous. But they would have to call him first thing in the morning.

How the hell was she supposed to sleep now?

Somewhere around 4 a.m., exhaustion must have claimed her. When she woke up later that morning, Nick wasn't there.

It took her a few moments to remember where she was. Another second to remember Keira. It was a punch to the guts.

She pulled herself out of bed and back into yesterday's clothes. Then the door to the room opened and Nick backed in with two cups of coffee. She didn't give him a chance to speak. 'Why didn't you wake me up?'

He looked tired. Maybe he hadn't slept as well as she'd been resenting him for in her restless hours of the night. 'I only woke up twenty minutes ago, love. I rang the ward and she's had a quiet night. We can go in and see her at 8 a.m. I wanted you to get some rest.'

What did a quiet night mean? Just a euphemism for no change? Julia picked up her mobile to check the time. 'It's 7.45. So, we can get back in to see her in fifteen minutes?'

'Yes. That's why I was coming to get you. Why don't you have a drink first? Give yourself a chance to wake up?'

She stood and took the cup from his hand. 'I'll drink it on the way. And we need to call Adam.'

On the way to the ward, between trying Adam's phone, which was obviously switched off, she filled Nick in on the results of her doom scrolling the night before. Nick's distaste for social media made his disgust as strong as hers had been. In the cold light of the morning, she could see that no one had meant any harm, but she kept trying Adam's phone all the same.

Keira looked exactly the same as when they'd left her the night before. She couldn't have moved. The nurses said that the doctor would do his rounds at 9 a.m. and he would be able to update them then. Other than that, they spoke in well-worn platitudes. Keira was *comfortable* and *stable* and had spent a *quiet night*.

Every ten minutes or so, Nick or Samantha tried to reach Adam, wanting to catch him as soon as he turned on his phone and not trusting him to see the text message they'd sent, asking him to call them back.

Five minutes before the doctor was due, Nick's phone vibrated in his pocket. He shook his head at Samantha's hopeful face to tell her that it wasn't their son, then took the call outside to the corridor.

The beeps of the machines were already becoming so familiar that Samantha barely heard them. She thought of their nostalgia of the night before: her evenings as a new mother, when she had been so tired she would almost cry as she willed Keira to go to sleep. She leaned in close now. 'Wake up, baby. Wake up. Please, wake up.'

Nick wasn't long on the phone. 'That was the police. They've found Keira's phone. It had been thrown into a bush on the edge of the park. They are going to take fingerprints, but are asking for our permission to look on it. Her messages. Her Instagram.'

'Of course, whatever they need to do.'

'Do you have her passwords?'

The rules of Keira having Instagram and Snapchat were that she gave them her passwords so that they could check her accounts whenever they wanted. In practice, they didn't check, believing that her knowledge that they could would be enough. Was that going to be proven to have been a huge mistake? 'Of course. Her phone pass code is her date of birth in six digits. Her Insta and Snapchat will both load automatically, but if they want them, they are both the same. Bella123.'

Bella was the name of the dog they'd lost last year: the small black rescue dog who had been Keira's best buddy and keeper of whispered secrets. Having her put down last summer had been the worst thing to ever happen to Keira.

Had been.

Nick was writing the passwords on the back of his hand. 'I gave the police her number yesterday. They've confirmed that the 999 call was made from Keira's phone.'

That was curious. 'But they are sure it wasn't Keira?'

He shook his head. 'Apparently, the caller repeated over and over, "She's bleeding. She's bleeding." So they don't think so.' Samantha flinched and Nick reached out his hand to clasp her arm. 'Sorry, love.'

'Do they think the person who called the police might be the person who attacked Keira?'

'No. They say it's pretty unlikely. Statistically, knife crime is overwhelmingly male, apparently. The police have asked if I'll listen to the call, in case I recognise the voice. But I said you'd be more likely to know who it was.'

She would definitely be more likely. Nick was a great dad, but he was away far too much to know any of Keira's friends very well. Aside from Grace, of course. It was going to be pretty tough to listen to the emergency call, but Samantha was ready to do whatever was needed to get the animal who had done this to her daughter. 'Of course. But will I need to go to a police station? I don't want to leave the hospital.'

'I'm not sure. I'll ask them in a minute when I give them the passwords. Are you okay here if I pop into the corridor again to call?'

'Yes, of course. And, once we've spoken to the doctor, we'll call Adam again.'

He nodded and left. She picked up Keira's hand.

Julia. That was one person she could trust. If she wasn't going to leave the hospital, she was going to need another change of clothes and some toiletries. Yesterday, the police liaison officer had offered to go and collect things, but Samantha had felt strange about her going through her wardrobe and drawers. Julia must still have the spare key and she would know what clothes Samantha would want.

She picked up her phone and tapped out a message.

TWELVE

JULIA

Julia had barely slept a wink.

Grace had been so upset last night that she had ended up lying next to her on the narrow single bed, holding her until she fell asleep. Even when her breathing had evened out and Julia had slipped away to her own bedroom, it had been difficult to sleep. Guilt lay heavily on top of her: for not talking to the police, for not having known that her daughter was being bullied the first time, for not knowing it was happening all over again.

Every time she closed her eyes, she saw the haunted look on Grace's face. It was the same expression she'd worn last year when it had all come out about the relentless verbal abuse she'd been enduring at school.

For weeks before that day, Grace hadn't been herself. Staying in her room. Barely looking at Julia when she spoke to her. Julia had begun to panic, imagining drug addiction, pregnancy, depression. She'd tried to talk to John about it. They may have split up, but they had always spoken about anything to do with

Grace. But he'd said she was just being a 'typical teenager'. He'd said she'd been okay when she stayed at his. But Julia knew from Grace that on weekends with her father she was often left to her own devices. Would he have even noticed?

It was when the school called to say that Grace had been spending a lot of time in the medical room with headaches or period pains or an upset stomach that alarm bells really began to ring. Grace loved school, loved her lessons.

And then she had refused to go to school at all.

That's when Julia had called John and told him that they needed to sit down and talk to Grace about it together. She'd asked him to come over, which he had, and to be patient with her, which he hadn't. He'd just sat opposite the two of them in the sitting room, his ever-present mobile in his hand. 'What's going on, Grace?'

What's going on? His favourite question. The tone of it made him sound like he was apprehending an unruly youth. When he'd used it on Julia, it had always made her feel like she had to account for herself and what she'd been doing. He was like it even when she'd been on maternity leave. He had no understanding of how hours could pass with a small baby. How you could achieve nothing and still be exhausted by 5 p.m.

Grace hadn't even looked at him. 'I'm not going back.'

He'd coughed out a dry laugh. 'That's ridiculous. It's school. You have to go.'

As always, Julia became the mediator. 'I think we need to get to the bottom of why she doesn't want to go, John.'

John had rolled his eyes and leaned forward so that his forearms were resting on his thighs. He was a tall, broad man and she would imagine he cut an intimidating figure when seated across the table from suspects. Now, his tone was patronisingly calm. 'Okay, Grace. Why don't you want to go to school?'

Still not looking at him, Grace had pushed her chair away from the table, burst into tears and fled to her room.

John scratched behind his ear and leaned back in the armchair. 'Well, that went well.'

It was exasperating. 'What do you expect? She's upset. She needs our support.'

He sighed. 'This is the real problem. You have always mollycoddled her. She's fallen out with her friends. It happens. You trying to clear every problem from her path is not helping one bit. She needs to toughen up a bit. Front it out. Go back to school.'

'This is not a police training camp. This is our daughter.'

John shrugged. 'You asked for my help, but you don't want to listen.' His phone dinged in his hand and he read the message. Smiled. She wanted to knock it from his hand.

'I'm going to make an appointment to go up to the school. Find out what's been happening.'

'Do that if you want, but I think you're making a mountain out of a molehill. She needs to just go back to school and find some other friends.'

He made it sound so easy. 'And how exactly am I supposed to get her there? She's refusing to go, John. And she's too big for me to pick up and carry.'

He raised an eyebrow that conveyed a world of judgement. 'Have you taken everything out of her room? Her computer? Her Nintendo? She might be less keen to stay home if there is nothing whatsoever to do. Anyway, I need to go. Angie has an appointment with the midwife and I promised to be there.'

Julia had bitten back the urge to ask why he was more interested in the child that wasn't there yet than the one that was in front of him, in pain. Falling out with John wasn't going to make any of this better.

Nina had been a lot more sympathetic, but she couldn't help either. 'Oh, love. That must be so tough. Poor Grace. And poor you.'

Julia had blown her nose and wiped her eyes. 'It's so hard,

seeing her so upset. And I just don't know what to do. Did you ever have this with the boys?'

'I think it's different for boys. I know that's totally sexist, but they don't seem to have the same friendship issues. Plus, my two are too thick-skinned to even realise, I reckon. Grace has a lovely, sweet, sensitive soul.'

She was trying to make Julia feel better, but it only made her feel worse. Was John right? Had she been overly protective? Was that why Grace was struggling so much?

In the end, it had been Samantha who was the most practical. Though they weren't spending as much time together by then, she always made Julia a coffee after she'd finished the garden on a Tuesday. 'I'd go and see the head teacher. Find out what the hell has been going on. You can't work out what to do if you don't even know what you're dealing with.'

And so, Julia had resolved to follow Samantha's advice. But before she'd even had a chance to call the head teacher, the head teacher had called her.

The last time Julia had looked at her bedside clock, it was past 2 a.m., so she was still asleep when her phone beeped with a message at 9 a.m. She peeled back her eyelids and reached for the phone, which she swore every night she would leave in the kitchen rather than bringing into the bedroom.

Samantha's name on the screen was as effective as a cold bowl of water.

> *Thanks for your message. It's not great news. She's still unconscious, but she's stable, at least. We're waiting to talk to the doctor. Thanks for offering to help. Would you mind going to the house and getting me some clothes and things? Dropping them to the hospital? I'll send you a list of what I need x*

Julia's heart started to thump in her chest. Of course she would help Samantha out. But she wished fervently that the help didn't involve going to the hospital and facing her. She tapped out a reply.

Of course, send the list. I'll be there as soon as I can.

She swung her legs out of bed. First thing she was going to do was check on Grace. A soft knock went unanswered, but a peep around the door confirmed that she was still fast asleep. That was one thing, at least.

Every hour that Keira didn't wake up made the secret that Julia was keeping worse. But it wasn't as if Grace's presence in the park would make any difference to Keira's recovery, was it? And Grace had helped Keira, looked after the girl who had – Julia now knew – made her life a misery.

Should she call John? He night be able to find out what was going on with the investigation, although there was no guarantee he would tell her anything. Many times in their marriage she had accused him, in the heat of argument, of being more in love with the police force than he was with her. Maybe that had been unfair, but he was definitely loyal and played by the rules. He wouldn't be revealing anything to her that wasn't in the public domain.

She felt as if she was being held by multiple ropes, being pulled in so many directions. She was angry with Keira for the way she had treated Grace, but that didn't mean she didn't still love the little girl who had been like another daughter to her. It was more than possible to hate the sin and love the sinner in this scenario. And Samantha was her friend. She was walking through her own hell right now and there was absolutely no way Julia could leave her alone in the fire. Of course she would go to the hospital this morning.

It wasn't going to be easy, though. The guilt of omission

already weighed on her and it would be worse when she saw Samantha in the flesh. She was going to have to look her in the eye, knowing that she had information about what had happened to Keira last night.

What else could she do, though? Grace was so fragile, so frightened. Last time, Julia hadn't listened to her daughter until it was almost too late. She wasn't about to make that mistake again.

She'd go to the hospital and get it over with.

THIRTEEN

WHEN THEY WERE EIGHT

November mornings in the park were not for the faint-hearted. Julia could see her breath in the air, the amount of steam increased by the hot chocolate that Samantha had brought in a flask. She had suggested they try an indoor play centre, but Samantha had looked at her as if she wanted to take the girls to a war zone.

Adam, now a long-limbed thirteen-year-old, was watching over the two girls on the climbing frame at the other end of the park from where Julia and Samantha were sitting on the bench. Julia was wearing her thick, functional outdoor jacket, but Samantha was in a deep red coat with a black fur collar, matching black gloves and hat. Julia often thought they must look such an unlikely pair.

'Adam is so good to play with the girls.'

Samantha smiled. 'He is a really good boy. I am lucky. I think he's secretly enjoying himself. Not that he'd admit it.'

Adam had that teenage gait – head down, lolloping slowly – which tried to prove his lack of interest in his surroundings. But Samantha was right – he was joining in with the girls' game, which seemed to be some sort of climbing frame tag. Not for the first time, she wondered what kind of teenager Grace would be. Would she stay her loving little sidekick, who painted stones for her to keep in her pocket 'so that you can think of me when you're at work'?

'Is he still doing well at school?'

'Yes. The grammar school was definitely the best choice we could have made for him. He's thriving there. And it won't be long before we've got to start thinking about the next stage for the girls.'

They had three years before they got to secondary school. Julia hadn't even thought about it. 'Will you consider a grammar school for Keira?'

Julia knew that Keira wasn't as academic as her brother, but she had a tutor every week already, so maybe they were getting her ready for the entrance exam.

'I don't know.' Samantha reached down into her large bag for the flask. 'I'm not sure it's the right environment for her. She's more artistic. We think we'll apply to St Anne's.'

It sounded as if Samantha and Nick had already talked about this. 'Maybe I should speak to John about looking into schools for Grace, then. I'm not even sure what our catchment school will be. That's if I can pin him down when he's actually home.'

Samantha concentrated on refilling her cup, then screwed the flask closed. 'Still not good?'

Last week, Samantha had caught Julia at a weak moment and she'd told her how difficult things had been between her and John lately. 'Not great. He told me this morning that he's going to be working Christmas Day.'

'Oh, no, poor Grace. What will you do? Do you have family coming?'

'I looked into flights to my mum and dad in Spain, but it's so expensive at Christmas. I guess it'll just be the two of us. We'll be fine.'

Samantha held out her gloved hands. 'Come to us.'

Julia really hoped Samantha hadn't thought she was hinting at that. 'No. You're very kind, but you don't have to do that. Haven't you got your own family coming over?'

She imagined Christmas at the Fitzgerald house to be a theatrical production with a huge cast, but Samantha laughed and shook her head. 'No, I have that joy on Boxing Day. I'll bore you with the dysfunction that is my family another time over a glass of wine. Do come. Adam is getting too cool for school about the whole thing since he became a teenager. Keira would love to have Grace with us.'

It was tempting. It wasn't that she and Grace couldn't have a lovely time together; it was more that John's absence would be so obvious if they sat down for Christmas dinner without him. But spending Christmas with someone felt pretty intimate. Although they'd known each other for nearly four years, their friendship – if you could call it that – centred firmly on their daughters and talking about them. Even so, Samantha was right, the girls would love to spend the day together, and wasn't that the most important thing? 'If you're sure, that would be lovely. I'll double-check with Grace, but I'm pretty confident I know what she'll say. What can I bring?'

Samantha looked genuinely delighted. 'Marvellous. Just bring yourselves. Do you have any favourite Christmas side dishes? I don't want to miss anything that makes your Christmas meal. At the moment I've planned turkey, gammon, roast potatoes, parsnips, pigs in blankets, Brussels sprouts with chestnuts and pancetta, broccoli, cauliflower cheese, spiced red cabbage, carrots and peas. Oh, and cranberry sauce, obviously. And Nick likes horseradish on his turkey because he's weird. Is there anything else you want?'

Julia watched Samantha count off the elements of a Christmas banquet with a smile. How was she going to cook all that lot at once? 'No, I think that's everything we could possibly want. What about dessert? Can I bring a dessert?'

Again, she shook her head. 'No need. I have—'

Julia held up a hand to stop her. 'Keep it a surprise. You're making me hungry just talking about it. I'll bring some wine, then.' Samantha opened her mouth to argue, so Julia raised her hand again. 'And that's final. Because if you don't let me bring *something*, we won't come.'

'Okay. Agreed. And John is welcome to join us when his shift finishes, of course.'

There was no way John would join them. Maybe Julia was being unfair, but she could imagine that John would be pleased that she and Grace would be somewhere else for Christmas. He'd probably take the opportunity to go for a drink with his colleagues when they came off shift. She didn't want to admit that to Samantha, though. It was hard enough admitting it to herself. 'Thanks.'

Adam loped over to them, rubbing his hands together. 'Can we go now, Mum? I'm getting cold. And I can't listen to any more stories about the new girl in the class.'

Julia tried to remember if Grace had mentioned this. She'd been so busy that week, sketching out plans for the next stage of her online gardening course. 'Is there a new girl?'

'Yes, Ava. Apparently Keira was asked to show her around, and she hasn't stopped talking about her.'

Julia turned to Adam. 'Can you go and round the girls up, then, and we'll make a move.'

Back home, once they had defrosted and dinner was on, Julia sat opposite Grace at the table, where she was concentrating on drawing a picture of herself and Keira on the swings. 'Is there a new girl in your class? Ava?'

Grace frowned. 'Yes. I don't like her.'

Julia had had a feeling that might be the case. 'Why's that?'

Grace continued to colour the picture. 'She wants to be Keira's friend.'

'Well, that's nice, isn't it?

Grace shook her head. 'It's not nice. Keira is *my* friend.'

When Grace was upset, Julia couldn't help but absorb her emotions like a sponge. Grace was a child who only had a small circle of friends, but where she loved, she loved deeply. From experience, Julia knew the pain that could bring and she wished that she could save her daughter from it. 'I know, sweetheart. But it's good to have lots of friends. Maybe you can be Ava's friend, too.'

Grace shook her head again and her bottom lip quivered. 'They want to be friends on their own. Ava wants Keira to go and play at her house.'

This was why Grace hadn't mentioned Ava. Instead, she had hidden the pain she felt at being excluded. Julia moved her chair closer to Grace's and put her arm around her. A tear splashed onto the page and blurred the crayon figures into one another. 'Keira will always be your friend, sweetheart. But you do need to share her with other people, too.'

Sometimes she wondered if being an only child was part of the problem. Grace had had Julia's complete attention her whole life; it was more than understandable that she didn't know how to share someone's love. Julia had desperately wanted another child but it just hadn't happened for them. And now that her marriage was hanging by a thread, it probably never would.

Grace pressed her face into Julia's shoulder. 'I just want to be Keira's best friend for ever and ever.'

Julia kissed the top of her head. 'I'm sure you will be, baby. I'm sure you will.'

FOURTEEN

SAMANTHA

Telling Adam had been unbearably hard. She and Nick had debated how best to do it. Video call, phone call, one of them, both? In the end, they had asked to use the relatives' room and Nick had FaceTimed him to check where he was and whether it was a good time to call. They didn't want to hit him with this if he was out with friends. He had to be at home, but ideally not alone.

They had obviously dragged him out of bed; he was shirtless and his hair pointed in about five different directions. Still, he grinned to see them and Samantha felt a pull on her heart in the knowledge that they were about to wipe that smile from his face.

'Blimey, Dad! FaceTime? Are you joining the rest of us in the twenty-first century?'

Nick was used to his son's teasing. 'Very funny. I'll have you know I was one of the first people in our area to have a mobile phone.'

Adam scratched behind his ear and yawned. 'Yeah, yeah, I know. And you had to carry the battery in a suitcase. Hey,

Mum. How's things? When are you sending me another food parcel?'

She'd got into the habit of sending him a box of treats every few weeks. All his favourites: her homemade granola, pineapple cake, ginger biscuits. The first time, he had laughed that she thought he was an Enid Blyton character at boarding school, but she knew he loved it. 'I'll send one up next week. Are you on your own, sweetheart?'

Adam rolled his eyes. 'Mum. We've talked about this. You said you didn't want to know about any of that.'

She had told him that. She knew that he was twenty now and was more than entitled to a sex life, but she didn't think his mother needed to know about it. 'That's not what I meant. It's better if... I don't want you to be alone.' She couldn't prevent her voice wavering and had to bite down hard on her lip to stop it from trembling. Nick reached for her hand out of sight of the screen and squeezed it.

Adam frowned, his tiredness evaporated. 'What do you mean? What's going on? Dad? What's happened?'

'It's okay, son. It's just that Keira has had... an accident. We're at the hospital and we didn't want you to hear about it from anyone else.'

Despite the usual sibling squabbles, Adam and Keira were close. Samantha knew that they sent text messages to each other, links to YouTube videos and incomprehensible memes. The concern on Adam's face was clear. She would have given anything to be able to reach into that screen and pull him home and into her arms. 'We don't want you to worry. She's going to be okay.'

Nick glanced at her. They'd promised not to lie to him and yet they both had. The parental instinct to protect is stronger that the truth.

Adam's expression was hard to read. 'What kind of accident? A car? Is it serious?'

Nick took a deep breath. He was going to be honest, and Samantha had to fight not to put her hand over his mouth. 'The thing is, son, she was attacked. There was a knife and—'

'Oh, no.' Adam's hand covered his face, which got paler as they watched. 'Where? How? What?'

'Slow down, mate. Take a deep breath.'

She knew they shouldn't have called him up like this. One of them should have gone to him. But damn social media had made it urgent and Durham was hours and hours away. She almost told him again that Keira was going to be okay, and then pressed her lips together. *No lies.*

She knew her son well enough to know that he was struggling not to cry when he spoke again. 'What actually happened? Was it someone she knew? Was it a random attack? A robbery?'

They didn't have the answers to any of those questions. As gently and briefly as possible, Nick explained that Keira had been stabbed in her side and that the knife had caught her liver. Her biggest issue had been the blood loss. Doctors were hopeful, but they were waiting for her to wake up.

Adam's face crumpled into tears. 'She's still unconscious? Oh, Dad. I have to come home. I need to be there.'

Samantha gave up trying to be calm and started to cry, too. 'Yes, darling, we'll get you home here. You mustn't drive yourself. Are you able to get the train? Or shall we sort out a taxi? Or a flight?' She could hear the desperation in her own voice. She would have mortgaged the house to get a rocket ship if it got him there quicker.

Nick put his arm around her shoulders, his voice calmly reassuring. 'I can book your train ticket if you want, son? Or you can get it and we'll pay for it.'

Adam used the heel of his hand to wipe his tears away. 'I can do it. She is going to be all right, isn't she?'

Nick nodded. 'We will keep you posted until you get here. Just be safe and take care.'

After they said their goodbyes, Nick stretched out his arms and held Samantha while she sobbed. All of Adam's questions had been the same as those whirling around her head. Did Keira know her attacker? Why had this happened?

They were on their way back to Keira's bedside when she heard Julia's voice. 'Samantha? Nick?'

There was her friend in the corridor. Samantha felt a rush of warmth at the sight of her: dependable, caring Julia. Her familiar face was grey and the imprint of raw concern was so strong that it started her crying all over again.

After accepting a hug from Julia, Nick left the two of them outside to talk while he returned to Keira. They sat beside each other on the row of hard plastic chairs in the waiting area; the overnight bag of clothes and toiletries that Julia had brought on the floor between them.

Though they weren't normally tactile, Julia was holding her hand, and her face couldn't have looked more concerned if it was her own daughter on the ward. 'How is she?'

Samantha wiped at her eyes with the perpetual tissue she had had since the night before. 'She's stable. That's all they keep saying. The operation to repair the internal wound was a success and she has no internal bleeding now, but she just lost so much blood.'

Julia closed her eyes for a second. Was she picturing the blood just as Samantha had done? Every time someone referred to it, that's all she could see. 'Is she awake?'

Samantha pressed her lips together and shook her head. 'Not yet. But her doctor said that's not necessarily a bad sign. Her body is healing.'

It was the 'not necessarily' that had frightened her, because of the implication that it could be a bad sign. The medical staff had been wonderful and they were keeping her regularly informed, but they weren't actually *telling* her anything. Nick had tried to gently explain that that was because they didn't know the answer to her only question. They couldn't tell them that Keira would definitely be okay. This had made her even more terrified.

Julia squeezed the hand that she was holding. 'Oh, Samantha. I don't know what to say. It's just so awful. I just can't believe that it's happened.'

Samantha couldn't believe it either; it was all so surreal. 'There's just so much I don't know. Not just about the... attack. About her life. She has a boyfriend and I didn't even know about it.'

Surprise had given way to hurt and confusion. She was the kind of mother that a daughter could speak to, wasn't she? What would stop Keira from telling her about this relationship? It wasn't as if she and Nick were Victorian parents who would forbid her to see him. Who was he? Had Keira been ashamed of him? Or of them?

As always, Julia was there with reassurance. 'That's the joy of teenagers. There's so much they don't tell us.'

Julia didn't need to explain what she meant. Samantha had watched, from the sidelines, the whole of last year with the bullying fallout.

When she'd first got to the hospital last night, the only person she had wanted with her was Nick. He was Keira's father, her husband and the only person who would feel the same way she was. He had been everything she'd needed since she'd found out about Keira, but it was only now, looking Julia in the face, that she could say aloud the guilt that was beginning to grow within her. 'I really thought I'd been a good mum.'

Julia looked surprised, but not shocked. 'You have been! You *are* a good mum. The best.'

Of course, she would say that. 'Then how come I didn't know about the boyfriend? How come she lied to me about being out with her friends? Why was she in the park on her own? Why didn't she call me to pick her up?'

As she spoke, Samantha thought again that maybe Keira hadn't been alone in the park. Maybe this boyfriend had been there too.

Julia was shaking her head. 'I don't know. I really don't know.'

'Has Grace said anything?' It was a long shot, but worth asking.

Julia looked up quickly. 'What do you mean?'

'About Keira? I know they don't see quite as much of each other, but they're still friends. Has she mentioned that Keira has a boyfriend?'

'Of course not. I would have told you.'

Was that true? Keira had said some things about Grace that Samantha hadn't passed on. But that was because she hadn't wanted to upset Julia. The events of last year had nearly broken her friend. At some point, Grace was going to need to learn to fight her own battles.

That was the thing: Keira *did* talk to her, all the time. Samantha had prided herself on the way they communicated. After her own experience of teenagerhood, she had been determined that her children would be free to say whatever they wanted. How had she got it so wrong?

With the phone call to Adam and now this conversation, she'd been away from Keira for over half an hour and she felt the pull to get back in and check on her. 'Would you like to come in and see her?'

Julia looked startled. She shuffled from one foot to the other. 'Isn't it supposed to be close family only, on a ward like this?'

'Maybe. But Keira is in a side room so we won't be bothering anyone. Anyway, we've known each other so long, you're close to being family.' She stood up, picking up the overnight bag. 'Come on.'

FIFTEEN

JULIA

The ward was quiet apart from the beeps of machines, the squeak of rubber-soled shoes and the quiet conversations of the nursing staff. Any moment, Julia was expecting someone to put a hand on her shoulder and tell her that she shouldn't be there, but one of the nurses nodded and smiled at Samantha as they walked past. It had been a long time since she had been in a hospital ward and she'd never been to an intensive care unit, so she wasn't sure what she was walking into. One thing she did know: sitting by Keira's bedside was the very last thing that she wanted to do right then.

Keira was in a side room which meant that they had more privacy than being on the ward. Nick was sitting beside his daughter, holding her hand. His six feet of height and broad shoulders made Keira look like a small child lying in the bed.

Keira. A few hours ago, Julia had burned with anger at the way she had treated Grace. In her head, she had painted her a villain. Now, with her face clear of make-up, eyes closed, she looked again the young girl who had splashed in the sea at Southwold, made cakes with Grace at the kitchen table, brought her bedraggled Ellie the elephant on a sleepover and tucked her in between the two of them in Grace's bed.

Nick turned as they came in, then stood up, still holding on to Keira's hand. 'All right, both of you? Are you staying for a little while, Julia? I just need to pop outside again for twenty minutes or so. It's supposed to be only two visitors to a bed, anyway, and I need to make some calls.'

Julia's throat was so dry, her voice was more of a croak. 'Of course. Yes. I'll be here.'

Like a tag team, Samantha took Keira's hand and Nick's seat. She nodded to the chair on the other side of the bed. 'You can sit down there, Julia.'

The chair she'd indicated was intimately close to the side of Keira's bed, so Julia pulled it away a little. Sat down. On the bed, Keira was so still. Without her animated expressions and hand gestures, she looked like a whole other person. Where was the essence of her right now? Hidden deep inside? Julia couldn't keep staring at her in silence, but what should she do?

Samantha helped her out. 'The doctor said that she might be able to hear us, so we've been talking to her like normal. Just about our day and stuff.'

That must be difficult when their day had been spent staring at their daughter. Still. Julia had to give it a try. 'Hi, Keira. It's Julia. I've come to visit.'

That sounded utterly stupid, but Samantha nodded encouragement to keep going. 'Hearing someone else's voice might help. Keira always loved listening to you, hanging out with you. You were much more fun than me.'

Julia felt her face flush at that. It was true that she'd always got on well with Keira. Keira was adventurous, where Samantha was hesitant. It had always been Julia who accompanied the girls on roller coasters, or swam in the sea with them. Samantha would be the one who laid out the blankets, remembered the towels and the good snacks. They used to joke that it was like a 1950s marriage. Without the obligatory missionary position.

Julia cleared her throat and tried again. 'Grace has been talking about you. We're both hoping you wake up soon so that we can talk to you.' This was true at least. Once Keira woke up and told them what had happened, Julia would be absolved of the weight of whether to speak to the police.

Last night, keeping quiet about Grace's presence at the park had seemed easier: her anger with Keira for allowing Grace to be treated like a leper had made Julia feel less charitable towards her. Now, looking at all the tubes going in and out of her, listening to the hiss of the oxygen machine, those feelings of resentment were dissolving. Who had done this to her?

Samantha was watching Keira's face, as if waiting for any sign of a response. It wasn't surprising that her own face was pinched and tired, but there was something else unfamiliar about her. It took a while for Julia to realise what it was: it was the first time in years that she'd seen Samantha without any make-up. It gave her a vulnerability that made Julia want to reach out and squeeze her. Instead, she focused on Keira. 'I've been thinking that we should book another holiday together. You and your mum, me and Grace. It'll be much more fun now you're older. For a start, your mum and I won't have to sit in the hotel bathroom drinking tea and biscuits and whispering while you and Grace are asleep in the double bed.'

She was rewarded with a smile and a crinkling of the eyes from Samantha. 'That feels like a lifetime ago. Taking it in turns to be the one who had to sit in the bath. These days, I reckon it'd be the two of them staying up and the two of us crashed out in the bed.'

'I think you might be right. Although at least now they're older and need less looking after, we can swap the tea for a glass or two of wine.'

Less looking after. If she could have stuffed those words back in her mouth, she would have done. With one daughter in a hospital bed and the other a virtual recluse, her words couldn't have been more tactless if she'd tried. Better to change the subject. 'Have the police told you anything more?'

Samantha shook her head. 'Not really. There's no weapon, so no fingerprints. They are searching the area. They have her mobile phone, so they've been searching through that. Messages. Instagram. That kind of thing.'

Julia hated social media with a passion. She'd deleted her own Facebook account years back when John's new girlfriend had started posting pictures of their wonderful life together. Deleting John hadn't helped. Every time the happy couple met up with friends who she also knew, his girlfriend – now wife – would tag everyone in a five-mile radius. Somehow, every loved-up picture of them had seemed to make its way onto Julia's feed.

Silence settled on them for few moments. Julia tried not to look at Keira's face. It was too hard.

'Do you remember' – Samantha's voice broke the silence – 'that time we took them to that children's petting farm and we almost lost them?'

'As if I could forget; it was terrifying.' When she remembered that day, Julia could still feel the panic. 'We were running around like lunatics, screaming their names.'

'And then we found them on the swings around the corner, calm as you like.'

'Grace wanted to know what I was shouting for and Keira was more concerned about what we'd done with the ice cream we promised. Their love for an ice-cream cone has bonded the two of them since they first met, hasn't it?'

It was stupid to think that this might make Samantha smile. Instead, her face crumpled as she reached out to stroke her daughter's cheek with the back of her finger. 'Oh, Julia. If she doesn't wake up, if we don't get her back, I couldn't bear it. She's my life.'

'She's going to be okay, Samantha. I know she is. Haven't you always talked about how strong-willed she's always been? Even as a tiny toddler. You said that she refused to wear matching shoes for about two months, do you remember? A red shoe on one foot and a blue on the other?'

Samantha gave a watery smile. 'Yes. Sometimes it would be a pink fluffy slipper and a yellow wellington boot. I was mortified because people kept pointing it out and thinking I'd made a mistake.'

Julia remembered Samantha's exasperation when her daughter refused to wear the beautiful coordinated outfits she'd chosen for her. 'There you go, then. Can you see that spirit doing anything other than fighting to come back to you?'

This time the smile was a little bigger, the eyes grateful. 'Thank you. For being here. For being a friend. It really does help to have you here.'

It had been a long time since Samantha had spoken to her like this. Wanted her there. Called her a friend. A warmth spread through Julia's chest before her brain caught up with her heart and guilt twisted her stomach. For a moment, she'd forgotten her deceit; the instinct to comfort had taken over. Samantha's eyes were so warm, so open: how could she look into them, knowing what she was keeping from her? It was awful. 'Look, why don't you and Nick go and grab a coffee together or something? I can stay with Keira till you get back. I'll keep up the chatter and I'll call you if she so much as moves an eyelash, I promise.'

She saw the indecision cross Samantha's face, the familiar maternal pull. The certainty that you are the only person who can properly watch your child. She was surprised when Samantha agreed.

'Actually, that would be great. I'm not sure what this phone call of Nick's is all about but he's been acting strangely about it. We can't really talk in here. It's so quiet, even with the door closed it feels as if everyone can hear what you say. Are you sure you're okay to stay here for a while? I really won't be long.'

It would be a relief not to have to look in Samantha's eyes. Not to hear what a great friend she thought Julia was. When she knew that she wasn't. 'Of course. Go. Go.'

Even now she was standing up, Samantha was wavering. 'Are you sure? I mean... will you talk to her, and will you hold her hand?'

Julia picked up Keira's hand. 'It'll be easier for me to talk when you're not here.'

Samantha looked relieved. 'Okay. I won't be long.'

After she'd gone, Julia shifted her chair closer to the head of the bed. She'd promised Samantha that she would keep chatting, and she intended to. Did it matter what she said? Could Keira hear her? She leaned forwards. 'We really need you to wake up, Keira, love. Grace is in a pickle and I don't know what to do to help. I know you haven't been close lately, but you were friends once. I know that you wouldn't want to hurt her and she wouldn't want to hurt you. Wake up and we'll get it all sorted out.'

There was so much more she wanted to ask. *What happened, Keira? Who were you with? And what did Grace actually see?*

Grace wasn't telling her, and Keira – poor, beautiful girl – couldn't. The only other people who might have some idea were Keira's other friends. Julia didn't know – or want to know – any of them, but she would be working in one of their mothers' gardens tomorrow. Constance Fielding, the queen of the St Anne's mums' court, had commissioned Julia to design and project-manage the landscaping of her garden over a month ago. After that, she'd insisted Julia do a weekly manicure of the raised beds – offering double pay when Julia had tried to refuse – during which time she had barely spoken to her.

Ordinarily, this was fine by Julia. Unlike Samantha, she had absolutely no interest in being adopted into their privileged coven. Tomorrow, though, she was going to have to push outside her comfort zone and firmly into theirs. Not for her sake. For Grace's.

SIXTEEN

WHEN THEY WERE TEN

Southcliff beach wasn't the prettiest of places, but Julia liked to close her eyes and listen to the sea lapping the shoreline. Only fifteen minutes from the girls' primary school, it had become something of a ritual to take them there for an hour on a Friday, as long as Keira didn't have one of her many after-school activities.

Julia took a deep breath of the cold, salty air. 'I think I prefer the beach in the winter, when there are fewer people here.'

Samantha pulled her jacket tighter. 'Me, too. Although I could do without that breeze today.'

Grace and Keira didn't seem to care, though. Both of them had taken off their socks and rolled up their jeans and were sticking their toes in the water, screaming if the water dared to splash their ankles.

At ten, they were no longer little girls. The top of Grace's head grazed the underside of Julia's chin, and Keira was half an inch taller. They were losing the softness of girlhood, too. Their faces more angular, their legs longer. Puberty threatened to claim them any day now.

Watching them together made the conversation they were about to have even harder. 'How are we going to tell them?

Samantha shook her head. 'No idea. They are going to be so upset.'

Both of them had visited all the secondary schools in the local area before completing the application form, even though Samantha had been set on St Anne's from the beginning. It was a lovely school. All girls. Very academic, but with a wide range of extra-curricular pursuits. When Julia had told the admissions office her postcode, he had shaken his head. 'You're welcome to apply, but we have a very small catchment area and we've never had anyone admitted as far away as your street.'

She had tried to explain this to Grace, but she didn't want to hear it. 'Just apply anyway. I want to go there.'

Sometimes as a parent, you had to do the hard thing. Julia wasn't totally sure how the application system worked, but she didn't want to risk a place at the best school in their catchment – The Grange – by putting St Anne's as their first choice. That meant that she'd known since last October that the girls weren't going to the same school. The emails she and Samantha had received that morning just confirmed it.

Down at the water's edge, Grace's hair was blowing in her face and Julia watched as she tried to plait it to keep it out of the way. Keira put down the shoes she was holding to help her. How much longer would they have of this unselfconscious fun? How long before they changed into the anxieties and uncertainties of early womanhood; conscious of their bodies, their looks, their effect on other people?

Julia took out her phone to take a picture. 'These are the ordinary moments I'm going to miss when she's older.'

It felt like a blink ago that the two of them had been starting school, and now they were about to embark on the next stage. The years were slipping away like sand through her fingers.

Samantha reached into her large bag and pulled out a

small towel. She was always better prepared than Julia. 'I know what you mean.' She shook out the towel, waiting for the girls' return. 'I keep meaning to ask you, how is the gardening course going? You must be over halfway through?'

Julia was embarrassed to admit that the course had got too much for her. This was now the third time she'd started an online course and then let it lapse. It wasn't that it was difficult; it was just finding the time. She'd planned to do it in the evenings, but she was just so tired lately. 'I've given it up. Well, postponed it. I'll try again when Grace is older and doesn't need me so much.'

'Oh, Julia. I thought that you had a plan to actually be a gardener rather than talking about it. Do you want to be a bank clerk your whole life?'

That stung. She kept her eyes away from Samantha's judgement. It was easy to make comments like that if you had a rich husband to indulge your every whim. 'I've had a lot on. With John.'

'Things are still not good?'

Julia looked down at the sand again, digging her fingers into it, the cold wet grains pushing under her fingernails. 'He's moving out.'

Samantha paused her repacking of the beach bag. 'Really? That sounds pretty final. When?'

'I don't know. He wants to go now. But I'm trying to work out when would have the least impact on Grace. With her starting a new school this year, it feels like too much change. John doesn't really get that. He says it'll be hard for her whenever we do it, so we just need to get on with it. He's barely home, anyway.' She paused and shook her hand free of wet sand. 'He's met someone else.'

It had been a long time coming. She and John had been growing apart for years. They couldn't even be bothered to argue anymore. Julia was sadder for Grace than she was for herself. For her, his moving out would actually be a relief.

Samantha tilted her head to one side. 'I was about Grace's age when my parents divorced.'

From a wine-fuelled heart-to-heart the year they'd spent Christmas together, Julia knew that Samantha had a pretty complicated relationship with her parents, both of whom had remarried quite quickly after their divorce. 'Do you have any tips to make it easier?'

Samantha laughed. 'I can tell you how to not make it impossibly difficult. Is that the same thing?'

Julia's stomach squeezed. She really didn't want this to be harder for Grace than it had to be. Although, how could it not be awful? 'I'll take whatever you've got.'

'Well, like Grace, I was an only child when my parents were still together. Maybe that's why I have such a soft spot for her. I remember what it was like to be an only one. I know some children are perfectly happy like that.' She nodded towards the two girls who were now crouching down, collecting 'pretty pebbles' for the burgeoning collections on their bedroom shelves. 'Especially if you find yourself a good friend.'

'I thought you'd mentioned a sister?' Julia also had a memory of a passing reference to a brother who lived abroad, but maybe she'd imagined it.

'Yes, I have two sisters and a brother. Half siblings, technically. My mum left my dad for someone else and took me with her. A new house. A new school. And then a new family – she had my sister about a year after we'd moved. She was the apple of her father's eye.' Samantha's face made it clear what she meant by that. Even though the spring sunshine was no longer bright, she flicked her sunglasses down from the top of her head so that they covered her eyes. 'And then my dad met someone and had a boy and girl. Twins. Pretty much the perfect family. Apart from when the older half sister came to stay and messed it all up, of course. When the twins were babies, it wasn't so bad because they shared a room. But as soon as they were old enough to have their own rooms, I had to sleep on a mattress on the floor of my sister's room.'

Julia wanted to say something comforting, but was prevented by Keira shouting up the beach at them. 'Is it time for hot chocolate yet, Mum?'

Samantha put her hands to either side of her mouth like a loudhailer. 'Good idea! Let's go!' She turned towards Julia and lowered her voice. 'Might as well sweeten them up first.'

The plan was always to tell the girls separately that they would be going to different schools at the end of the year, but they hadn't factored in that some of their school friends would already know. Once they were seated in the warm cafe, both girls sitting behind large hot chocolates, surprised that they were allowed both cream and marshmallows this close to dinnertime, Grace was the first to ask the question. 'Did you get the school email? Are we going to St Anne's?'

Julia swallowed. She'd already lied once. 'No. I'll check when we get home.'

Two set of eyes swivelled to Samantha, who corroborated the story. 'Yes. Me, too.'

Keira shrugged as she licked the cream from the long spoon. 'Well, you can look it up now. On your phone. Everyone else at school knows already. Their mums looked it up this morning.'

Damn. They'd been stupid not to think that the whole year group would be buzzing with this today. This was definitely not the time or place for breaking their hearts. 'There's no rush, is there? Why don't you finish your hot chocolates and then we can go home and find out.'

Grace frowned. 'What's going on, Mum? We did get in to St Anne's, didn't we?' She reached out for Keira's hand. They were both staring at her, fear on their faces. There was nothing else left but to tell them the truth.

'Grace, honey. You know that we aren't in catchment and it was always going to be a long shot that you would—'

She was cut off by a howl from her daughter, followed by an explosion of tears.

It took them another five minutes to get Grace to calm down; she was absolutely devastated. Keira's protest was more belligerent than emotional. Once Samantha confirmed that she did have a place at her chosen school, she crossed her arms. 'Well, if Grace isn't going to St Anne's, neither am I. I'll go to The Grange, too.'

Samantha's voice was uncharacteristically stern. 'No, you will not.'

Julia hoped that Samantha's tone was more about Keira's attitude, than judgement on the school she'd chosen for Grace. 'It won't make any difference. You will still be friends. You'll still see each other.'

She moved her chair closer so that she could put her arms around Grace, but her daughter shrugged her off. 'It's not fair. You're pulling us apart. We're best friends.'

'This doesn't stop you being friends.' Samantha reached across to take Keira's hand and smiled at Grace. 'You can see each other outside school whenever you want.'

Keira had a face like thunder. 'It's not the same. School lasts for hours.'

Grace nodded. 'And Keira has to do her piano lessons and her tutoring and horse riding. That doesn't leave any time.'

Samantha reached out for Grace's hand too. 'We'll have weekends. You are always welcome at our house.'

After Samantha's insight into her own childhood, this kindness was even more meaningful. 'And Keira, love, you are always welcome to ours.'

'Anyway.' Samantha picked up the tiny biscuit on the

saucer of her coffee cup. 'Your mum is going to start her gardening business soon and I will be her first customer. So that's another reason we'll have to stay in touch.'

She looked at Julia with a raised eyebrow. She was right. It was time to go back to the course and get it finished. With John out of the way, there was no reason not to pursue her dream. As long as it didn't affect Grace, of course.

SEVENTEEN

SAMANTHA

Outside the ward, in the echoing corridor, three plastic chairs had their backs against the wall, ready to catch grieving family members. In the middle seat, Nick was leaning forwards with his head in his hands. He hadn't heard her push through the doors to leave the ward and it squeezed at Samantha to see him so vulnerable. She'd taken his solid support for granted since last night: Keira was his daughter too. She took the seat to his right and placed a hand on his back. 'Hey. How are you doing?'

He took a moment to sit up, and she had the distinct impression that he needed the time to rearrange his expression. She knew he was trying to be strong for the two of them. But he didn't need to be. He leaned towards her and pressed his warm lips to her cheek before replying. 'Same as you, I guess. Scared.' He waved his phone. 'Adam just sent me a text. He's checked the trains and the combination of Sunday services and engineering works are making his journey impossible. I've forbidden him to drive himself down, so he'll be on the first train out of Durham in the morning.'

Tomorrow? She wanted to see him as soon as possible. 'Why don't we just pay for a taxi?'

Nick raised an eyebrow. 'From three hundred miles away? That would cost an absolute fortune. No, he's happy to get the train tomorrow and it'll give him time to pack a bag and email his tutors to explain.'

It wasn't like Nick to quibble about spending money, but she wasn't about to start changing the plan if it was easier for Adam this way. He would be with them by tomorrow, and at least he wasn't driving himself while upset. Even so, the whole time he would be en route tomorrow, it gave her another thing to worry about. 'Can you switch on that thing on your phone, so that we know where he is? The one we used to use when he was at home?' She didn't add that it was the same app they used for Keira. Keira hated it – the fact that they could see where she was at all times. Not that it had done any good. Even if they had checked it, how would they have known that the park would have been so unsafe for her at eight o'clock at night?

Nick smiled. 'Adam is one step ahead of you. He's told me he'll send me a location link so we can follow his journey. He knows what his mother is like.'

That didn't surprise her. Adam had always been such a thoughtful boy, so understanding that she would worry about him when he was out at night. He hadn't given them much to worry about, though. He was so focused on his studies, and the few friends he had were good, sensible boys – just as happy with a quiet beer in the summerhouse at the bottom of the garden as they were with a night at the pub.

That was why parenting Keira had been such a surprise. The polar opposite of Adam, she was always pushing boundaries, wanting to walk herself to school, to camp out with her friends, to get the train to London. Whatever Samantha and Nick agreed to, the next week it was something else. Samantha had always been relieved that at least she had a nice group of friends. Or so she had thought. 'You said that Adam sent you a text? So it wasn't him on the phone?'

Nick shook his head. She had known him long enough to be able to tell when he was keeping something from her. He obviously thought he was better at hiding it than he was. 'It was nothing important. Just work.'

That irritated her. 'Work' already got so much of him. There were so many birthdays and events he had missed because he was flying off somewhere or coming back from someplace else. Surely someone in the office could cover his job while his daughter was unconscious in hospital? She tried to keep her voice calmer than she felt. 'Do you really need to speak to them now? Can't Adrian field your calls?'

'Adrian doesn't work for the company any longer.'

'What?' Adrian had worked with Nick for about six years. They'd been promoted at the same time, and their friendly rivalry at work spilled over onto the squash court and tall tales that they both liked to tell at the barbecues and meals out that she and Nick had had with Adrian and his wife, Amanda. Why hadn't Nick mentioned he was leaving?

Nick seemed to come to some sort of decision. He took a deep breath and turned to her. 'The thing is, love... I won't be working for that company much longer, either.'

Now her head was spinning. She had no clue what he was talking about. 'Have you just been fired?'

'Made redundant. There will be six months' money and a nice handshake. But, yes, I've lost my job.'

'What, now? Just now? They called you in the hospital to tell you that they were making you redundant? Do they not know what we're going through right now?' She knew that her voice was getting louder and louder but she didn't care. Nick worked hard. He had sacrificed a lot for that firm. Yes, they paid well, but they got their pound of flesh for it. How dare they treat him like this?

It wasn't until he put his hand on her arm that she realised that her whole body was shaking. 'Hey, love. Calm down, it's okay. It's going to be okay.'

As always, her first flush of anger gave way to tears. 'It's just not fair. And it's wrong. To tell you that now.'

Nick sighed. 'They didn't tell me now. I found out a month ago. That was an agency on the phone. About another job. Obviously they didn't know about Keira.'

A month ago? He had known for a month that he had lost his job and he hadn't told her? This time she was actually speechless; she opened her mouth, but nothing came out.

'I know I should have told you and I'm sorry. It's just that I know how much you hate change and upheaval. I was hoping that I would be able to find another job quickly and then I could present it to you as a done deal. Lost one, won one.' He held out his hands, palms up, and moved them up and down like a balancing scale, trying to lighten the effect of his announcement.

It wasn't working. 'I can't believe you lied to me! All this time, I've thought you've been going off to work, and there wasn't even a job.'

He held up a hand. 'I didn't lie. I have been going to work. Ordinarily, we'd have been put on gardening leave immediately, but they wanted Adrian and me to finish the project we've been working on. They know us. They trust that we're professional and will get it done.'

Well, she was mightily glad that his company knew him, because she was finding it hard to trust that she did right now. 'I still can't believe you kept this from me.'

Although, deep down, she knew why he had. They had met when she was nineteen. Nick had graduated from university the year before, and she was interning at a fashion house after her A levels. He had made a comment about the colour of her boots and she had mocked the 'squareness' of his pinstriped shirt. He had asked her out and she had said yes, and they had fallen in love faster than she had believed possible.

He knew that she'd had unhappy teenage years. After her parents' acrimonious divorce when she was ten, she had spent the next eight years living between two houses, two families. Seeing new half siblings arrive. Whichever house she was in, there was a step-parent for whom she was second best. Not their child. And she had felt it. That was why, when she met Nick, she was living on the floor of her friend's flat. And also why, when they got together, she told him in hesitant, hushed conversation late at night, that she dreamed of a house and a husband that was hers. Of children who would feel safe and loved and secure. And never second best.

Nick must have been thinking the same thing. 'You know why. I just didn't want you to be scared.'

But she *was* scared. Their house was lovely, but she wasn't naïve about the size of the mortgage payments required to keep them in it. 'Do you think you'll find another job?'

'I'm sure it will be fine. But we don't need to worry about that right now. All we need to worry about is Keira. When she wakes up, she needs us both focused on her.'

Nick stood and held out both hands to pull her up. But she felt as if he had actually just pulled the ground from under her feet. If Nick could have hidden something as huge as losing his job and she hadn't noticed, what could Keira have been hiding from them? Could she trust no one in her life?

She thought of Julia. Good, dependable Julia, sitting with Keira. They might not have spent much time together lately, but at least she could trust her.

EIGHTEEN

JULIA

On Monday morning, Grace refused to go to school.

With the covers pulled over her, she had turned to face the wall. The smiling faces of her music posters looked down on Julia as if to mock her feeble attempts at parenting. 'Come on, Grace. You can't stay home.'

From beneath the covers, Grace's voice was muffled, but no less determined. 'I don't want to go. They hate me there. Everyone hates me. I'm not going back.'

How could they be going through all of this again? When Grace had still been at The Grange, there had been days and days like this. Every morning had been a battle to get her dressed and out of the door. Julia always felt as if she'd done a day's work before she even got into her van in the morning.

This morning, there was no energy left in Julia to fight. 'Okay. You can stay home, but you need to do some revision. And I have to go to work.'

In the circumstances, she would have cancelled any appointments for the day, but she was hoping that her booking with Constance Fielding was going to yield more than the twenty pounds an hour she was paid to pick leaves out from her bedding plants.

Constance Fielding was always well mannered. There was nothing Julia could put her finger on to criticise the way Constance spoke to her, but there was a just a tone, or an expression, or a... *something* that made her feel as if Constance was looking down on her from a great height. How Samantha could tolerate spending time with her, Julia would never understand.

The first time Julia had been there to tidy the raised beds, Constance had – after a polite offer of a cup of tea or coffee – left her to her own devices. The garden was huge: a vast green lawn. She'd wanted, she told Julia, with a vague wave of her manicured hand, a bit more character to it. Julia had drawn up some plans with various zones and plants of different heights and widths and colours. The art was choosing plants that would flower at different times – keeping the garden full of life as long as possible.

She had enjoyed working on the garden alone, without interruption. Aside from aphids and caterpillars, there was nothing worse than a client who hovered around you as you worked, asking the names of plants, of tools, of methods.

Today was different. On the way over, she had tried to come up with a reason as to why she would need Constance's presence. To show her something new that was starting to poke through the soil, maybe. Or to explain that the wisteria would need some aggressive cutting back. The next problem would be how to get from conversations about plants to people and, more explicitly, what Constance's daughter knew about Keira and her movements.

In the event, she didn't need to engineer anything. Although she didn't look particularly interested in Julia's planting techniques, Constance was definitely hovering. 'It's just so terrible, what's happened to poor Keira. Everyone is in shock.'

Julia nodded as she made a hole in the soil with the handle of her trowel. 'I know. It's awful. Poor Samantha. It's so hard on her.'

'Have you spoken to Samantha, then?' Constance frowned, clearly surprised that Samantha would lower her standards so far as to be friends with Julia. *Charming woman.*

'I was there when she got the call. And I saw her at the hospital yesterday. Briefly.' That last was added as an afterthought and not strictly true, but Julia wanted to be the one finding things out, not gossiping about Samantha.

Constance took a step closer, pushing her sunglasses onto the top of her head. 'Really? I wondered about going to the hospital to take some flowers, but I wasn't sure whether I'd be getting in the way.'

The last thing Samantha needed was the Mothers' Mafia turning up. 'Probably best to leave it. You can't have flowers on the intensive care ward, anyway.'

'I'll have some sent to the house for Samantha, then. When is she coming home?'

'I assume she'll be there as long as Keira is.' She would need to come home at some point, though. Julia wasn't sure how long they let relatives stay overnight at the hospital. Surely it was only when the patient was in immediate danger? And Keira was going to be okay, wasn't she?

'How long do they think Keira will be in? I mean, is she conscious?'

Julia felt a nasty rash of discomfort at the turn this conversation was taking. Constance was clearly pumping her for information. 'It's not really my place to—'

'Oh, no, of course not.' Constance took a step back. 'I wasn't trying to pry, it's just that we're all so worried. Cleo is beside herself. They are such close friends. It's hard to know what to tell her.'

Julia wondered if Cleo, Constance's daughter, was one of the nasty pieces of work making Grace's life a misery. 'I'm sure it's a shock for all of them.'

Constance picked up a ball of gardening twine and began twisting the end with a manicured finger and thumb. 'In some ways. Although it was always likely to happen. You must see how much freedom the girl has? Cleo said she's been spending time with some proper wrong 'uns.'

If Julia hadn't been so irritated by her judgemental comments, she would have laughed at Constance's slip into the Estuary English that had been her mother tongue before she'd married a City boy and reinvented herself as the local aristocracy.

She wanted to defend Keira, but with Grace's recent revelations in mind, and the need to find out what she could about Keira's movements, her curiosity overpowered her loyalty. 'Really? Like who?'

Constance clearly took this as a signal that she could speak openly. She pulled a garden chair over to where Julia was working. 'Well, apparently she's been seeing a boy from another school. He might even be at the *college*, but I'm not sure.' She said the word 'college' like it was a home for juvenile delinquents.

The information about the boyfriend might be useful, especially given Samantha hadn't known there even *was* a boyfriend, but Julia didn't want to fuel any falsehood fires. 'Really?'

Now Constance was leaning off the edge of the seat, her eagerness to gossip no longer hidden. 'Cleo says that he's quite rough.'

Cleo wants to shut her mouth. What was it with these girls who were supposed to be Keira's closest friends? And their mothers, who were supposed to be Samantha's? Julia had never been comfortable at the school gate and had been relieved once Grace was old enough to take herself to school. It wasn't that she didn't like female company, but there was something about a group of women with children the same age that made her feel like she was lacking in some fundamental way.

Samantha, on the other hand, was the most well-connected woman she knew. PTA, school governor, fundraising committees: she had done it all. She knew everyone at the school and everyone knew her. She slid through social situations like a warm knife through butter; she was popular with everyone. Or so Julia had assumed, from a distance.

Constance was back to twisting the gardening twine. 'Samantha is very relaxed as a parent, isn't she? I've always wished I could have her ability to not stress out about it all.'

Constance's tone of voice made it clear that she wasn't really paying Samantha a compliment. Julia kept focusing on the planting. 'Hmm.'

Constance clearly took that as agreement. 'You've got a teenage daughter, too. You need to be on it with them, don't you? Give them an inch, and all that. They need to know where the boundaries are.'

Constance could learn a thing or two about boundaries herself. Was she really judging Samantha's parenting in the middle of all this? 'It's easier said than done, isn't it?'

'Well, of course. I'm just saying that this will be a short, sharp shock to a lot of parents around here. Those that let their kids just run wild.'

Just once, Julia wished she had the guts to tell this woman in no uncertain terms what she thought about her sweeping judgement of 'some parents'. She was sick of people who thought they'd written the book on successful parenting. Particularly when they were women like this, who didn't have to worry about juggling a job and a child. Or about where the next mortgage payment was going to come from. Or about finding the time to clean the house and cook the dinner and help with homework in the two free hours they had each night.

But she wasn't that person. 'They're all growing up, aren't they? I guess we have to loosen the reins a little and see how they cope.'

Constance raised an eyebrow. 'There's loosening the reins, and then there's opening the door of the stable completely.'

Julia couldn't listen to this any longer. She'd wanted to find out where Keira might have been going that night, and instead she'd got pulled into the murky waters of playground politics. 'I've left some tools in the van. I'll be back in a moment.'

Before collecting the 'forgotten' tools that she didn't need, Julia sat in the front seat of her van and took a few breaths. This was all getting to be too much to hold inside. She pulled out her phone and checked it. How much longer could she leave it before calling the police?

There were no messages from Samantha, and she could only hope that no news was good news. If Constance had seen Keira lying on that hospital bed, would she have been so quick to judge? Life was fragile, and none more so than that of a child. Fifteen-year-old girls might look like the adults they emulated, but they were still children. They still needed help in the choices they made.

Like the choices Grace was making?

She fired off a text – *All okay?* – then sat and waited for Grace to reply. Hopefully, Constance would get bored waiting for Julia to return and call a friend to dissect the blame with, instead. She only had about an hour's work to do today anyway; the rest could wait.

Grace's reply was short.

I'm fine.

But it was accompanied by a picture of her holding up a packet of her favourite chocolate biscuits. At least Julia knew she was safe at home.

Before she could talk herself out of it, she sent another text.

Hi John, it's me. Can you let me know when you have time to chat? I need to speak to you about something.

When Julia got home, Grace was listening to that depressing music which usually signalled that she was best left alone. But as soon as the front door opened, she appeared in the small hallway. 'Hi, Mum.'

'Hi, love. How are you feeling?'

If anything, Grace's face was greyer than it had been the night before. She shrugged. 'Have you heard anything from Samantha? Everyone is saying that Keira is in a coma. Why hasn't she woken up yet?'

Julia struggled into the kitchen with the bag of groceries she'd picked up on the way home, set them down on the table and sank down onto one of the kitchen chairs. 'I don't know, love. I guess it just takes time. I'm sure she's going to be fine.'

She knew nothing of the sort and Grace would know that, too. This wasn't like the times Grace would break a toy as a child and give it to John to 'Daddy Fix', or when she would graze her knee and Julia would ease the pain with a cold compress and kisses. Neither of them knew what Keira's prognosis was, however much they tried to cling to a positive outcome.

Grace crossed to the kitchen counter and picked up the kettle. 'Would you like tea?'

She was so thoughtful, so kind. How had they come to this? 'Yes, please, love. Then I'd like to talk to you about something.'

Julia could see Grace freeze, even though she was at the sink filling the kettle. She turned off the tap. 'What?'

'I've been thinking today, while I was working. We don't have a choice, love. We *have* go to the police and tell them that you were the one who found Keira.'

Grace's head snapped around. 'No.'

'Just listen to me a minute. Apparently, Keira had a boyfriend. A bad sort. She hadn't been spending much time with her friends. I'm not sure the police have a lot to go on, and it might help if you can tell them any little thing that you remember.'

As she was speaking, Grace's eyes had grown wider and wider. Now, her whole body was trembling, her voice barely above a whisper. 'No, Mum. Please don't make me do that. You don't understand.'

That phrase usually infuriated Julia, implying, as it did, that she was never young, had never experienced anything in life. Now it just made her heart ache. 'I do, love. But this might be so important. Do you know who this boy might be? Samantha seems to think he's not from the school. Have you seen Keira with anyone?'

Grace looked as if she was about to be sick. 'No. There was no boy there. It wasn't a boy who did it.'

Julia's heart thumped loudly in her chest. 'What do you mean, it wasn't a boy? How do you know that?'

Grace screwed her eyes shut, scratching at her pale, thin wrists. When she opened them again, Julia couldn't read what was in them. 'I know that it wasn't a boy who stabbed Keira. Because I was right there when it happened.'

NINETEEN

WHEN THEY WERE TWELVE

Full of vibrant colour and lush green leaves, Samantha's long back garden looked incredible. Julia was wandering around, plucking up any petals that had dared to fall to the ground, when Samantha made her jump by laughing just behind her. 'Do you want me to bring out my vacuum cleaner?'

Julia crumpled the offending petal in her hand and laughed too. 'No. I'll stop now. I just want everything to be perfect.'

It had been very kind of Samantha to suggest this: a garden party where Julia could show off her gardening skills to all of Samantha's new St Anne's friends in the hope of securing some business. For the last year, she had been working as a gardener on her two days off and at the weekends, but now she wanted to hand in her notice at the bank and to do that, she would need more clients. 'Thanks again for this, Samantha. I really do appreciate it.'

Nina had pulled a face when Julia had gushed to her about Samantha's generosity. 'She just wants an excuse to show off to her new rich friends. I'm assuming she's never bothered to introduce you to any of them before?'

There was no reason for Julia to have met them; they were

the mothers of Keira's school friends. Julia and Grace were outside that group.

Now, Samantha waved away her thanks. 'It's my pleasure. I'm just going to pop back inside and check on the caterers. Are the girls upstairs?'

'Yes. I think Keira wanted to show Grace her new coat.'

Samantha rolled her eyes. 'She managed to wangle that one out of her father. A Valentino coat for a twelve-year-old. Ridiculous.'

Julia had no idea how much a Valentino coat would cost, but she would imagine it was a lot more than she could afford. The last couple of times the girls had got together, Grace had come home wide-eyed with stories about Keira's new friends and the places they went on holiday, or the restaurants they ate in with their parents, or the fact that at least two of them owned their own horse.

A minute after Samantha returned to the kitchen, Nick appeared out of the back door, carrying two glasses of something bubbly. 'Samantha has sent me out with one of these for you, and I have strict instructions to stop you from ironing the lawn.'

Julia grinned. She liked Nick. He wasn't there that often, but when he was, he always made a point of being kind to her and – more importantly – to Grace. She held up her hands in mock surrender. 'I'm not touching another thing. I promise.'

After handing her one of the glasses, Nick stood sipping the other and looking around the garden. 'You've done a fantastic job, Julia. You really have.'

John always used to complain that Julia couldn't take a compliment, but she was happy to accept it today. She had worked so hard there over the last couple of months and had spent hours researching at home for the perfect combination of shrubs and flowers. Nick was right; she had done a fantastic job. 'Thank you. Let's hope all your friends think the same.'

Nick looked down into his glass. 'Ah. I don't think I can call them friends; I hardly know them. More Samantha's department, really, school mums. Although I think I'm about to be dragged to a dinner party in the near future.' He sipped his drink, then looked at her. 'I'm glad Keira and Grace have stayed friends. It's good for Keira to have someone like Grace in her life.'

What exactly did he mean by 'someone like Grace'? Julia didn't get the chance to ask as, just then, Samantha swept through the French doors into the garden with four other people. 'Come through! Come through! Nick – come and meet Constance and Jeremy. They're Cleo's parents.'

Before striding over to his wife, Nick winked at Julia. 'Your prospective clients have arrived.'

Julia had been anxious about this party since Samantha had first conceived it, but before long she was actually really enjoying herself. Her initial awkwardness fell away as she spoke to people about her course and her passion for plants, and explained the layout of the garden they were standing in. She was grateful for Nick's suggestion a couple of weeks ago that she get some professional leaflets printed. She had already given out over half of the pile she'd brought.

When there was a lull in the conversation, she excused herself to go the downstairs bathroom. Even though nerves meant she'd only drunk that first glass of Prosecco that Nick had brought, she'd been shuffling from foot to foot for the last five minutes, needing to empty her nervous bladder.

The downstairs toilet was at the back of the house and the fanlight at the top of the window was open, so she could still hear the music that Nick had rigged up to play in the garden. While she was washing her hands, a couple of shadows walked past the frosted glass and a shrill voice carried into the bathroom.

'The garden looks simply fabulous, Samantha. Really gorgeous.'

It was wrong to eavesdrop, but compliments like this were making Julia believe that she was actually going to be able to make a proper career out of this. She took longer than was strictly necessary to wash her hands as she listened.

'So, how did you find her? I've been trying to get a decent gardener for months. Was she a recommendation from someone?'

The way she was being described, Julia felt like a new restaurant. She waited for Samantha to explain how long they had been friends. Actually, she wouldn't be surprised if Samantha took a little bit of the credit for Julia becoming a gardener in the first place. To be fair, Julia might never have actually stuck out the course if it hadn't been for Samantha's little shove in that direction.

But Samantha's response was actually much vaguer than that. 'Her daughter was at primary school with Keira.'

There was a pause before the strident voice replied. 'Oh, really? Well, that's useful. Is that the girl who's following Keira around like a lost puppy? In the supermarket jeans?'

Whoever this woman was, her braying laugh made Julia's fingers itch. How dare she speak about Grace like that? Surely Samantha would put her right?

But Samantha's hushed voice did nothing of the sort. 'Julia's a single parent, so of course I suggested that she bring her daughter with her.'

Julia felt sick. Had Samantha just effectively denied their friendship? Worse than that, she'd let this woman look down on Grace and not corrected her, nor told her to stop being such a nasty snob. Were these the kinds of people Samantha spent time with now? Maybe Nina was right. Maybe Julia had never been introduced to them before because Samantha was ashamed of her.

When she put her hand on the door handle, she could see that it was trembling. She needed to get a hold of herself before she went outside. She wasn't going to speak to Samantha about this now; it wasn't her style to make a scene. But she couldn't stay there talking to these people if they were looking down on her and Grace. It was horrible.

She took a deep breath and opened the door, nearly falling over Grace in the hall.

'Mum. I've been looking for you. Can we go home?'

She could tell by the look on Grace's face that she was upset. 'What's up, baby?'

Grace shook her head. 'Nothing. I just want to go.'

She looked as if the merest nudge would make tears spill from her eyes, so Julia didn't push it. 'Okay. I'll just say goodbye to Samantha and Nick and then we'll go. Do you want to wait outside at the front for me?'

Grace nodded gratefully. 'I'll get our jackets from the rack.'

Julia's face grew warm. 'Actually, our coats aren't on the rack. Samantha took them upstairs.'

When they'd come, Samantha had taken their coats up to her room because she said she wanted to leave the coat rack empty for the other guests. At the time, it had felt like intimacy – they were the real friends – but now she realised that it was more likely to be that Samantha was embarrassed to have their 'supermarket' coats on display.

'Oh, yes. I think they are in Keira's room. I'll go and get them.'

In the kitchen, Samantha was looking in the cupboards for something. Julia steeled herself, then coughed to get her attention.

Samantha's head appeared from behind a cupboard door.

'Julia, hi. I'm just looking for some plates for the canapés. The caterers haven't brought enough.'

'We're going. Grace has a headache.' This could easily be the truth, based on the pained expression on Grace's face a moment ago. Julia wasn't about to tell Samantha what she'd overheard, but she didn't want to be there a moment longer.

If she had thought that Samantha would be upset that she was leaving the party early, she was much mistaken. 'Oh, that's a shame. I hope she feels better soon.'

Clearly, she had served her purpose there today and was now free to leave. Nina had been absolutely right; this whole thing had merely been an opportunity for Samantha to display her home and garden to maximum effect. 'Okay. Goodbye, then.'

She thought her voice sounded suitably curt, but Samantha didn't even seem to notice. 'I think you should get at least two new customers tonight. And there might be more when word gets around at the school.'

Was Samantha waiting for her thanks? However she felt right now, Julia definitely needed the business. 'That's great.'

'Aha!' Samantha pulled out a long white dish with a silver edge. 'That's what I was looking for. Take care, Julia.'

Within seconds, she had handed the plate to someone in a black uniform and flounced back out to the garden, where she leaned against Nick's shoulder as he talked to a broad, dark-haired man in an open-necked shirt.

How had Julia ever thought that they were actually friends?

'I've got our coats, Mum. Shall we go?'

She turned to Grace with a smile. 'Yes, sweetheart. Let's get home.'

They walked down the street slowly, arms linked. 'The garden looked so good, Mum. I'm really proud of you.'

Julia's eyes misted at that. Bless her little girl for being proud. 'Thank you. That means a lot to me.'

They walked on in silence for a while. Julia was still trying to calm down from the eavesdropped conversation. Then she remembered that it had not been her who had wanted to leave the party, it was Grace. 'Why did you want to go so soon? Weren't you having a good time?'

She felt Grace's arm jump in hers as she shrugged. 'I don't like Keira's new friends very much.'

Julia's stomach twisted. 'Were they mean to you?'

She shook her head. 'Not exactly. It was more Keira, to be honest. She acts different around them and I didn't really like it. Do you know what I mean?'

Julia unlinked her arm from Grace's and put it around her shoulder instead, pulling her closer.

'Oh, my lovely girl, I know exactly what you mean.'

TWENTY

SAMANTHA

The first she knew that Adam had arrived was when she felt his hand on her shoulder. 'Hi, Mum.'

Samantha turned around and was shocked all over again that this man in front of her was her son, her little boy. She stood and held out her arms. 'Oh, Adam. I'm so glad you're here.'

Adam squeezed her for a moment, then turned to look at his sister. 'How is she?'

Already, seeing Keira like this was feeling strangely normal. But, for Adam, it must be a huge shock. She watched him take in the machines, the tubes, the oxygen that was keeping his sister alive. 'No change. But that doesn't mean we have to worry. Her body is healing. She lost a lot of blood. She just needs time.'

He nodded and it was obvious that he was trying to keep his emotions under check. *You can cry*, she wanted to say. *It's okay to cry.*

'And can we do anything? To help her, I mean?'

She smiled. He was his father's son. If there was a problem, they wanted to fix it. It was one of the reasons Nick drove Keira crazy sometimes. *I don't want your advice, Dad. Stop telling me what to do.* Samantha had learned the hard way that it was always better to leave Keira to it; to wait for her to come and sit on the end of the bed and get it off her chest without giving her the solution. There was always a bittersweet side effect to Keira's upset: Samantha got to cuddle with her and stroke her hair and pretend for several minutes that she was her baby girl again.

But not this time. 'We just need to keep talking to her. It's possible she can hear us. We just need to keep telling her that we love her and that we're here when she wakes up.'

When. It was so much more comforting than *if.*

She was trying hard to stay positive, to stop the scary thoughts from crawling into her brain. *What if the doctors are wrong? What if she wakes up and there is permanent damage? What if she doesn't wake up at all?*

Adam took Nick's usual seat. 'I left Dad outside; he had to make a phone call. He said we're only allowed two to a bed so I should come straight through because you were desperate to see me.'

'Your dad was right.' Just seeing Adam was a salve to her soul. His strong shoulders, long legs, mouth that was usually so quick to smile. She was so damn proud of him.

Keira used to accuse Samantha of making Adam her favourite. 'Golden Boy', she used to call him. Or 'He Who Can Do No Wrong'. It had only been a joke, but it was true that Samantha found Adam easier. He was calm and thoughtful; his mood pretty constant and level. Keira, on the other hand, was tempestuous and emotional. She could be the most wonderful creature alive and also drive Samantha crazy with the way she behaved. Perhaps it was their different personalities that had kept her children close friends? Had Adam – living hundreds of miles away in Durham – known more about Keira's life than Samantha had?

Now Adam was talking to Keira, telling her all about his train journey down that morning. The strange people he had met. Keira was a natural mimic and she had the mimic's fascination with anyone eccentric or just different. Once the story had gotten as far as Southcliff Central Station, Adam tailed off and sat back in his chair with a sigh.

'You're doing great, darling. It's so nice to have you here. If she's going to listen to anyone, it'll be you.'

His smile was brief and more for her benefit than his. He turned back towards Keira before he spoke. 'Dad said she was in the park on her own. That's weird, isn't it?'

It was weird. So much so, that Samantha no longer believed it. 'The police are trying to find her on CCTV to see where she'd been and who she was with. Did you know she had a boyfriend?'

In the moment, she wasn't sure what she wanted his answer to be. Adam looked back at her from where he'd been studying the numbers on the screen above the bed. 'Keira? Yes, she did mention it.'

Something prickled in Samantha. Was it jealousy? Why hadn't she been told? 'It was a surprise for me and your dad. Do you know anything about him? Where he's from, where she met him, how long they've been together?'

She didn't want to ask her main question – *Why did she keep him a secret?* – partly because she didn't want to make Adam feel awkward, and partly because she was scared of the answer. Either way, Adam shook his head. 'No. She was pretty cagey about him, actually. Said it wasn't serious. That's probably why she didn't tell you.'

Bless him for trying to make her feel better. How often had he been the peacemaker between the two of them? When Nick was away or working late, it would be Adam talking Keira back from a slammed bedroom door, or reassuring Samantha that he would keep an eye on his headstrong sister. Had she been unfair to let him assume that position? Now he looked uncomfortable, but she wasn't sure if it was on her behalf, or whether there was something else he wasn't telling her. 'What is it?'

He glanced at Keira as if to ask her permission, then pulled his phone from his pocket. 'Okay, don't get upset about this, but, on the way here, I had a look at her Instagram. To see if I could work out anything from what she's been doing.'

Samantha and Nick had looked at her Instagram, too. As had the police. 'There's nothing there.'

He nodded. 'I know. But then I looked at her friends' Instagram accounts. It was easy to find them because they all tag each other in their photographs. And that's when I found it. Another account. She has a separate account that I've never seen before.'

Samantha's chest tightened. Why would Keira need a secret account? 'Is it on there now? Can I see it?'

Again, he hesitated. 'I was going to show Dad first.'

What the hell was on there? Adam might be a man, but she was not a child. She held out her hand. 'Adam, give me the phone.'

Samantha wouldn't call herself an expert on Instagram, but she posted most days and knew her way around. She also followed Keira's account. It was always just pictures of her and her friends, often at odd angles, almost always pouting.

But this account was completely different. Keira's friends were barely on it. It was mostly Keira with people Samantha hadn't seen before. At parties, in the park, at unfamiliar houses. And recently there were plenty of her with a boy who, judging by the way she was draped across him like a silk scarf, was the boyfriend. He was quite a bit taller than her, thin, and there was something in the expression on his face that made Samantha shudder. 'He looks *mean*. How did she meet someone like that?'

Adam's face was set – he wasn't giving anything away. 'Have you got to the ones from last week?'

Flicking through the images with her finger, Samantha looked longer, closer this time. She stopped at a picture of Keira and this guy at a party: he had an arm around her shoulders, they were laughing. His other hand was in his pocket. *No*. She looked closer. It was on the handle of something in his pocket. Something that looked very much like a knife.

Her hand flew to her mouth. 'Oh, no. No. Her boyfriend carries a *knife*?' She looked up at Adam.

He looked on the verge of tears. 'I don't know, Mum, but it looks like that. We need to show Dad.'

'Yes.' She held out the phone to him, not wanting to have it in her hand any longer. 'And we need to show the police.'

TWENTY-ONE

JULIA

Julia sat down before her legs gave way beneath her. 'What do you mean? You were there? When Keira was attacked? What the hell, Grace? Why did you lie to me?'

So slowly that Julia wanted to shake her, Grace took the chair opposite. The table was only small – it had to be, in the size of their kitchen – but they seemed a mile apart from each other. Grace's face twisted with emotion. 'Hold on, Mum. Just let me explain.'

Explain? How was she going to explain why she had kept this vital piece of information a secret? It was one thing keeping it from Samantha – and the police – when Julia had thought that Grace had nothing important to add to the investigation. But now her daughter was telling her that she was there. She saw the attack?

It was hard not to throw these thoughts at Grace, but that wasn't going to get her anywhere. She needed to know exactly what happened – what Grace had seen – and the only way to get that information was to listen and let her tell it in her own way.

She took a slow breath in and a long breath out. 'Okay. I'm listening.'

The few moments it took Grace to begin were interminable. When she spoke, her voice was quiet, small. 'School has been bad. Really bad. The friends I've told you about, Safa and Jasmine, they're in my form and I hang out with them at break time, but they aren't in any of my lessons. Keira's friends are, though.'

Because Grace had transferred schools once the timetables were already in place, the head had explained that she wouldn't necessarily be able to be placed in the correct set that year. They would have to put her in a lower set because that was where they had the smaller class sizes and space for an extra student. Even in a school as prestigious as St Anne's, lower sets seemed to include less engagement and more poor behaviour, but the school had reassured them both that she would be able to move at the end of the academic year.

'They are so horrible, Mum. I can't even answer a question without hearing them laughing about me. In lots of the lessons, the teacher directs questions at me because the rest of them don't seem to know the answers, but it makes it worse every time I answer.'

A familiar guilt spread across Julia's shoulders. Why hadn't Grace told her about this before now? 'I can ask again. About you going into a different class.'

Grace shook her head. 'It's not just in my class. The thing is' – she took a deep breath – 'Keira told them stuff about me.'

'What kind of stuff?'

'About last year. What happened at The Grange.'

Anger replaced guilt. 'She told them you were bullied?'

Grace wasn't looking her in the eye. There were toast crumbs on the table and she was pushing them into a small pile with her finger. 'I have – *had* – this blog. I didn't tell you, but I started up a blog so that I could write down everything that happened. I read this thing online that said more people should speak out about... that kind of thing. So I did. It was all anonymous, but I wrote it all down in this blog.'

Why had Grace not mentioned this before now? They could come back to that later. 'How does this connect to Keira?'

'I told her about it. Last year, when we were still friends. I told her and she read it.'

Julia could see where this was going. 'And she told her friends?'

Grace nodded. 'They keep repeating bits of it to me. I almost took it down, but there were comments on it from girls who said it had helped them and I wanted to be brave for them.'

A rush of pride swept over Julia. There was so much she wanted to ask, but they needed to stay focused on the attack right now. 'You are so brave, sweetheart. I want to talk about this some more, but I need you to tell me what went on in the park. I need to know what happened, Grace.'

Grace nodded. 'I only went to the park for a walk; I just wanted to be alone for a while. You know you always say that a walk makes you feel better—? But I'd only been there a little while and I saw Keira. I tried to swerve her, walk back towards the play area, but she saw me and she started up again.'

'Started up with what?'

'Having a go at me about coming to her school. "Why did you have to transfer to my school? You're ruining everything. They think we're friends. Why do you have to be such a freak?"'

Every phrase stabbed at Julia's heart. Why did kids have to be so cruel? What was it that made them turn on each other like this? 'And you were walking away?'

Grace nodded. 'Yeah, to start with. But then I got really angry. I've had enough, Mum. I've had enough of people thinking that they can talk to me like that.'

Julia couldn't disagree with the sentiment; it made her gut-wrenchingly angry, too. 'So, what happened?'

'I turned around and started shouting back. Asking her who the hell she thought she was. Why was she so bothered what her friends thought? Why was she so pathetic that she had to fit into the sad little world that they think is so important?'

As Grace spoke, Julia could hear and feel the anger emanating from her daughter. And why shouldn't she be angry? Fight back? Although verbal fighting was one thing; what had happened next was another matter. 'Okay. So, you were yelling at one another. Where did the knife come in?'

'It was Keira's. I had no idea that she had it. I was so angry with her that I was up in her face, yelling, throwing my arms about. But I wasn't meaning it violently. I wasn't going to hit her or anything. Honestly, Mum, I never ever intended to do anything to hurt her.'

Her face pleaded with Julia to believe her. Julia knew that Grace didn't have a violent bone in her body. This was the girl who cried when kids at school pulled the legs from crane flies. She reached out for her. 'I know that, sweetheart. Just keep going. I need to know it all.'

'I was yelling so much that I could barely see her. She stepped back from me and then held the knife out. Told me to stay away.'

Julia felt sick. 'That must have been a shock—?'

'Yeah. It was, but I was kind of beyond being scared. Does that make sense?'

Julia wasn't sure it did, but she nodded. With every second of this story, she felt a creeping sense of dread. Like pulling out a wobbly tooth, she just needed it over with, as quickly as possible. 'What happened, Grace?'

Grace covered her face with her hands. 'Oh, Mum. It's just so terrible. I'm so scared to tell you. You will hate me.'

Julia was terrified too, but there was nothing, nothing, that would make her hate her daughter. 'You know I could never hate you. You are the most precious thing in the world to me, Grace. You know that. Just tell me the truth and I can help you.'

This had been her mantra since Grace was tiny. *Tell Mummy the truth and you won't be in trouble.* It hadn't worked last year, had it? When Grace had gone through all that alone. It had been the first thing she'd said to her. *Why didn't you tell me?*

Grace dropped her hands from her face. 'I laughed at her. Told her she was pathetic for carrying a knife. I don't think it was even hers. The way she was holding it was all wrong; it was obvious she'd never used one before.'

Julia wanted to know how Grace knew the 'right' way to pull a knife on someone, but she knew it was better to keep quiet and let Grace finish.

'I kept telling her how pathetic she was. How much of a coward she was for not standing up to her friends. I... I called them some names.' She bit her lip. 'Not nice names.'

Bad language was the absolute least of Julia's worries at that moment. 'It's okay. You were hurting.'

For the first time, there was a glimpse of hope in Grace's eyes, as if she had only now had the thought that her mother might believe and support her. That hurt Julia even more than the crease of pain on her daughter's brow. 'I was. It was like I had all this anger stored away and now all the boxes were flying open and it was rushing out. I didn't care that she had a knife. I didn't care that she was waving it around in my face. I just kept shouting at her, telling her how awful she was.'

'And then?'

'Then I tried to take it.'

'The knife?' How was that even possible? Julia had tried to persuade Grace to take self-defence classes after the bullying at her last school. Someone had suggested it as a way to build her confidence. But Grace had lasted about three lessons: it wasn't for her. And now she was saying that she'd managed to disarm Keira, like a character in an action movie?

Grace obviously knew that she was surprised. 'I didn't actually get it. I kind of grabbed her arm with one hand and held the hand with the knife with the other. Then I waved her arm around. I was taunting her with it. Trying to show her how stupid she'd looked.'

This was going somewhere she didn't want to go. All of sudden, Julia no longer wanted to know how this ended. But she didn't have the luxury of that choice. 'And there was no one else around? It was only eight o'clock. Was there no one there?'

She could hear how pleading her voice was. *Please let there have been someone else.*

Grace was on the home stretch of the story now. She looked past Julia as if the whole event was playing out before her eyes. 'We were kind of wrestling with it. She managed to shake me off and then she started mocking me about last year. About what happened. She called me a slut, a whore, a prick tease and I just couldn't bear it. The anger. It just got hold of me and... and...'

She started to cry. Huge, hard sobs that made her frail body quake.

Julia mouth was dry, but she managed to push out the words. 'And what, Grace?'

'I rushed at her. I think I was going to push her or, I don't know, grab the knife or... I wasn't thinking. But she stepped towards me with it and somehow, somehow...' She looked up, her face contorted with agony. 'It was me, Mum. I did it. I stabbed Keira.'

TWENTY-TWO

WHEN THEY WERE FOURTEEN

The afternoon Julia had got the call from the head teacher, Nina had been trying to persuade her to join a dating site for the first time. Having spent the morning doing some heavy lifting for a new client who wanted their garden fully remodelled, Julia had arranged to meet Nina for lunch on Nina's day off. In the ten minutes it took for their paninis to arrive, Nina had been asking her what she had done 'for fun' in the last two weeks. When she couldn't come up with more than the movie night that she and Grace had had last Friday, Nina had launched in with her opinion that Julia should start looking for a new man in her life.

'It's been two years since you separated from John; it's time you got back out there.'

She meant well, but Julia was not of the same romantic persuasion as her pal. 'I don't have the energy for someone else. It's enough looking after Grace and the business.'

'And there's your problem. You are always worrying about Grace and not thinking of yourself. I hate to be the bearer of bad news, Jules, but once she goes off to university or work, it'll just be you in that flat. You need to start meeting more people.'

She didn't like to think about that. 'I've got you. And Samantha.'

Nina rolled her eyes at that. 'Samantha? For the odd coffee when she can fit you in, you mean?'

Julia had never told Nina about the conversation she'd overheard at Samantha's garden party, partly because she was embarrassed and partly because she had to see Samantha anyway, because the girls were still kind of friendly. That said, Keira seemed to be too busy to meet up with Grace very often, these days.

She smiled her thanks at the waitress who was laying knives and napkins in front of them. 'Okay. Well, I've still got you.'

Nina gave a dramatic sigh. 'Yes, of course you have. But I'm not going to let you put your cold feet on the backs of my knees in the middle of the night, am I? Don't you want some – y'know – in your life?'

She did know, but she wasn't sure she had the energy. 'Even if I did want to meet someone, eligible men don't fall from the trees, do they?'

Nina had a gleam in her eye as she pulled her phone from her pocket. 'I've been asking the younger girls at work about internet dating. We agreed that Tinder wouldn't be right for you, but they have suggested something called Bumble. I even got them to show me how to set up an account.' She swiped at her phone screen, then held it up in front of Julia's face. 'He looks all right, doesn't he?'

Julia couldn't help but laugh. 'You'd better delete that before Rob sees it and thinks you're leaving him. And I can't believe you've been discussing my love life with your work colleagues. How can you be lecturing me on internet dating, anyway? You and Rob met at school. You've never had to do any of that business.'

Nina was frowning at her screen as she swiped a few more times and held up another picture of a random man. 'Exactly.

That's why I want you to do it. So that I can live vicariously through you.'

Julia was interrupted in her reply by her own phone ringing. It was the school. Her heart always answered the sight of that number by thumping twice as hard. 'Hello?'

'Good afternoon. Is that Mrs Kennedy?'

Julia didn't like the fact that she still had John's surname, but she didn't want a different one from Grace. '*Ms* Kennedy. Yes. Is this about Grace? Is she okay?'

'That's what we wanted to check. Is Grace with you?'

Now she felt sick. Grace should be in a classroom right now. 'No. Is she not with *you*?'

'She hasn't turned up for afternoon registration. We thought she might have come home at lunchtime and not come back for some reason.'

Julia could see by the concern on Nina's face that her own must look panicked. She didn't have the time for any niceties. 'I'll call her now. Let me know if she turns up there.'

She terminated the call and scrolled through her favourites to Grace's name. 'She's not in school,' she told Nina, as she listened to it ring. Once. Twice. Three times.

'Hi, Mum.'

Oh, thank God. She was okay. 'Where are you? I've just had the school calling me.'

'I'm at home. I left at lunchtime.'

Now Julia knew she was safe, Grace's unconcerned tone was more than annoying. 'Why are you at home? You can't just walk out of school.'

'I didn't feel good this morning and they just sent me back to class. So, I walked out at the end of period four.'

This was not like Grace. She was the girl who never put her hand up in class. Who teachers always told her needed to 'speak out' more. What in heaven's name had possessed her to just walk out? To *truant*? 'You can't just do that, Grace. I was imagining goodness knows what. Stay there. I'll be home shortly.' She threw her phone into her bag and rummaged around to find her purse and car keys.

Nina reached out to stop her. 'I'll get this. You go home to her. Just take a breath before you get in the car.'

'I just can't believe it, Nina. You know Grace. Can you imagine her taking it into her head to just walk out of school?'

Nina rubbed her arm. 'I know. But maybe there is something more to this than she's telling you. You did say she keeps complaining of headaches and tummy aches. If one of my boys had a tummy ache it was usually because they were worried about something. You know her better than I do, but might it be worth asking her what is really going on?'

When Julia pulled up outside the flat, her phone rang with the school number again. She had already let them know that Grace was safe. What could they be calling about now?

'Hello?'

This time it was a male voice. 'Hello? Mrs Kennedy?'

'Yes, that's me. Grace is at home. I called ten minutes ago and I'm just about to go and speak to her.' She stepped out of the van and slammed the door closed.

'That's good. I'm Mr Proctor, deputy head here at The Grange. I was wondering if we could have a conversation about Grace?'

All she wanted to do was get inside and speak to her daughter. 'Now?'

'Actually, I hoped you would come in. There seems to be an issue with some of the other girls in her year group and I'd like to nip it in the bud as soon as we can.'

This was the first she'd heard of any of this. She stood at the front door to the flat, her key in the lock. 'I'm sorry, I don't understand. What issue?

There was a pause on the other end. 'It's quite delicate. It's to do with a boy, apparently.'

A boy? What boy? This was getting worse by the minute. 'Of course. I need to speak to Grace first, but we could come in shortly. About an hour?'

'Three thirty? That would be great. I'll see you both then.'

Julia took a deep breath before turning the key and pushing the door open. 'Grace? Are you there?'

'In the kitchen, Mum.'

Her voice sounded normal. Bright, even. Julia hung up her coat and bag and slipped off her shoes. The kitchen door opened as she walked towards it and Grace stood there, flour down the front of her shirt. 'I've made you a cake.'

This wasn't an unusual occurrence. But in the circumstances, it wasn't what Julia had expected. 'I thought you didn't feel very well?'

'Oh.' Grace turned back towards the sink, where she'd clearly been washing up. 'I feel better.'

Julia sank down onto one of the kitchen chairs. It was one they called 'purely decorative' because it wobbled, but she didn't have the energy to get up again. 'Grace. What's going on?'

Grace continued to rub at the mixing bowl with a sponge. 'I didn't feel well and they wouldn't let me come home or call you, so I just left after period four. That's all.'

Julia let the silence settle for a few moments, then tried another tack. 'Grace. You never lie to me. We said no secrets, ever. Remember? If you don't tell me what's going on, how can I help? Just tell me the truth.'

Then, just as she'd been since a small child, once Grace started, the whole lot came tumbling out.

'No one is speaking to me.'

'Why? What's happened?'

'A boy made up a story and everyone believed it and now they don't want to know me.'

Cold dread crept over Julia. She prayed this wasn't where her mind was going. 'What story?'

At this point, Grace became reluctant. 'Just something. It doesn't matter.'

Julia tried to keep her voice calm, not show how desperately she needed to know what had happened. 'It does matter, sweetheart. I want to help you. But you need to tell me. I love you and there's nothing you can say that will change that. Please, darling. Trust me.'

Grace looked down into her lap, twisting the bottom of her school jumper between her fingers. 'Lee Phillips. He told everyone that I... I did something *to* him at a party.'

Lee Phillips? Wasn't he the boy who was always in the school newsletter for scoring goals for the football team? Who the hell did he think he was, going anywhere near her daughter? Julia had been so naïve. So sure that Grace was still her little girl. 'Did what to him? He's a big lump of a lad. I can't imagine anything you did would have hurt him?'

Then Grace looked up at her, her eyes dark wells of pain and humiliation. 'Mum, he said I did sex stuff with him.'

Julia was unable to stop her face from flushing, but she tried to hide her shock. 'Sorry, I'm an idiot. I see. And it's untrue? Nothing happened between you? Because it's okay if—'

Grace recoiled. 'It's all lies. Nothing happened. He made it up because I told him to leave me alone. He's going out with Evie Oakley and he came on to me and I told him to get lost and then he made it all up.'

Julia wanted to find out where that boy lived and march round and sort him out. Right then, though, she needed to focus on comforting Grace. 'Oh, honey, that's awful. Surely all your friends know that he's a liar?'

Shaking her head, Grace started to cry harder. 'He has been

saying awful things... It's all lies but people are believing it... Oh, Mum, it's been so awful.'

What an absolutely vile person this boy must be. Julia folded Grace into her arms. She couldn't understand why her friends weren't supporting her. The girls she'd had around here for dinner, bought birthday gifts for when she could barely afford to buy herself a new pair of shoes. 'What about Sarah and Rachael and Kareena? Aren't they sticking up for you?'

She shook her head. 'They're friends with Evie, too. She's told them not to speak to me.'

Not for the first time, Julia was angry with the way that these girls could be. Wasn't it difficult enough to be a teenager, without your friends making life worse? 'Well, I'm going to go up to the school in an hour and—'

'No!' Grace's face was full of horror. 'You can't do that. You can't. It'll make everything worse.'

In that moment, Julia wasn't sure how the situation could possibly get any worse.

But it had.

TWENTY-THREE

SAMANTHA

It was strange that Julia wasn't answering her phone.

Time lost all meaning in that room, but Samantha and Nick had just spent a third restless night in the relatives' room, which made it Tuesday morning. Adam had stayed with a friend so that he didn't have to sleep in the house on his own. Julia would be at work, but she usually kept her phone in her back pocket. Since that awful call last year from the school about Grace being missing, she left no call unanswered. So why were all Samantha's calls going to voicemail?

It was a long shot asking Grace about Keira's new friends, the ones in the new Instagram pictures. It hadn't been her first thought to ask, because Samantha knew that the two of them hadn't been close since Grace had started at the school. But she'd try anything at this point.

Nick appeared in the doorway. 'I've spoken to Detective Inspector Brown about the Instagram page we showed them yesterday. They are still looking into it.'

He looked tired: his hair stood in tufts on his head where he had been running tight fingers through it; a sure sign of stress.

When he sat in his chair, the legs squeaked on the floor with the weight.

'Did they say whether they'd got any leads from it?'

Even saying those words aloud made Samantha feel silly. Like a minor character in a crime show. Sitting in this room with Keira felt surreal: things like this didn't happen to people like them. She felt bad for the thought. What did 'people like them' even mean? And when had she become it?

Nick rubbed at his cheeks with the palms of his hands, as if to warm them. 'No. They've spoken to Keira's friends again, but they are drawing a blank. They've given them a first name for the boyfriend, but with no surname or address, it's going to take some time to track him down.'

'The Instagram pictures should help—?'

He nodded. 'Yes, that's what Detective Brown said. If he's known to the police that'll help, too. It'll just take time.'

Time was something they had too much of at the moment. Sitting there, staring at Keira, at each other. The minutes dragged themselves into hours and nothing seemed to change.

Samantha had spent far too much of that time scrolling on social media. The posts about Keira were growing longer and longer as more and more random people commented on them. Like a fertile branch, there were so many offshoot conversations about knife crime and policing and how the area was 'going downhill fast'. Some were even commenting on her parenting. *Why are young girls like this out at night?*

It was 8 p.m., Samantha wanted to scream. And why couldn't young girls go out? Why did no one question the young boys who were out?

Nick had told her several times to stop looking, but there was a macabre fascination to it. If the roles had been reversed, would she have been one of the many people on there, offering 'love' to a family she didn't know?

Nick closed his eyes. He looked as if he might fall asleep any minute.

'Why don't you go home and rest for a couple of hours. Or take a shower?'

He yawned and shifted in his seat, straightened his back. 'I was going to suggest the same to you. You haven't left this building since Saturday night.'

How could she leave? Until Keira woke up, she didn't want to go anywhere. 'I'm fine. You go. You can check and see if there's any post, and water the plants. But no working on the quiet.' She wagged a finger and tried to make her mouth smile. It was a standing joke in the family. If they were on holiday and couldn't find Nick, they would accuse him of sloping off to check his emails.

He smiled back. 'I won't. Scout's honour. Anyway, work knows what's going on, so they won't be expecting anything from me. And I've told the agency not to call me until I call them.' He looked down at his hands and picked at a nail. 'That was after they'd already sent me a message, though.'

He was being uncharacteristically cryptic. 'What message?'

'About a job.'

She rolled her eyes. 'Well, I didn't think it was a tip-off for a horse race.'

'It's not important right now, anyway.'

Now he really was being strange. 'What job, Nick?'

He sighed. 'Look, I'm not even thinking about it right now. There's nothing as important as focusing on Keira.'

Why was he being so evasive? 'What job?'

His shoulders dropped. 'Glasgow. The job is in Glasgow. It's a really good package. Relocation costs etcetera. But I've told them there is no way I am interested in talking about work right now.'

Butterflies fluttered in Samantha's stomach. Glasgow? 'Wow. Scotland. I didn't even know you were looking that far.'

'I wasn't. But there aren't that many roles at my level around at the moment, so the agency are "casting their net wide". Their words, not mine.' He smiled at her again. They both had a healthy distaste for corporate speak.

'I see. And this company in Glasgow, they want you?'

'I've told them that I can't talk about anything right now. But the agency said they are really keen on me. There's a couple of guys there that I've worked with before and they've been singing my praises, apparently. The agency said that they're not in any rush to employ someone – they just want to make sure it's the right person to fit in with the team. So, they are going to back off and wait until I'm available for an interview.'

She frowned, not liking the idea of faceless suits discussing their family. 'You've told them what happened to Keira?'

His eyes widened. 'No. Of course not. I told the agency that my daughter is in hospital. That's all. They don't even know how serious it is.'

How serious it is. Those words were like cold water in her face. This whole time, Nick had been the one telling her that everything was going to be okay. 'I can't think about any of that right now.'

'Of course not. Me, neither. I'm just telling you what they said because, well, because I screwed up not telling you about the redundancy earlier.'

She nodded her understanding, then turned back to Keira. It was all very well saying she didn't want to think about it right then, but what else did her brain have to work on? There was the fact that her daughter had been lying to her about where she'd been, the identity of a boyfriend Samantha knew nothing about, or this.

Glasgow? She couldn't get over the expression on Nick's face when he'd mentioned it. Whatever he said, she could tell that he was excited at the prospect of living hundreds of miles away. In his job, it was usual for people to relocate to where the projects were – often even abroad. That was why he had had to travel so often for his job in the last fifteen years: it was the trade-off for staying in the same place.

And why had he stayed in the same place? For her. For the kids. She had been adamant that she didn't want them uprooted every couple of years: new houses, new schools, new friends. Although, now that Adam was at Durham, they would actually be closer to him in Glasgow. Had Nick been thinking that, too?

This was ridiculous. Why was she even thinking about this with Keira lying there? 'Anyway. Are you going to go home and get a couple of hours' sleep?'

'As soon as the doctor has been, I will. I'll wait for the update. Do you need anything bringing back?'

'No. Julia brought me enough clothes for a couple more days.'

Julia. She'd try her again. Julia would understand almost as well as Nick why Samantha wouldn't want to move. And maybe it wasn't such a long shot to ask Grace about Keira. She may have heard something at school.

She sent Julia a text.

Can't get through on your phone. Can you call me?

Then she had a thought. It was Tuesday. Julia would be coming to do the garden that afternoon. 'Julia might be there when you get home. If you see her, can you ask her to give me a call?'

'Julia?' Nick frowned. 'Sorry to say this, but gardening services is one of the things we might need to cut until I've got a new job. Sorry. I know we love Julia, but needs must.'

Once the doctor had given a brief summary of 'no change', Nick left to go home. Alone by Keira's bedside, Samantha couldn't help looking at her mobile again. There were some more WhatsApp messages, including one in the St Anne's group from Karen, Katie's mum.

Yes. Maybe we should keep them at a distance in future.

She stared at it for a while. What did that mean? She scrolled upwards to check, but there was nothing before it that Karen could be replying to. *Yes* what? Who was she agreeing with? And who were they suggesting they keep at a distance? Herself and Keira?

As she watched, the message disappeared. Replaced with the words: *This message was deleted.*

Heat filled Samantha's face. Clearly, Karen had posted that message by mistake. It was meant for another WhatsApp group. One to which Samantha hadn't been invited. One in which – it seemed – she and Keira were being discussed. This must be the same WhatsApp group that Pippa had messaged her about on that first night. Humiliation and anger fought for supremacy, until she looked at her daughter.

Let them have their private little gossip. It didn't matter. They didn't matter.

Her phone vibrated in her hand. A reply from Julia.

Sorry. Something has come up and I don't think I can make it to do your garden today. Hope Keira is okay.

It wasn't about the blasted garden; she wanted to talk to her friend. Even if part of it was to tell her she couldn't keep employing her.

Don't worry about the garden. But can you call me? I need to talk to you about something.

TWENTY-FOUR

JULIA

She knew.

As soon as she read Samantha's text that morning, Julia's heart galloped ahead and her mind wasn't far behind. Samantha wanted to talk to her about 'something'. What else could it be? She must know that Grace had been there, in the park. Did she know that Grace had been the one holding the knife?

Her stomach lurched. She couldn't even think about it without the contents of her stomach threatening to reappear. *Grace*. The kindest, quietest, most beautiful creature in the world. How could she have been involved in this? How could she have...?

Julia shook the thought out of her mind and pushed her mobile away from her. Initial panic over, she reasoned that Samantha couldn't know too much, otherwise she would have called. Or she would have already told the police and they would be knocking on the door. Julia would think of something to reply with in a minute. *Once I've got through reading this*. She opened her laptop on the kitchen table.

She'd been shocked at the discovery that Grace had a blog about everything that had happened. Not that Grace had written it – she had always had a notebook full of stories and thoughts and sketches – but that she hadn't mentioned it to Julia. When she was tiny, she would show Julia every scribble she made on the reams and reams of paper she used to get through. *Look, Mummy, a house. Look, Mummy, a doggie. Look, Mummy, it's me and you and I drew a big heart because we love each other.* As she got older, the drawings gave way to stories that she insisted Julia read *right this minute.* They would be about a girl and her dog, or a girl and her horse, or a girl and her cat: that girl had lobbied hard for a pet of her own. Once she was in secondary school, she had become less likely to parade her writing skills, but Julia only had to ask and Grace would flick to something creative she had written that she was proud of. Reddening, but smiling, at Julia's effusive praise.

But she hadn't said a single word about writing a blog.

Last night, after Grace's revelation, they had sat up together late into the night. It had been too late to call the police anyway. Or that's what Julia had told herself. They would have to tell them eventually, of course they would. That was what had kept her tossing and turning into the small hours, imagining what would happen. Grace arrested. Grace in a police cell. Grace in prison. Were there any circumstances in which this might not happen?

That morning, after a night in which she'd barely slept, she had taken Grace a cup of tea in bed. 'I want to see the blog.'

Grace had looked as if she hadn't slept either. Dark circles caved under her eyes, almost bruise-like in her pale face. 'No, Mum. You'll just get upset.'

That had made her feel even more awful. And more determined. 'Grace. I'm your mum. You don't need to keep secrets from me. I thought we'd talked about that.'

Grace had chewed on her lip. 'But you're going to feel awful about it.'

Ever since the divorce, she'd been like this. Not wanting

Julia to be upset, she hadn't told her when John had got engaged to his girlfriend, or when they had announced a few months later that they were going to have a baby. When John himself had mentioned it on a phone call about summer holiday arrangements, he had been surprised that Grace hadn't told her. But Julia wasn't. Sometimes Grace seemed more like the mother than she did.

'Grace, I'm more upset that you feel you need to keep things from me. Please. Just let me know what it's called.'

Reluctantly, Grace had given in and given Julia the name of her blog: *Girl down the Drain*. Even though Julia knew it was a play on words of one of her favourite thrillers, it had sent a shudder down her spine.

She typed the name into the search bar on her laptop now, fingers trembling. What was she going to find out? What secrets or half-truths was Grace hiding?

She scrolled through the Google suggestions: a song on Amazon music, a news story about a young child who had fallen down an actual drain. Eventually, she found it: girldown-thedrain.wix.com

Holding her breath, she clicked on the link.

The front page – if that was the right word – had a picture of a drain on it. Then there was a one-sentence introductory paragraph.

This is about the year that screwed up my life.

Underneath, there was a list of entries. The first was from about a month before the first phone call from the school. It was titled 'The Party'. Julia clicked.

So, I read an article that said you need to find a way to talk about the things that hurt you. This is me talking. It's for me, but if it helps you, too, then I'm glad.

Julia pressed her palm to her chest. This was her girl; always wanting to help, thinking of others, a huge heart on legs – that's what John used to call her when she was little and cried at the adverts on TV about starving children or hurt animals.

A few months ago, I was at a party. I didn't even want to go, but my friends were going and Mum said it would be good for me to get out of the house. Everyone was drinking. I don't really drink, but my friends kept on at me, so I had some of the 'cocktails' they'd made by filling up a plastic bottle with spirits from home and topping it up with coke. It was disgusting, but I drank it anyway. What else was there to do?

Was this what Grace was worried about Julia seeing? She wasn't pleased that her daughter had been drinking at fourteen, but there were much worse things. She read through the next few sentences, which described other people dancing and messing around, until she got to a name she didn't recognise.

Jacob (that's not his real name) wouldn't leave me alone. He kept saying all these things about liking me and that I was really pretty without my glasses and how he thought I was really clever. I knew he was going out with someone but (and I'm not proud of this) I've never had a boy talk to me like that before and it was nice. I let him keep talking to me. People have said I was flirting and I don't know if that's true or not. I don't really know what flirting looks like.

With every sentence, Julia' stomach clenched tighter and tighter. Her poor, vulnerable, innocent girl.

I honestly didn't notice that he had his arm around me. He had got closer and I could feel his breath on my neck and it tickled so I laughed. That's when he kind of pushed forward and kissed me. Kissed my open mouth. It was a shock, but I didn't stop him, so I suppose some of what they've been saying is true. I didn't stop him kissing me. But I honestly don't remember how we ended up in the bedroom.

Julia fists clenched on top of the keyboard. It was as if she was on a rocking boat, and nausea lapped at her stomach. *No, please, no.*

I know I said I was going to write about what happened, but my memory of what went on is really patchy. I remember his mouth on mine and his hands and then everything is a bit weird. He remembers, though. He said it was me touching him, that I wanted to do those things. But all I remember is feeling really sleepy and him talking to me all the time, taking my hand and moving it where he wanted it. Even those few memories make me so ashamed. I know that you don't know me, but I'm not like that. I haven't even properly kissed a boy before.

Julia closed her eyes. This was excruciating. Anger and guilt and heart-breaking sorrow were fighting for dominance. How had she not known any of this? Her baby girl had carried this alone.

By Monday, it was all over school. Everyone was talking about it. 'Jacob' had been dumped by his girlfriend and she was in tears in the toilets. Some of her friends were yelling at me in the playground. Calling me a slut and a whore. I didn't see Jacob, but one of my friends said he was strutting around like a god. I just wanted to curl up and die.

So did Julia. She'd known about the bullying, that Grace had felt alone with no friends. That these nasty little bitches had made her life hell. But she'd thought that the lies had been complete fabrications; she'd had no idea that any of this had actually happened. She had a vague memory of the party, of encouraging Grace to go – something she would never forgive herself for now – because she'd wanted her to make more friends and spend less time in the house. Grace hadn't stayed at home that night; she'd called and said she was staying over with her friend Beth. What an idiot Julia had been. Why hadn't she realised that it was suspicious?

That was the end of the first blog post. Julia clicked on the next one. It was just titled 'After'.

That week, every day was worse than the last one. Everyone seemed to know what had happened that night. People were looking at me in the corridor. Making sex signs at me. You know the ones I mean. Jacob's girlfriend and her mates made my life absolute hell. One of them spat at me in the playground. They made it clear that anyone who spoke to me wasn't a friend of theirs. They were awful to my friends too. I suppose I can't blame them for not sticking up for me. Who would want to get treated like that? They were nice to me outside school and everything, but – in school – there wasn't much they could do.

Wasn't much they could do? They were supposed to be her friends. To support her. Have her back. And they did nothing? Not even tell a teacher what was going on?

Unbidden, Samantha's face popped into Julia's mind. Maybe they hadn't been close in a long while, but Julia wasn't being a good friend either, was she?

Word by painful word, she read through the entries which recounted the rumours that had circulated. The things this vile boy had said about Grace's body, so that she had felt as if everyone was staring at her as she changed for PE. The things that had been written about her in notes passed around and then left on her desk for her to see. A condom removed from its packet, which someone had dropped in her bag. Why had no one seen this? Where the hell had the teachers been looking? Where the hell had *she* been looking, not to know what was going on?

> *When it gets really bad, I go to the medical room. I've told the nurse that I get really bad migraines and she lets me sit there for a while. Sometimes, if it's period four or five, she'll call Mum and Mum will come and get me. Mum wants to take me to the doctor, or the opticians, but I told her I'm okay. Sometimes I nearly tell her about it, but when I'm at home, I feel so much better. I don't want to talk about it. I don't want my mum to know what happened. I don't want to even say their names in my flat.*

Tears were rolling down Julia's face. If she had known, she could have done something. Demanded that this boy be held to account. Told John. Surely what he'd done was *rape*? Grace had been drunk and he'd taken advantage of that. She'd been fourteen. What kind of boy did that to a fourteen-year-old girl?

Behind her, down the hallway, she heard Grace's door squeak open. 'Mum?'

In seconds, she was down the hall with her arms around her trembling daughter. 'I'm sorry, Grace, I'm so sorry. I'm here now. It's going to be okay. I promise, I am going to make everything okay.'

She'd let her down before, but she wasn't going to let her down again. It might not be right, or legal, or moral, or being a good friend, but she was going to keep her mouth shut until Keira woke up and then they would work out how to deal with it. Right now, her priority was the sobbing girl in her arms.

She said a silent prayer that the 'something' Samantha wanted to talk about had nothing to do with Grace. Later, she'd call her and find out.

TWENTY-FIVE

SAMANTHA

She hadn't wanted to come home at all.

Nick had been persistent. 'She's stable. And I am here. And so is Adam. I feel a lot better for an hour at home this morning. Now it's your turn.'

One of the nurses had joined in to support him. 'Your husband is right. You'll make yourself ill otherwise, then how are you going to help Keira when she wakes up?'

It was Adam who swayed it. 'Come on, Mum. Dad's right. You look exhausted. Go home and have a nap, a shower, a coffee and then come back. I'm going to tell Keira all the things I've been getting up to at university, and I don't want you listening in.'

He looked really worried about her. Maybe she could risk an hour or two. 'Okay, but if anything happens' – she pointed a finger at Nick – 'and I mean *anything,* you call me and I'll be straight back.'

Nick looked relieved that she was going to go. 'I promise. Shall I drive you home now?'

She shook her head. 'No. You stay with the kids. I'll get a cab.'

. . .

Both Nick and Adam had been back to the house and they had mentioned that there had been deliveries of flowers and home-made cakes, but she wasn't ready for the sheer volume of blooms. Many of them were still in their wrappings, with the bottom shoved into a vase of water. Once they'd run out of vases, either Nick or Adam had filled the sink and just propped the flowers up in there.

Dropping her bag onto the kitchen floor, Samantha read some of the cards that were attached.

So sorry. Let us know what we can do. Thinking of you.

People were kind. But, after seeing the deleted message from Karen, she couldn't help but wonder how sincere some of these were.

In the cab on the way home, she had sent Julia a text asking her to come over. Here in this empty kitchen, she had the urge to see her like you'd want a glass of water on a hot day. Julia was so calm and logical; she'd help her to make sense of all the different thoughts buzzing around her head.

Over the years, there had been times that they'd done this for each other. When the girls were small, it had been helpful to have someone with a child the same age to run things by or ask for advice. In their relationships, too, they had been a friendly ear for one another. Julia's divorce had been a big one. She and John had done their best to keep it amicable, but anything involving lawyers and finances was bound to bring worry, indecision and resentment. Samantha remembered Julia pacing up and down her lounge, waving a glass of wine as she expostulated about the costs involved in making sense of it all.

Over the last few years, though, Julia had become quite distant. Of course, she'd had to focus on Grace, and had been wrapped up in dealing with all of the fallout from that bullying business. Thinking how little she'd been in contact around that time nipped at Samantha's conscience. But if Julia had needed someone to talk to, surely, she'd have asked her?

Samantha knew how lucky she was to have Nick. Much as she complained about the amount of time he spent at work, he was always there for them – even if it was at the end of the phone. But Nick was a solutions man, a fixer. And sometimes there were problems that couldn't be fixed. Sometimes she just wanted to rant about something – or someone – without him advising her to stop taking on so many commitments or drop someone from her life. That was where Julia was so good; she would nod her head and agree with Samantha and then make her laugh. She was exactly what Samantha needed right now.

In the text, she'd asked Julia to come over at midday so that she could have a shower first, so she was surprised when the doorbell rang at 11.45 a.m. Even more surprised when it wasn't Julia.

She opened the door to the back of a very stylish blonde head, which whipped around in surprise. 'Samantha! I didn't expect you to be in, darling. I just rang on the off-chance that your cleaner might be here. I wanted to drop these off for you all.'

Karen waved a box with a ribbon which bore the name of a local biscuit shop in swirly writing. She clearly wasn't yet following through on her deleted suggestion to keep her distance, then. But this wasn't the time or place for Samantha to get into it with her.

'Thank you. I've only popped home for a minute. To have a shower.'

She's assumed this was enough of a signal for Karen to say her goodbyes, but she stayed on the doorstep, as if waiting to be asked in. 'How is poor Keira? We're all so worried about her. Katie is in pieces.'

Samantha pressed her lips together tightly. There was no way she was supplying Karen with any more social media fuel, but she had to say something. 'She's still unconscious at the moment. But we are hoping she'll wake up soon.'

Karen's face was full of sympathy. 'Can I do anything? Do you want me to come in and make you a cup of tea while you take a shower?'

That was the last thing Samantha wanted. 'Thanks, but I just need to take a shower and get back to the hospital.'

Karen looked disappointed. 'Okay. Is there any news about who did it? We're all in complete shock.'

Seriously? Did this woman think she had the time to talk about that? Enough was enough. 'I saw your message, Karen. Before you deleted it.'

She frowned. 'What do you mean?'

'Your message. About keeping your distance. You posted it on the wrong group and then deleted it. I know you're all talking about me. And Keira.'

Karen paled. Shifted to her other foot. 'I don't know what you mean. We're not... There isn't another...' She could obviously tell from the look on Samantha's face that she wasn't believing a word. 'I mean, there *is* another group, but it's just so that we can talk about how to support you both.'

Samantha didn't have time for this. 'I don't care, Karen. I need to get back to the hospital.'

She closed the front door and rested her back against it, closing her eyes. She'd thought Karen was her friend. That all of the women who had been messaging her were her friends. She expected to feel rejected, disappointed, sad. But what she actually felt was more like relief.

The only person she wanted to see was Julia. And she would be there in ten minutes. Better get into the shower. She sent Julia a text.

Getting in the shower. Just let yourself in.

Though she would never admit it to him, Nick had been right. The shower had made Julia feel more herself, more in control, ready to get back to the hospital and be strong for Keira. She didn't want to give the St Anne mums any more headspace and she knew that Julia wouldn't take offence if she only spent ten minutes with her. If it had been Grace in the hospital, she would be exactly the same.

When she got downstairs, Julia was in the kitchen and the kettle was on. She held out her arms and Samantha walked into them. Julia gave proper hugs. Not those polite, fingertips on the shoulders, barely touching hugs. Proper, hold you close and squeeze you tight hugs.

When she let go, there were tears in Julia's eyes. It meant a lot that she was so upset about Keira. 'How is she doing?'

'Still asleep. No one seems to be concerned at the moment. They just repeat the fact that her body has had a huge shock and they are monitoring everything. She'll do it in her own time, I guess.'

The kettle stopped rumbling and clicked off, so Julia turned her back to fill the cups on the counter. 'It's like when they were little, isn't it? And you worry about them sitting up, crawling, walking. That's what everyone says, isn't it? They'll do it in their own time.'

Samantha took a cup of black coffee from her. It was lovely to think of Keira when she was small. She was always such a fierce bundle of energy. Like a tornado, she would sweep up anything and everything in her path and leave a trail of destruction behind. 'Remember when they were little? It was always Keira getting Grace into trouble. I'm amazed you wanted to stay friends with us.'

As usual, Julia wouldn't let Keira take the blame. 'Grace was more than happy to follow. Keira gave her confidence. She never would have done half the things she did if she hadn't had Keira to do them first.'

Samantha wrinkled her nose and laughed. 'You say that as if it was a good thing.'

It had been a good thing, though. The girls had been good for each other. Not going to the same school, they had really enjoyed seeing each other every time they met up. Keira would always be full of something adventurous, and would take the shy Grace along with her. Grace had brought a calm restraint to Keira's wilder plans. Sometimes they would joke that she was like a second mother.

Again, Julia's eyes filled. 'It was a good thing.'

It was a shame they had grown apart. And it was something she and Julia had not really talked about. She glanced at the clock on the wall, shocked to see that she'd been away from Keira for almost two hours. 'I need to get some things together and get back to the hospital. Sorry.'

'Of course.' Julia frowned into her mug as if she was about to read the tea leaves. 'You wanted to talk to me about something?'

She'd almost forgotten. 'Yes. Well. I was going to ask if you would speak to Grace about whether she'd heard anything at school about Keira having a new group of friends. I know it's a long shot, but I just want to check every avenue.'

Julia sipped at her tea. Nodded. 'Of course, yes. I'll ask.'

She obviously though it would be fruitless. Still, it was worth a try. 'And I also have some other news. It's Nick. Well, his job. He's been made redundant. I'm sure he'll get something soon, but in the meantime, we need to reduce our outgoings. It means I can't afford to have you do the garden for a while at least. I'm so sorry.'

Julia looked almost relieved. What had she thought she was going to say?

'I'm so sorry about Nick's job. You don't need to be worrying about me, though. Look, I'm here now, anyway. I'll give the garden a good going over, cut everything right back. No need to pay me.'

This was Julia all over. So many times, Samantha had told her that she would never make any money from her business if she kept doing favours and little extras for people. It was amazing how many people would take advantage of her time and expertise. Samantha wasn't one of them. 'I can't let you do that.'

Julia looked almost desperate. 'Please. I want to. I wish I could do something more important to help. At the very least, I can do this.'

About to protest again, Samantha could see that she really meant it. Like Nick, Julia was a fixer, a mender. It was their love language. 'Thank you. I really appreciate it.' She slid off the kitchen stool and gave Julia another hug.

When this was all over, she would make Keira invite Grace over. Maybe they could get the girls back to being close again.

TWENTY-SIX

JULIA

As she pulled the back door closed behind her, Julia sighed with relief. Samantha's text had really been about the gardening, not about Grace. Relief quickly gave way to guilt at the thought of the Judas hug she had just given Samantha. If Samantha knew what secrets Julia was keeping, she would not have been so glad to hold her close. Julia had meant it about wanting to do the garden for free; it was an act of penance.

Gardening was more than just a job; it was a passion. Nothing could beat the feel of a new shoot poking through the soil, the delicate smell of jasmine, the vibrant yellow of a rose. With her fingers deep into the damp soil, whatever stress or concerns Julia had would be worked out of her as she kneaded or patted the area around the plants, giving them space to breathe. Nurturing a garden to its full potential was a joy, an honour. Samantha's garden was particularly beautiful, and keeping it that way was the very least she could do. In actual fact, she'd do the garden every week for free for the rest of her life if it meant keeping Grace safe.

Grace. She would be at home, worrying, anxious to know

what Samantha had to say. Julia fished her phone out from the pocket on the side of her work trousers and sent her a quick text.

> *Hi Grace. Everything is okay. It wasn't about you. She doesn't know you were there.*

Julia's head was as busy as a hive of bees. Working in this particular garden was a reminder of how supportive Samantha had always been of Julia following her dream, including hosting that awful garden party for her. But it was also the place she'd dismissed Julia as if she barely knew her. Let that awful woman speak about Grace as if she was nothing. She had been one person to Julia's face and another behind her back.

The irony of these thoughts wasn't lost on her. Who was she to cast the first stone? Wasn't that exactly how she was behaving right now? Only worse.

She snipped more viciously than necessary with her secateurs. When she was with Grace and could see the fear and pain in her eyes, she would lie to anyone in order to save her. But here, at Samantha's house, the deception was under a brighter light. What could she do? Of course it wasn't right keeping quiet about what had happened with Grace and Keira. This was a terrible crime. Of course she should take Grace to a police station right now and get her to tell them what had happened. Not doing so was making it worse every minute, because everyone was going to find out once Keira woke up, anyway.

If Keira woke up.

She shook the evil thought from her head. Yes, she was angry about the way Keira had treated Grace, but she definitely did not wish her dead. What was she wishing for, then? That Keira would wake up and say nothing? Or not remember? Or that she would say that it was a terrible accident and she didn't hold Grace responsible? Would the police even care about that, or would they arrest Grace immediately?

She snatched at another branch and severed it from its stem. She still couldn't get her head around Grace's version of events. Why had Keira had a knife in the first place? The outfits she wore to go out in were too skimpy and tight to hide a pair of nail scissors, let alone a knife big enough to put someone in hospital.

And why had they both been in the same park – alone – at exactly the same time? Grace, she could understand; she had always like to have time to herself. But Keira was the centre of every social bubble. Why had she not been with her friends?

Even Grace's account of the accident (she couldn't think of it as an attack) didn't add up. There was something missing in the story and she couldn't put her finger on it.

Against her leg, her phone buzzed and she pulled it out. John.

'Hi, Julia. Did you want me?'

She was grateful that they had managed to find a way towards an amicable relationship. Being a single parent was hard enough without the wrangles with your ex that some people talked about. John had been a pretty poor husband at the end, but he was generally a good dad. 'Hi, John. Yes. I need to talk to you about Grace.' She glanced around. Samantha had gone upstairs to pack a bag when Julia had come outside, but it was too risky to speak about it there. 'Is there any chance we can meet up this afternoon? Or tonight?'

The irritation in his voice was so familiar. 'I'm at work right now. Is it important? Urgent?'

Julia walked further into the garden, away from the house. 'I can't talk right now. What time do you finish?'

'Three o'clock. Unless something kicks off just before.'

The joys of a police job. Their marriage had been full of cancelled events and burned dinners. 'Would you mind meeting me then? I wouldn't ask if it wasn't important.'

'Okay. Shall I come to the house?'

At the moment, Julia didn't want Grace knowing that she was talking to her father about this. In Grace's current state, she dreaded to think what she might do. 'Yes. But park down the road and text me when you're there. I'll come out.'

'You're worrying me, now, Julia. What is going on?'

'Just come and meet me. I'll explain everything then.'

She held the phone to her chest for a few moments after the call ended, staring into space, her heart a mixture of relief and trepidation. Relief, because John would know what to do. Trepidation, because she worried about the position her revelation would put him in. Was he more loyal to the police force or his daughter?

Grace hadn't replied to her text yet, which was strange. Normally she would text her back pretty quickly; she knew how much Julia worried about her. Maybe the text had arrived while she was talking to John. Julia scrolled to her daughter's name. Not only was there no reply, her original text was wasn't there, either. That was odd. Why hadn't it sent? Was there a draft folder for text messages?

A terrible possibility crossed her mind and she scrolled up, feeling sick and hot. There it was. She had sent the message. Just not to the right person. How had she done that? Why hadn't she double-checked? *Oh, no. Oh, no.*

The back door squeaked as it was pushed open and Julia looked up to see Samantha standing in the doorway, holding up her phone, her face like thunder. 'What wasn't about Grace? And where the hell *was* she that I don't know about?'

TWENTY-SEVEN

SAMANTHA

The look on Julia's face was all she needed to confirm it. Grace had been there when Keira was stabbed. 'What the hell is going on?'

Julia held up her hands in submission. 'Please. Let me talk to you. I can explain.'

How was she going to explain keeping this to herself for the last three days?

Samantha wanted to get back to her daughter. But she needed to hear this first. 'You'd better talk quickly.'

Julia nodded. 'Can we go back inside?'

This time, there was no cup of coffee or tray of biscuits between them. Sitting across the kitchen table from one another, it was more like a police interview. Not ten minutes ago, Julia had been an anchor Samantha could cling to; now she was a stranger.

'Tell me now. Was Grace there? In the park? Does she know what happened?'

Julia nodded slowly. 'Yes. Grace was there. She was the one who called the ambulance. And she waited with Keira until the ambulance came.'

None of this was making any sense. 'So why haven't you told the police it was her? Why haven't you told me? I can't believe you've kept this from me, Julia. Grace might be able to help them find the person that did this.' Her mind was whirring. 'Oh my... Does she know who it is? What did she see?'

Julia was trembling, but Samantha didn't care. She needed to know why her so-called friend had lied to her. Why she was sending messages to her daughter as if she was in the clear for something she'd done? Slowly, the wheels of Samantha's brain started to move. Julia was watching her face, as if waiting for her to work it out for herself. There was a truth there, but her mind just wasn't grasping it.

Julia was speaking unbearably slowly, as if she was speaking to a three-year-old. 'There was an argument. Between the girls. At the park. Keira's friends... and Keira... they've been making Grace's life hell.'

'What do you mean?'

'Bullying. It's been going on for the last couple of months. I didn't know about it.'

Samantha couldn't work out why Julia was telling her this. Her daughter was still unconscious, and Julia wanted to talk about the girls falling out with one another? 'Julia, my daughter is not a bully and I don't have time to listen to this. I need to get back to the hospital. Whatever Grace saw, you need to tell the police right now. Or I will call them as soon as I get there.'

She stood up and the legs of the dining chair squeaked across the granite tiles.

Julia reached out for her. Grabbed her arm as if she was drowning. 'Please. Just two minutes.'

This was ridiculous. 'No, Julia, I have to—'

'Grace was holding the knife!'

It was as if all the air had been sucked from the room. There was a whooshing in Samantha's ears, like the sound in a seashell when you hold it to your ear to hear the sea. The room seemed to move in front of her face and she felt hot, really hot.

Now Julia was standing and she moved Samantha downward so that she was sitting in the chair again. 'Are you okay? You've gone very white. Let me get you some water.'

The last three days had been one shock after another. But Grace? This just didn't make sense. She took the water that Julia gave her. The cold glass in her hands helped to bring her back into the room. 'I don't understand.'

Julia sank down opposite her. 'To be honest, neither do I. Grace is not making a lot of sense. All I can get out of her is that they were arguing, there was a knife and then, somehow, Keira got hurt.'

Initial shock over, anger coursed through Samantha like lava. 'Grace stabbed Keira? Is that what you're saying? Your daughter is responsible for my daughter lying in that hospital bed?'

Her voice got louder with each word. She could feel herself shaking. It was as if she was there, but not there. Nothing made sense. She was looking at Julia, but she was also standing outside, wondering what the hell was going on.

Julia reached for her arm, but she shook it off. She didn't want her touching her now.

Julia sighed. 'Grace thinks that she might have been holding the knife, but there's no way that she can be sure because she says there was a struggle. A fight.'

'A fight? Are you kidding me? Keira doesn't fight. If there was a struggle, Grace must have been the one who started it.'

Even those words coming out of her mouth sounded strange. They didn't talk like this about their children. Samantha had cared for Grace, sympathised with Julia, tried to help them both. She felt sick to the stomach.

Julia was twisting her hands. 'Please, Samantha. You know as well as I do that Grace isn't violent. For goodness' sake, how often have we both tried to help her to stand up for herself? With all that awful business last year? And it's much worse than I even knew. There was a boy, and—'

'No!' Samantha felt the word roar out of her. How dare Julia ask her to listen to another sob story? 'I don't care what Grace has been through! We've been here before, haven't we? Poor little Grace and her problems. And we were there for her. I even gave you all the information about the damn school. And now you tell me that she has attacked my daughter! I have to call the police. I have to call them right now.'

She pushed her chair back and practically leaped across the kitchen in the direction of her bag to get her phone.

But Julia got there first. She grabbed Samantha's bag and held it against herself. 'Please, Samantha. Just think for a minute. This is Grace. If they arrest her, I think it'll kill her.'

Samantha grabbed for her bag. 'My daughter is fighting for her bloody life! How *dare* you ask me to think about your daughter? The person who put her there!'

Julia had tears coursing down her cheeks. 'Please, Samantha. I'm begging you. Telling the police about Grace now is not going to help Keira get well. Let's focus on her and then when she wakes up, we can—'

'We?' Samantha was surprised at the volume of her own voice. 'There is no *we* any longer. You aren't a friend, Julia. You don't get to talk about Keira or offer to help or even breathe the same air as her. All you care about is yourself and Grace. Give me my bag.'

She reached out a hand, but Julia took a step back, keeping it clutched tightly to her chest. 'No, please. Just wait a little longer before telling the police about this. Speak to Grace, see for yourself how awful she feels, how sorry she is—'

'Sorry?' Spit flew out with the word, but she didn't care. '*Sorry?* That's a word she should use for breaking a toy or arriving late. You can't just be *sorry* about something like this.

They're not children playing a game – my daughter is fighting for her life. And you think she can just say...' There were so many conflicting feelings flying around that Samantha was fighting to stop them overwhelming her. She started to pace, to pull at her own hair. She wanted to yell and scream and hit something. If the finger she pointed at Julia had been a gun, she didn't know what she might be capable of. 'This is your fault. You've done this. You've mollycoddled her, made her pathetic and weak. Grace, the eternal victim. She's stabbed someone else, but we all have to feel sorry for *her*. No one wants to be her friend, so she can do what she likes, hurt who she wants because she's jealous of them.'

Julia straightened. 'That's out of line. If your daughter wasn't such a manipulative, nasty little madam, she wouldn't be in this position. You have no idea how horrible she's been, because you have no idea what she gets up to, clearly. You didn't even know where she was on Saturday night. If you hadn't let her stay out at all hours, dressed like she was ten years older than she is, then she wouldn't have been in the position to have this happen.'

If she had been a different kind of woman, Samantha would have flown at Julia for that. A part of her that she hadn't known existed wanted to scratch her face. 'You are blaming my daughter for being attacked? Is that what's happening here? Your mousy, miserable daughter has attacked her, and you are saying it's Keira's fault? Listen to yourself, Julia. How much longer are you going to protect Grace from any consequences whatsoever?'

'And when are you going to *give* your daughter any consequences whatsoever? She was supposed to be Grace's friend and all she did was make her life even worse.'

'And you were supposed to be *my* friend. Just shows how wrong a person can be.' Samantha didn't have time for this. Keira was in hospital and she needed to get back to her. Nick could call the police as soon as she got there. They could deal with this.

Julia's laugh was harsh and cold. 'Friend? *Now* you call me your friend? Even though you pretty much denied even knowing–'

Samantha lunged towards her, wrenching the bag from her hands. It must have been open, because her phone fell onto the floor. Before she could pick it up, it started to ring.

It was Adam. He didn't even let her get to the end of her hello. His voice on the other end was frantic, breathy, scared. 'Mum? It's me. You have to come back to the hospital. Right now. Mum, you need to come.'

TWENTY-EIGHT

JULIA

However angry you are, whatever is going on, there are moments when everything has to be put to one side.

All Julia had to go on was Samantha's questions barked into her phone. 'What's happened? Is it bad? I'm coming. I'm coming.'

It was clearly not good news. Julia switched to autopilot, gathered up the tissues and mints which had also fallen from Samantha's bag and pointed towards the door, keeping her voice low so as not to interrupt Adam in Samantha's ear. 'Get in the van, I'll drive you to the hospital.'

All colour had drained from Samantha's face, the red of her anger replaced by a deathly pale. Five minutes ago, she would probably have refused, but now – Julia knew – nothing mattered except getting to her daughter. She nodded and followed Julia like a small child, still speaking to her son at the other end. 'And they've told you nothing? Where's your dad?'

Outside, Julia opened the passenger door for Samantha and then closed it behind her. Adam must have started to cry at the other end because the tone of Samantha's voice changed. 'It's okay, baby, I'm coming. Tell Dad I'll be there really soon. Okay, okay. I'm coming.'

As Julia slid behind the steering wheel, Samantha dropped the phone onto her lap and stared out of the window. Rain began to tap on the windscreen as Julia pulled off the drive, and the scrape of the wipers filled the gap where she would normally have asked what had happened, whether Keira was okay. Apart from their recent conversation at the hospital, it had been a while since she and Samantha had really opened up to one another, but she still cared about Keira. Still cared – she realised with some surprise – about Samantha, too.

After the argument they'd just had, though, how could she? They were on different sides now; both with the same fierce desperation to ensure that their daughter survived this awful situation. Even though the drive to the hospital was less than ten minutes down residential roads, it felt as if it they were on a journey into an underworld; their mutual silence heavy with unspoken accusations, remonstrations and guilt.

Julia had swapped her Ford Fiesta for this van only a couple of years ago, but it was nearly as old as the girls, and the poor suspension meant that they felt every bump in the road. With every ounce of her, she wanted to reassure Samantha, support her, tell her that she'd be there whatever happened. But how could she, now that Samantha knew about Grace? She wanted to beg her again on Grace's behalf, but that was out of the question. Right now, she needed to get Samantha to the hospital; everything else could be dealt with afterwards. Once Keira was okay. *Please God, let her be okay.*

When Samantha did speak, it was so quietly that Julia barely heard her. 'I can't lose her. I can't.'

Julia almost gasped with the pain in her chest. She took her left hand from the wheel and reached for Samantha's, which were clasped around the mobile phone in her lap. 'She'll be okay. I know it.'

Samantha pulled her hands away, still gazing out of the window. 'You don't know anything.'

Her voice was laced with such hate that it stung Julia like a slap. She couldn't blame her for that. If their roles were reversed, wouldn't she have felt the exact same way? Protection was in a mother's DNA. 'What did Adam say?'

There was such a long pause that she thought Samantha was going to ignore her, but eventually she spoke. 'Just that one of the machines had sounded an alarm and people had appeared from everywhere. They'd been pushed out into the corridor. He didn't know anything else. Nick was trying to speak to someone while Adam called me.'

That didn't sound good. Not good at all. Julia's throat was tight and dry, but she tried to keep her voice calm. 'Why don't you call him again?'

In her peripheral vision, she saw Samantha look down at her phone as if she'd forgotten it was there. Her head bowed forward; she was frozen. 'I'm scared to call.'

Julia's insides felt as if someone was gripping them and twisting them hard. There is no fear so great as that of losing your child. The thought of losing Grace was so horrific that she couldn't even think about it. News stories about the deaths of children were too devastating to read. Without Grace, she wouldn't want to live. Samantha's fears would have been her fears: she wouldn't want to call, either. Not knowing was agony, but knowing the worst thing imaginable had actually happened would be the end of everything.

She turned into Nightingale Road. They would be there any moment. 'I'll take you right to the door. Is there an entrance closer to Keira's ward than the main reception?'

Samantha was staring out of the passenger window again. The rain was now heavy enough that she wouldn't be able to see anything. It sounded like gravel was being thrown at them. 'The main reception is fine.'

The windscreen wipers squeaked across the windscreen, clearing a sightline through the water. Julia wanted desperately to comfort her friend. Whatever had happened – and not happened – between them, this was Samantha. She was in appalling agony and Julia should be there for her. Wanted to be there for her.

But how did she do that when it was her daughter who had caused this to happen?

The barrier to the car park took an age to lift. Then they were in and Samantha was taking off her seat belt as Julia drove as close as she could to the main reception entrance without actually driving through the door. Samantha's hand was on the door handle before Julia had even stopped the van.

As she began to let herself out, Julia had to say something. 'Please tell me how she is. Whatever has happened, I'm still your friend.'

After slamming the ancient door closed, Samantha didn't even stop to look back.

Julia was trembling so much that she didn't trust herself to drive home again until her hands had stopped shaking. She pulled into a parking space and turned off the ignition. As the van's engine shuddered off, she leaned forwards, her forearms on the steering wheel, and gave herself up to the hard, painful sobs which she'd suppressed the whole way there.

It would have been indulgent to cry in front of Samantha. Because Julia's daughter wasn't the one whose life was in danger. But Grace wasn't okay, either. Julia hadn't been exaggerating when she told Samantha that going into prison would kill her daughter. The events of the last year had taken more and more from Grace until she looked as if a strong wind might blow her away forever.

Earlier, once she'd calmed down and washed the grief from her face, Julia had tried again to talk to Grace about the revelations in her blog. About that nasty excuse for a boy and what he'd done to her. It had been incredibly difficult to stay calm, not to scream and shout about the injustice of what had happened. But it was impossible to find out more because Grace had closed down the conversation like a slammed door.

'I don't want to talk about it.'

Julia wanted to make her realise how important it was not to push this down inside her, where it would fester and then leak its poison into her view of her self.

'But it was wrong, Grace. What he did. You didn't make this happen. You were drunk and—'

The pain in her scream had pierced Julia's ear drums and her heart. 'I said I don't want to talk about it!' And then she had slammed the door.

When Julia raised her face again, the rain was still crashing onto the windscreen. She sat up, opened her glove compartment for a tissue and wiped her face. Even this made her think about Samantha. She always used to carry tissues – and, once upon a time, baby wipes – everywhere she went. When the girls were young, she'd been so organised with snacks and antiseptic wipes and plasters and colouring books. Julia had never been as prepared as Samantha was.

She also hadn't been prepared for how much harder parenting got once the problems weren't physical ones. Emotional pain couldn't be soothed with a tube of antiseptic 'magic' cream and a lollipop. When Grace was young, she would climb onto Julia's lap for a cuddle. Julia would hold her tight, rocking her gently, talking softly into the top of her head. When Grace had become a teenager, Julia had yearned to do the same for her, but the more pain Grace was in, the more she had locked herself away, unreachable.

Of course, Julia was worried for Keira. But she had a whole medical staff fighting to keep her safe, watching her, caring for her. Grace's emergency was silent, hidden. There was no one helping her except Julia, and she didn't know what to do. When she looked back over Grace's childhood, she realised how many times she'd spoken to Samantha for advice. How often Samantha had provided another perspective, or a push when needed.

Not that she could ask her now. She turned the keys in the ignition. It was time to get back to Grace. Between now and home, she was going to have to work out how to break the news about Keira and what might be going on at the hospital.

How was Grace going to react to the knowledge that her friend's life was back in danger?

TWENTY-NINE

WHEN THEY WERE FIFTEEN

Without Grace knowing, Julia had been to speak to the deputy head at The Grange. Mr Proctor had clearly been concerned and had done his best to resolve the situation, but he was no match for the juggernaut of popularity that was Evie Oakley. According to Grace, the power couple that were Evie and Lee were back together and she was the one who was taking the weight of the blame. For something she hadn't even done. No amount of sitting in a circle with the head of year as facilitator was going to resolve the situation. Grace refused to go to school, to shower, even to eat. It had been the darkest and most terrifying few months of Julia's life.

They had the same conversations over and over. At the kitchen table. In the sitting room. Through a slammed bedroom door. 'Grace, your exams are just over a year away. You only need to go in and do your lessons and then I'll pick you up again. You were doing so well. Don't throw it all away because of some horrible people.'

'I don't care. I'm not going back there.'

John had tried to speak to her, too. 'There are people in this world who are not good, Grace. Believe me, I know. But you need to stand up to them. Make them realise that you are not someone to be treated like this.'

Grace had listened to his advice mutely. He'd taken this as a sign that he was getting through to her. Julia knew that her tightly pressed lips and tapping toes said otherwise.

'I'm not some youth offender that he can counsel into doing what he wants.' Her rant had started as soon as he'd gone. 'Why are you both trying to make me go back there? Send the work home. I'll do it. I'll teach myself on YouTube; it'll be more interesting than half my teachers, anyway.'

Her anger was so out of character that it had pushed Julia even more out of her depth. Where else could she go for help? Nina was a great pal, but both of her boys had sailed through school. Samantha's two were the same. What had she done wrong?

She hadn't challenged Samantha about the overheard conversation at the garden party; there hadn't seemed much point. Maybe she had read more into their friendship than there ever was. She knew that Samantha could be – in Nina's words – a 'stuck-up cow', but she had thought that they had become good friends over the years. After the shock of what she'd heard that day, their relationship had become more distant. She'd realigned her regard for Samantha as that of an acquaintance rather than a friend. And you don't ask an acquaintance for advice about how to deal with your daughter.

And then there had been that terrible, terrible day.

She wouldn't normally have walked straight into Grace's bedroom without knocking, but she'd thought she was in the bath. When she did open the door to see Grace sitting at her desk, her back bent in concentration, Julia thought she was doing some of the work the school had sent home.

'Sorry. I didn't realise you were...'

Grace's head whipped around so fast, her eyes so wide, that

it took Julia a moment to realise what she was seeing. She dropped the basket of laundry that she'd been about to put away. She opened her mouth, but it took the words a moment to come; as if the world was in slow motion. 'Grace, what are you...?'

Grace had pulled her legs up under her black hooded top, dropped what looked like a small blade. 'It's nothing.'

'It is not nothing.' Sickness and confusion and anger and sheer terror made Julia's limbs heavy. It was like being in a nightmare where you can see someone is about to get hurt but you can't get there quickly enough; your legs sluggish, as if walking through treacle.

Somehow, she made it to the desk. 'Grace. What are you doing?'

'It's nothing.'

'Grace.'

'It's not serious. It helps.'

'Show me what you've done.'

Grace looked as if she was going to refuse again. But her shoulders slumped and she extended her leg down onto the floor. Blood had been smudged across three precise incisions. As Julia stared, she saw that they weren't alone. Other, older, scars criss-crossed the top of her pale, tender thigh.

She pulled her gaze away and looked into her daughter's defiant, yet frightened face. 'Oh, Grace.'

'It helps me, Mum. It helps.'

'How can hurting yourself help? How can it?'

If she had felt out of her depth before, now she was drowning. They were on the edge of a deep, dark whirlpool and it was sucking them in.

That day, holding her baby in her arms as her slight body shuddered with sobs, Julia vowed to her that she would never set foot in that school again.

. . .

To give him credit, John had been really good. He was the who had dealt with The Grange and had even pushed them to offer some counselling for Grace.

And – when Julia had bitten back her pride and called her – so had Samantha.

Julia hadn't gone into details about what had happened. It was up to Grace to decide how much she wanted to tell other people. But, when Julia explained that there had been some unpleasantness from other girls, Samantha had been really supportive. 'How dare those little witches pick on Grace? I'll send Keira round with carrot cake.'

When Keira came the very next day, it was pure joy to hear their chatter and laughter from Grace's bedroom. Since the garden party, Samantha and Julia hadn't seen much of each other outside the quick coffee Samantha made for Julia after work, and the girls hadn't either. But they seemed to be able to pick up exactly where they'd left off.

They even went out together as a foursome to a local cafe. It was like the old days, when the girls were small, the two of them joking about old memories.

Then Samantha suggested they start to make it a regular thing. 'I don't know why we haven't done this in such a long time.'

Keira agreed with her. 'Yeah, it's really nice to see you, Grace. I've missed your laugh.'

Were they being kind and charitable, or did they mean it? Julia found that she didn't really care. They were putting a smile back on Grace's face, and that was all that mattered right then. 'We should do it more often. Maybe we could even reprise a trip to the beach one day?'

Grace's face darkened a little. 'As long as we don't run into anyone from school.'

Keira linked her arm through her friend's. 'If we do, they'll have me to deal with.'

Watching Grace grin her appreciation at her friend took Julia right back to their nativity play all those years ago. And it gave her an idea.

Back home, she broached the subject as gently as she could. 'It was nice being with Samantha and Keira today, wasn't it?'

Grace nodded. 'Yes. Really nice. I'd forgotten what it was like to all be together.'

'But it was good? Being together?'

'Really good. Just like old times.'

Julia had to suppress a smile at her fifteen-year-old daughter talking about 'old' times. 'If it was possible for me to get you into St Anne's where Keira is, do you think you'd want to give it a try?'

When John had last spoken to The Grange about Grace, the head had suggested something called a 'managed move' to another school. It was a system the local heads used to virtually swap pupils to give them a fresh start, if they needed it. On the way home from the cafe, Julia had cooked up the idea that they could ask whether he could get Grace into St Anne's. But only if Grace wanted to, of course.

From the look on her face, it seemed as if she might. 'Really? And I could get in? I could be with Keira?'

For the first time in months, fresh shoots of hope pushed up inside Julia. 'Well, we can definitely try.'

They agreed not to say anything to Keira or Samantha until they knew if it was possible. Julia called John that night and he said he'd call the head teacher at The Grange first thing in the morning. 'It's a great idea. She needs to be back in school. And at least a girls-only school will eliminate any hassle from boys.'

When she'd said goodnight to Grace that evening, Grace had smiled up at her. 'I feel so much better, Mum.'

Julia kissed the top of her head. The girls would be back together. And she had enjoyed Samantha's company today, too. Maybe she should give their friendship another go? Samantha was who she was. Around other people, she changed. But that didn't mean they couldn't be friends. It was all going to be okay.

THIRTY

SAMANTHA

From the end of the corridor, Samantha could see that Nick had his hands on Adam's shoulders, his face close to their son's. She tried to walk faster, call out to them, but her voice wouldn't come. As she got closer, she could see that Adam was crying. *Oh, no. Please, no.*

Nick turned at the sound of her shoes in the echoing corridor. Leaving one hand on Adam's shoulder, he reached out for her. 'Thank God, you're here.'

He pulled her in and she wrapped her arms around him and Adam. She wanted to ask, but she was afraid of the answer. Adam was at last six inches taller than her, but he bent to press his face into the bottom of her neck like a small boy. 'Oh, Mum. It was so scary.'

She looked at Nick. Years of marriage meant not always having to ask a question to be understood. 'We still don't know anything. They said they would come and get us.'

For the next ten minutes, they stood, then sat, on the row of plastic chairs, always touching: a held hand, an arm around a shoulder, a palm on a knee. They were in limbo; holding on to one another to prevent themselves being sucked down into hell.

Half of Samantha's heart was on the other side of those doors, fighting to stay alive; the other half was next to her, pale and terrified. She slipped an arm around Adam's back. It had been a long time since she'd been able to hold him on her hip with one arm. When they are small, everyone tells you how quickly it goes, but you never really believe them. 'She's going to pull through this, Adam. You know how strong she is.'

Julia's words came back to her. *She's going to be okay. She's strong-willed.* They had been comforting at the time, but now... Now, she couldn't think about that.

Nick followed her lead. 'Your mum's right, son. Remember all those times she used to drive you crazy, demanding to come into your bedroom when your friends were there? She'd stand outside your door with her arms folded and refuse to move.'

Adam was old enough to realise that they were trying to give him – and themselves – something positive to focus on. 'I used to have to pick her up and carry her back to her own room.' His face crumpled into tears. 'I'd do anything right now to have her follow me around and refuse to go.'

Samantha's heart was tearing with the strain of holding her own grief and trying to comfort Adam. Then Nick's arms were around them both, surrounding her, pulling Adam in. She was squeezed so tightly between them that she could barely breathe.

'Mr and Mrs Fitzgerald?'

They turned to see one of the nurses from Keira's ward, her face a study in conveying nothing. 'Shall we find somewhere quiet to talk?'

Nothing good ever started with those words. Not parents' evenings, not business appointments and certainly not conversations in hospitals. Nick was the first of them to be able to speak. 'Of course. We'll follow you.'

In absolute silence, they followed the nurse back into the ward but, instead of proceeding to Keira's side room, they took a sharp left into a small room with a PVC sofa and chairs, a low coffee table and a water dispenser.

The nurse glanced at Adam and then back to Samantha. 'I want to let you know what's happening with Keira. Are you happy for me to go ahead?'

Samantha took one of Adam's hands in both of hers once they had all sat down. When she spoke, her voice was a mere croak. 'Yes. Please. How is she? What's happening?'

'Keira's blood pressure dropped quite dramatically, which is what caused the machines to bleep and everyone to come running. That can be caused by several different factors, but, because she experienced trauma to the head when she hit the ground, we wanted to get her down for a CT scan immediately.'

Nick had sat down with them, but now stood up again. Samantha knew that he wanted to pace the room, but there wasn't enough space. Instead, he ran his hands through his hair, rubbed his chin, then went back to his hair. 'Okay. What does that mean? When will they know what's causing it?'

The nurse spoke so slowly and calmly that Samantha wanted to shake her. 'It seems that a blood vessel in the space between the skull and the brain has been damaged. This means that some blood is collecting between the skull and the surface of the brain.'

Blood collecting in her head, near her brain? Samantha was hot, her vision hazy at the edges. She couldn't pass out now. 'Is that dangerous? It sounds dangerous. Is it dangerous?'

Nick put a hand on her shoulder, rubbed it with his thumb. She had a sudden memory of a tearful Keira, aged about three or four, telling Nick she had bumped her knee and needed a 'special thumb rub' to make it better. Nick had laughed. He hadn't even realised until that point that it was something that he did unconsciously.

Again, the nurse paused before replying. It must be part of their training. To give relatives time to take in the information that might blow their world apart. 'It can be. From the scan, Keira's appears to be small, and the team is monitoring it closely. It may be that it heals itself. But we have a neurosurgeon on standby in case it needs to be operated on.'

Operated? Neurosurgeon? Samantha understood the words, but they seemed to float around the room like unexploded bombs. When she covered her mouth with her hand, it was trembling.

Even Nick took a moment to compose himself in order to be able to ask more. 'And what is the surgery? How do you do it?'

Again, the nurse glanced at Adam before she spoke. 'The neurosurgeon would drill what are known as burr holes into Keira's skull, then a flexible rubber tube would be inserted to drain the haematoma.'

This was surreal. The room seemed to be slowly spinning. Samantha could feel herself swaying in her seat. Nick sank down beside her and held her still; it wasn't until she saw the fear in his face that she felt truly terrified.

'I know that this is a lot to take in. But if Keira does need surgery, we want to be able to move quickly, so I have the surgical consent form here for you to sign.'

She lowered the clipboard that she'd been holding close to her chest. Samantha recognised the form from the last one she'd signed – for her C-section for Keira. She knew that on that sheet somewhere were the list of risks involved in the surgery. They were going to have to sign to give the surgeon consent to drill into Keira's skull.

Nick took the clipboard from the nurse and stared at the incongruously bright yellow paper with unseeing eyes.

This time, it was Adam who spoke. 'Is it very dangerous?'

The nurse neither nodded nor shook her head. 'I know it sounds invasive, but it is actually a straightforward procedure. But, yes, there are always risks to any surgery. There is a full list on the consent form. Further bleeding, infection and so on. There is also a very small risk of a stroke.'

This time it was Nick who leaned forwards, his elbows on his knees. 'Oh, my God.'

Reflexively, Samantha put her hand across his back where it lay, uselessly. What comfort could any of them give?

'I can come back if you'd like some time—?' The nurse's voice was kind. Although this must be relatively routine for her, she wasn't rushing them.

'No.' Nick sat up. 'We have to sign it, don't we? If she needs it, she needs it.' He looked at Samantha for confirmation. Her throat was too dry to speak, so she merely nodded. He took the pen joined to the metal clip of the board with a twisted string and signed in the generous flourish she knew so well.

'Thank you.' The nurse took the board back and stood. She must have a million other things to do. 'You are welcome to stay in here. Can I get you something to drink? If you want to go to the canteen or go home, we will call you as soon as we have any news.'

Home? As if they were going to be anywhere else but right there. 'We'll be fine here for a while, thank you.' Nick was back to himself, back to polite smiles and taking charge. Samantha felt as if she were floating above this whole situation, tethered only by the grip she had on Adam's hand.

When the nurse quietly clicked the door closed, she crumpled onto Nick's chest.

Though they'd planned to stay in the room together, it was far too small for comfort. Nick needed to move; he was like a caged tiger. Even Adam had suggested three times that he go and get them coffee, water, paracetamol for the headaches that were pounding through all of them. He was his father's son: he needed something to do.

On top of everything else, Samantha couldn't cope with their combined pent-up energy. 'Why don't the two of you go to the canteen? You can get something to eat. I know it's been at least three hours since you've eaten, which must be some kind of a record.' She poked Adam in the side, her thin attempt at a joke rewarded with an equally thin smile.

'Why don't we all go? The nurse said she'd call us as soon as there was news.'

Samantha shook her head. 'I have somewhere else I want to go.' When she'd asked at the nursing station whether there was a hospital chapel, they had given her directions to a new multi-faith room.

Aside from the plastic sign on the door, she wouldn't have known it from any of the other doors on the second-floor corridor. She knocked on it gently, then a little louder. When there was no response, she pushed it open.

Larger than she'd expected from the door, the room was set out like a church: four rows of chairs faced a table with a white tablecloth, on which there was a candlestick and a display of flowers. There was no one else there. She slipped onto a chair at the back, the first one in from the aisle.

She'd never been particularly religious; her own parents were both atheists, as far as she knew. But her grandmother had been a Methodist and she had been the nicest person Samantha had ever known. Sitting in that room on the ward, she'd felt so helpless. Who knew if prayer made any difference? She was willing to try anything.

She closed her eyes. Waited for inspiration. Behind her, she heard the door slide open across the carpet tiles. She turned to see a broad-shouldered man, about her height, with a black shirt and dog collar. He nodded to her but didn't speak.

She cleared her throat. 'I hope it's okay for me to be here. The nurses said I should just come in.'

'Of course. You are very welcome. Each of the local faith

leaders takes a day here, and today is mine. I'm Father David and I'm here if you'd like to talk, or want someone to pray with you. But you are very welcome to just sit and rest in the peace.'

There *was* an air of peace about the place. In the quiet, maybe she could get her mind around everything that was happening. 'I'm not really... I mean, I don't go to church.'

His face was so kind. 'It's okay. We don't ask for membership cards.' When he smiled, his left eye winked at her like a kindly uncle.

On an impulse, she decided to ask for help. 'Could you pray with me? I don't know how it works.'

He took the chair across the aisle from her. 'It would be my pleasure. It's just a conversation, really. Between you and your god.'

She didn't even know if she had a god. 'How do I start?'

He held out his hand, his elbows resting on his knees. 'Well, some people like to start by saying thank you for something. And then sorry for anything they feel remorseful about. And then they might ask God for something that's important to them right now. How does that sound?'

Samantha swallowed. 'I'd like to say thank you for my beautiful daughter. Well, both my children, really.'

Father David nodded, but he didn't interrupt.

'And I'd like to say sorry for, for being a bad mother, for not taking better care of her.' Her voice was wobbling and her eyes were filling again.

Father David didn't try to placate her by dismissing her self-criticism, but just by sitting there quietly, he was a comfort. When she didn't continue, he gently prompted. 'And is there something you wanted to ask for help with?'

She nodded, the hot tears spilling from her eyes. 'For her to be okay. Keira, my daughter, I just want her to be okay. Please, God, I'll do anything. Just let her be okay.'

THIRTY-ONE

JULIA

When she opened the front door, she could hear Grace's music whining down the hall. Samantha's cruel words came back to her. *Your mousy, miserable daughter... pathetic and weak.* Even if she wasn't already wound as tightly as a ball of twine, this music would have put her nerves on edge, the depressing dirge reinforcing the mood she was about to walk into. And she was going to make it worse.

Her knock on the bedroom door was answered by a pale blotchy face. Frightened eyes scanned Julia's expression. 'So, does she know? Is everything still a secret? What's happening?'

It felt like an age ago since Julia had sent the text to Samantha by accident. With everything that had happened in the last couple of hours she had completely forgotten that she hadn't sent Grace a message after all. Exhaustion washed over Julia so hard that it made her want to lie down on the floor right there and give into it. 'I need to talk to you. And then we need to speak to your dad.'

Grace looked as if she might throw up there and then. 'What's happened? What has Keira said? What did Samantha say?'

'Let's sit down, love.'

Grace let Julia guide her towards her bed. Julia resisted the urge to fold the piles of clothes and shake out the bunched-up duvet. What did any of that matter, now?

Grace picked up a notebook which was open on her bed and held it, closed, against her chest. 'Just tell me, Mum. What did Samantha say?'

Was that journal the keeper of the truth in all this? Samantha had told her that a couple of the school mothers had confessed that they would secretly read their daughters' journals, check their phone messages. Julia had never done that with Grace. Had preferred to trust her, give her privacy for her thoughts. Had that been the wrong thing to do?

She took a deep breath. Where to start? 'I'm not sure how Keira is doing.'

Grace frowned. Had she been so sure that Keira was going to recover? At fifteen, was she still so young that she thought everything was going to turn out okay? 'Did Samantha not tell you? I thought the operation was successful? I thought she was going to be all right?'

Julia took a deep breath. 'There's another problem, sweetheart. Samantha had to rush to hospital. Keira's not in a good way, I guess. But I'm sure she'll be fine.'

Grace looked a little less scared for a moment. 'And I'm still safe? No one knows I was there?'

This was a harder question to handle. 'Samantha knows.'

Grace's intake of breath was so sharp it made Julia jump. 'What? Oh, no. What did she say? She'll tell the police. They're going to arrest me.' Arms flying everywhere, she was whipping herself up into a panic.

Julia had to calm her down. 'We don't know what she'll do. She's focused on Keira right now. Let's talk to Dad and—'

Jumping up from the bed, Grace started to pace. 'No! No! I don't want to talk to Dad. He'll make me speak to the police.

It'll all be worse. Mum, please, please don't call Dad.' She turned to face Julia, pulling at her sleeves, scratching at her arms; it was awful.

She hadn't always been this anxious. Yes, she had been shy as a child, but she was always happy. Contented. That was the word Julia's mother had always used to describe her when she was crayoning a picture or playing make-believe with her stuffed animals. *She's such a contented little soul.*

When had it changed? When had that kindness and sensitivity become... oversensitivity and anxiousness? Had that awful experience at the party triggered everything else, or was there more? Was Samantha right? Had Julia mollycoddled her? Had she spent so much time making sure that Grace was okay that she'd left her unable to cope with life? Was this her fault?

'Please sit down, sweetheart, we can work this out.'

Grace spun around. Her eyes were wild. 'No! We can't! You don't understand. You don't *know*.'

That was the second time Julia had had that levelled at her in the last hour. It felt as if any way she turned, someone was throwing her lack of knowledge in her face. 'What don't I know? Tell me. If you don't tell me, Grace, how the hell can I help you?'

She hadn't meant to raise her voice. Hadn't meant to let Grace see her frustration. But she felt like the water butt in the garden after a heavy rainfall; one drop too many and she was overflowing.

Grace didn't answer. Instead, she grabbed a bag, pulled open the top drawer of her chest of drawers and began to pull out clothes and shove them into the bag. 'I need to leave. I need to go. Everything will be okay if I'm not here.'

Fear loomed over Julia, over the whole room. She had no idea what was going on at the hospital right now. She'd asked Samantha to tell her how Keira was, but the slammed car door had made it clear that Julia would be the last person to know.

What if the unthinkable happened? What if Keira didn't make it?

Would that make Grace a murderer?

She watched her pale, slight daughter – the girl who would rescue the tiniest of spiders and release them in the garden. How could she be responsible for taking someone's life? It didn't make sense on any level. She didn't even know if Samantha had told anyone yet. Nick? Adam? The police?

Julia tried to take Grace in her arms. 'Stop. Baby, please stop. Look at me.'

Grace shook her off. When she turned, her eyes were dark, impenetrable pools. 'No. Listen to *me*. I don't want to be here anymore.'

There was a weight, a frigidity to her tone that meant Julia did not need to ask her what she meant. Sometimes you didn't need to see someone in a hospital bed to know that they were at risk.

In that second, she made a decision. 'Okay. Let's pack.'

THIRTY-TWO

SAMANTHA

After leaving Father David, Samantha met Nick and Adam in the canteen, where she managed to swallow half a cup of peppermint tea. They were back in the relatives' room when they got the news.

'Mr and Mrs Fitzgerald?'

Samantha, Nick and Adam looked up like three baby birds about to be fed. Nick recovered first and stood up. 'Yes.' He coughed, cleared his throat. 'Yes, that's us. How is she?'

The nurse smiled. Was that a good sign? Samantha also stood and slipped her right hand into Nick's, her left still in Adam's.

'I'm sorry you've had such a frightening time. After consulting with the neurosurgeon, she's confident that Keira's haematoma won't need surgery. We've moved her back on the ward.'

Nick squeezed Samantha's hand tightly, but his face stayed focused on the nurse. 'Can we see her?'

She smiled again. Samantha was scared to hope, but that must be a good sign. 'Yes, of course. She's very sleepy, but she's awake.'

Samantha wanted to grab her, shake her, make her say it again. *Awake?* Had she heard her correctly? Keira was awake? There was a high-pitched keening noise. It took a minute for her to realise it was coming from her own mouth.

Nick let go of her hand and wrapped a strong arm around her; she was so weak, it was all that was holding her up. He coughed out a sob, wiped the back of his wrist across his eyes, then squeezed her again. 'Come on, let's go and see our girl.'

In the circumstances, the nurse relaxed the two visitors to a bed rule. As soon as she'd keyed in the code to get them onto the ward, Samantha let go of both Adam and Nick and almost ran in the direction of Keira's bed. There were several nurses, doctors and visitors in the corridor and it was all she could do not to barge them out of her way. *Let me get to my daughter.*

And then, there she was, propped up slightly, her eyelids heavy but open. She was awake. It was really true, she was awake.

Tears dripping from the end of her chin, Samantha reached out and stroked Keira's soft cheek with the back of her fingers. 'Hello, my darling. Oh, hello, my beautiful girl.'

'Hello, Mummy.'

Keira hadn't called her 'Mummy' for years. Resisting the urge to scoop her into her arms, Samantha pressed her lips gently to her warm cheek. 'How are you feeling, sweetheart?'

'I'm tired.' Her eyelids fluttered as if they might be about to close.

But Samantha wasn't ready to lose her to sleep again so soon. 'Are you in pain?'

Nick came in and took Keira's other hand. Adam hovered at the end of the bed. Keira shook her head. A tiny movement. 'No. I don't think so. Maybe. I don't know.'

They probably had her on morphine. Samantha could remember that from her C-section. There was pain, but it felt as if it floated around you rather than inside you. 'You just rest, my darling. Mummy and Daddy are here. We're not going anywhere.'

Keira closed her eyes and went to sleep. Samantha was no doctor, but she could see how different it was from earlier in the day. Her breathing, the twitch of her mouth. This was a gentle, healing sleep. She leaned forward and rested her forehead on Keira's hand, and gave in to the tears of relief.

An hour later, Keira was alert and talking to them. It was incredible.

She had been in and out of sleep; each time she opened her eyes she was a little less foggy, a little more talkative. Samantha hadn't left her side. She would have climbed onto the bed and used her own body to cover her daughter like a blanket, if the nurse would have allowed it. She never wanted to let Keira out of her sight again.

Though she wasn't sure why, she still hadn't told Nick what Julia had told her. There was a part of her that didn't want to spoil the joy of this moment. Also, she had no way of knowing what Keira could hear when she had her eyes closed, and she wasn't about to leave her to speak to Nick outside in the corridor. Right now, Keira was here, she was safe. She would talk to her first, before she called in the police to speak to Grace.

Nick stretched his arms and yawned. They had sent a protesting Adam home in a cab half an hour ago, telling him to get some sleep. Now that the worst was over, exhaustion was creeping over all of them. Nick stood up and stretched his legs. 'Can I leave you two alone for ten minutes while I hunt down some decent coffee?'

Keira actually rolled her eyes. 'You and coffee, Dad. Maybe we can ask one of the nurses to hook you up with a caffeine drip?'

She must be feeling better if she was back to 'roasting' her father, as she called it.

And maybe this would give Keira an opportunity to talk to Samantha, if she wanted to. They'd sidestepped around talking about the attack. Thankfully, the doctor had told the police that they couldn't talk to Keira yet, which meant that they could just be with her for a while, in a bubble, not thinking about what came next.

Nick leaned across the bed and pressed his lips to Keira's forehead. His voice was gruff. 'We missed you, kiddo.'

Maybe it was the lack of make-up, or the dishevelled hair, but Keira's smile made her face look the same as it had when she was a little girl. 'Good to be back, Dad.'

Once he was gone, Samantha pulled her chair nearer to the head end of the bed. 'You're going to need to speak to the police soon, love. When the doctors think you are up to it.'

Keira's smile disappeared. 'No. I don't want to.'

'It's okay. No one's going to rush you if you're not up to it. I just didn't know if you wanted to get it out of the way. Just tell them what you remember, that's all.'

Her mouth was a tight line. 'There's no point. I don't remember anything.'

It was so obviously a lie, but Samantha wasn't about to push her. 'Okay, love. That's absolutely fine. I'll tell them that. But what if someone else remembers something?' She paused. 'The thing is, I know what happened. All you need to do is confirm it, and I can tell the police for you.'

She instantly regretted her words when she saw how frightened Keira looked. 'What do you mean? Who remembers something?'

She looked agitated. Samantha could have kicked herself. But now she'd started, she might as well get it over with as quickly as possible. 'I know about Grace. Julia told me. I know it was Grace who hurt you.'

The colour that had started to come back to Keira's cheeks drained away. 'Grace? Grace said she did it?'

Her shock was confusing. Had she been telling the truth when she said she didn't remember? 'She told Julia. She said you were arguing, fumbling over a knife, and that it was an accident.'

'An accident?' Keira was searching her face as if there was more to this story than Samantha was telling her. 'That's all she said? That we were arguing and it was an accident?'

Slowly, Samantha nodded. What was Keira not telling her? 'Is there any more to it than that?'

Keira shook her head. 'No. She's telling the truth. It was her.'

Until that moment, Samantha hadn't fully believed that this was the whole story. For all the fury she'd vented at Julia, she still couldn't reconcile the quiet, timid Grace with something like this. But, if it really was true, the police needed to know sooner rather than later. 'If you're not feeling up to it, maybe I can speak to the police about what happened? Then you can give them the details when you feel stronger.'

'No.' Keira shook her head. 'You can't tell them.'

'Why not?'

'Because there's stuff you don't know.'

'So, tell me.'

Keira shook her head. 'I can't. But you cannot tell the police about Grace. Please, Mum, I'm begging you.'

She was getting agitated. Samantha stood up. 'Hey, shush, shush. Don't get upset. There's nothing to be worried about. You can tell me anything, baby. Anything at all. I'm your mum. I love you.'

Keira's hand still had a catheter in the vein and she almost pulled the tube out in grabbing for Samantha's hand. 'If you love me, you'll tell the police I don't remember. And Dad. And

Adam. You need to tell everyone that I don't remember. Promise me.'

Samantha was scared that she was going to put back her recovery by getting so stressed. She would have agreed to anything for now. 'Okay, okay. I promise. But it is true? It was Grace?'

Keira looked at her for a few heartbeats, then nodded. 'Yes. It was Grace. But it was my knife.'

THIRTY-THREE

JULIA

Even as she packed clothes into a suitcase, Julia knew this was a ridiculous idea. For a start, where the hell were they going to go? But she needed to buy some time; the look on Grace's face had terrified her. *I don't want to be here.* She knew what she meant.

For a long time, she had been hypervigilant around Grace, terrified that she might start to hurt herself again. It had been absolutely exhausting. Julia wasn't completely naïve: she'd heard the term self-harm before, but had never thought it would be something that would happen in their family. Grace was loved, she knew that she was the centre of Julia's world and they had always had such an open relationship, able to talk about anything. When she'd turned thirteen, fourteen, nothing had changed. Her music had got moodier and her clothes darker, but she was still her Grace.

What had terrified Julia the most was that she hadn't known it was going on. She'd known how unhappy Grace was, that she was spending so much time alone. Yet she hadn't seen it coming.

Starting at St Anne's had seemed like a chance to get it

right. To start again. That first morning, Grace had been nervous but excited.

'How do I look, Mum?' She had given Julia a twirl in the hall at home.

The uniform had cost an absolute fortune, but it was worth it to see that smile. 'You look fabulous.'

Grace's smile had wavered a little as she picked up her new school bag. 'I hope they like me.'

'How could they fail to like you? And anyway, Keira is there. She'll look out for you.'

Julia had considered asking Keira to walk in with Grace that first morning, but then the head teacher at St Anne's had invited Julia and Grace to a meeting in her office before morning registration. Just knowing that Keira would be on the playground reassured Julia, though. She would make sure that Grace was okay.

The first couple of weeks had been fine. Keira had shown Grace around and – even though they weren't in the same classes – had met up with her in the playground. Julia wasn't sure why this had started to change.

'Did you see Keira today?'

'No. I think she had hockey practice at lunchtime.'

'Who did you walk home with today?'

'Just on my own. I wanted to get back quickly to get my homework done.'

Julia had been concerned, especially when Grace had started to spend more time in her room again. But Grace had told her that everything was fine. That she didn't need to worry. Had Julia believed her because she was convincing, or because she couldn't bear to think that it was all happening all over again?

Now, here they were. Yet again, Julia had let her daughter down, leaving her to suffer through those feelings alone.

This time, she had to find a way to make this all okay.

But how the hell *was* she going to make it okay?

Packing to leave was just buying time. Grace had been so relieved that she wouldn't have to speak to the police that she hadn't even asked where they were going. She'd just trusted that Julia would have a plan. A way to sort this out, so that everything would be fine.

Julia did not have a plan. All she had was an absolute determination to keep her baby safe. Safe from the police. From Samantha. From herself.

Her phone ringing in the back pocket of her jeans made her jump. It was John. *Dammit.* In the events of the last couple of hours, she'd forgotten that she'd arranged to speak to him.

Grace's head poked out of her bedroom door. 'Who is it? Is it Samantha? The police?'

Julia shook her head. 'It's your dad.'

Grace's eyes widened. 'Don't answer it.'

'I have to, Grace.'

Grace stepped into her bedroom. 'No, you don't. You know you'll end up telling him. And then he won't be able to stop himself from reporting what's happened.'

Julia reached out and held the top of her arm. How much did she want to pull up those sleeves, check that she hadn't hurt herself again? 'Grace, I'd called him and told him to come over. His car will be outside. If I don't answer, he's going to knock anyway.'

Grace shuffled from one foot to the other while she seemed to be weighing this up in her mind. She loved her dad. If she was this worried about seeing him, it was a clear sign that she wasn't well. Once this was all over, Julia needed to get her some more help.

After a few moments, Grace came to a conclusion. 'Don't be long with him. I want to leave soon.'

John's car was parked around the corner from the flat. As she slipped into the passenger seat, it struck Julia how ironically clandestine this was: meeting her ex-husband for a conversation in his car.

John must have been struck with the same thought. 'Did she see you leave? Did we get away with it?' He smiled at his theatrical whisper. Julia was about to ruin that playful mood.

It was easier not to answer his question directly. 'Grace is upstairs. She's really upset about this business with Keira. It's made her scared to go out.'

John raised an eyebrow. 'Really? It's not as if she goes out much, anyway. Aren't you always trying to encourage her out of the house?

She felt a pang of guilt. She *was* always trying to do that. Trying to get Grace to meet up with friends and spend some time away from her bedroom. If only she had realised. All the time Grace was in her bedroom, she'd been safe. 'I've tried to tell her that this is a rare thing to happen. People don't just get stabbed in this area.'

John laughed his gruff, humourless laugh. 'I wish that were the truth. It's happening more and more frequently. For a while, we could get away with blaming kids coming on the train from East London. Now we've got our home-grown wannabe gangs.'

If only that were the case in this instance. 'Have you had a lot of trouble with them, then?'

'Not me personally, but yes. They've tried knife amnesties, but there are still a lot of youngsters out there carrying knives. It's for their "protection"; that's what they say when they're brought in. It's a losing battle.'

'And what happens when they're caught? What happens to them?'

'Oh, they'll get a sentence, but they won't serve it all. Not if it's a first offence and they behave themselves inside.'

'But they would definitely go to prison? Whatever the circumstances?'

John raised an eyebrow. 'Yes, of course.'

'Even if it was self-defence?'

John sat up in his seat and looked at her intently. When Grace was young, she used to tell him not to look at her with his 'police face' on. 'Why are you asking me all this, Julia? What do you know? Has Grace heard something? Because you have a duty to report it if she has.'

She didn't want to give herself away. 'No, no. Sorry. It's just been on my mind, I guess. Stupid question.'

'Anyway, we're not here to talk about someone else's crime. You wanted to talk about Grace. What's going on?'

She wasn't going to tell him now. Grace was right. It would be his duty to report it. Telling him would put him in an awful position. 'I'm worried about her. I think it's all starting up again. The bullying.'

'At the new school? Again? What is it with her? Why can't she just find some new friends? We can't keep moving her to new schools.'

She was irritated at the 'we'. They'd made the decision together, and he *had* been good at dealing with The Grange. But when it came to St Anne's, it had been Julia who'd attended all the meetings with the new head teacher, filled out the reams of paperwork, kept Grace's spirits up when she'd taken her shopping for school uniform.

It wasn't John's fault, though. He didn't know all that she knew. About why the bullying had started, and continued. About the awful experience that Grace had had. Should she tell him that, at least? He was Grace's father and they had always talked things over that related to her, even when they were in the very midst of their divorce. But Grace was fifteen now. Was it her decision whether to tell her father?

'I know. You're right, she can't keep moving schools. But I just wanted you to know that she isn't doing so well at the moment. She needs help. Counselling. Therapy. I know the school offered her a few sessions, but she needs more than that. We might have to pay for it privately.'

This, as well as being true, was a good cover for why she had asked him to meet her. Admittedly, they could have talked about it over the phone, but John was too concerned about Grace to raise that. 'Really? That bad? Shall I come in and see her?'

'No, she doesn't really want to talk about it at the moment. Not even to me. I really think she needs to talk to someone professional.'

John nodded. 'Okay. Of course, I'll contribute. I can find out who we recommend to youngsters, if you like?'

'Thank you. Yes. That would be great.'

As she let herself back inside the flat, Julia almost fell over the bags that Grace had dragged into the hallway. Grace was sitting in the lounge, waiting for her. When Julia opened the door, she sprang up out of her chair. 'As soon as Dad has gone, I think we should leave.'

Julia still hadn't worked out what they were going to do. Maybe she could check them into a hotel, just for a night. Give Grace a chance to calm down and realise how futile it would be to run away. Before she had a chance to say anything, though, there was a knock on the door. Had John ignored her suggestion that they leave talking to Grace for tonight?

Grace was already at her bedroom door. 'If it's Dad, just tell him that I'm asleep.'

Julia waited for the click of her door closing before opening the front door. It wasn't John standing there.

Samantha looked different; her face not quite so taut with fear. Still, she wasn't smiling.

Julia hadn't heard from her since dropping her off at the hospital earlier. 'How's Keira?'

'She's awake.'

Relief coursed through Julia with such force that it nearly knocked her over. In its wake, it left fear. 'Has she said anything? About what happened that night?'

If Samantha had told the police what had happened, it would be them knocking on the door now, not her. What had Keira told her that had stopped her from calling them?

'She has. Can I come in? I need to speak to Grace.'

THIRTY-FOUR

SAMANTHA

There was a pile of mismatched bags in the hallway. What was going on? 'Where's Grace?'

'She's... not here at the moment.'

Not here? Keira was lying in that hospital bed and Grace was... where? With her friends? Out for ice cream? 'When will she be back?' As she spoke, she followed Julia through to the kitchen.

Julia had pulled out a seat for her. 'Do you want a coffee? Tea?'

'This isn't a social call.'

'I know that. But they give you a glass of water even when you're being interviewed by the police.'

Was she trying to make a joke? Because that was going to go down sideways. Still, Samantha sat down, even though she felt as if she had done nothing but sit for the last few days.

Julia turned her back to make the drink that she hadn't even accepted. How could she be so calm? So untroubled? Samantha had come here to get to the bottom of things, but now she had half a mind to let the police do it and to hell with Grace. If it hadn't been for her conversation with Keira earlier, she would have done just that.

It was my knife. The look on Keira's face when she said it spoke volumes. Up until that moment, everything had been about that night, that attack, that moment. But Keira's side of the story had been about so much more than that.

Samantha had been almost winded by the revelation. 'What do you mean, it was your knife?'

'I carried it with me. For protection. When I walked across the park.'

There was so much she wanted to unpick in that statement, Samantha didn't know where to begin. 'Where did you get it?'

Keira had lowered her gaze, twisted the top of her bedsheet. 'I don't remember. Someone gave it to me.'

Another obvious lie, but Samantha didn't want to push her too much yet. 'I still don't understand why you were in the park on your own. Why weren't you with your friends?'

'There was some trouble at Adventure City. We got split up.'

She was clever. If Samantha didn't know – from the police talking to Keira's friends – that this was also a lie, she would have believed it. It was one of the reasons Samantha didn't like her going there. The theme park on the seafront was full of families during the day, but as the afternoon gave way to early evening, the atmosphere changed. Anywhere full of teenagers was liable to have its moments of trouble. The *Southcliff Gazette* regularly had reports of fights in and around that area.

'Why didn't you call me to pick you up?'

A year ago, Samantha had complained to Nick how she was little more than a taxi service for Keira's social life. She realised now that it had been happening less and less. When was the last time Keira had called her for a lift rather than finding her own way home?

Keira had shrugged, still not meeting her eye. 'I felt like a walk.'

In different circumstances, Samantha would have laughed at this. 'Okay, I'll buy that. But why didn't you call your friends? Meet up with them again? You told me you were going to get pizza with them.'

'They were with some boys. They're not nice. I didn't really want to be with them.'

This reminded Samantha of the Instagram pictures. 'Were you with a boyfriend?'

Keira shook her head. 'No. I don't have a boyfriend.'

'Sweetheart, there were pictures. On your other Instagram. The police have seen them.'

Keira seemed to freeze for a second. 'He's not my boyfriend. He's just someone from that group. He wasn't with me. He stayed with them.'

If all this was true, why wouldn't she look at Samantha? 'Keira. You need to tell me the truth. I can't do anything unless you tell me the truth.'

When her daughter looked up, her eyes were full of tears. 'I'm so sorry, Mum.'

Samantha stood and put her arms around her. 'Oh, baby. It's okay, it's all going to be okay. I'm just trying to understand what happened.'

And the police would be asking these questions shortly, too.

She held Keira in her arms while she cried. A nurse stuck her head around the door and mouthed, 'Everything okay?' and Samantha nodded and smiled. Everything was not okay, but this particular issue was not a medical one.

Once Keira had stopped crying, she sat back in the bed and accepted a tissue from the box Samantha held out, blowing her nose noisily.

Samantha rubbed her arm and gave her a moment to

compose herself. She needed to get to the bottom of this before she handed it over to the police. 'Just tell me what happened, from the beginning.'

The scrape of Julia pushing a mug of coffee in her direction brought Samantha back to the moment. Julia sat down opposite her. 'What has Keira said? I'm guessing you haven't spoken to the police yet.'

Samantha's instinct was to tell Julia everything, spilling every fragment of Keira's story, every emotion she was feeling across the kitchen table for them to pick through and piece together. There had never been any filter between her and Julia, no need to gloss over events to hide the ugly truth. But this was different. 'She's told me a few things. I want to talk to Grace about them. To find out her side of things. Before I call the police.'

She added the last sentence to poke at Julia, to remind her how serious this was going to get for her daughter. Maybe that would break through this curious calm that she was operating under.

Julia stared down into her black coffee as if she was about to tell her own fortune. 'Grace is really fragile right now. Let me ask her what you want to know.'

Again, a rage burned in the pit of Samantha's stomach. How dare she call *Grace* fragile? 'She must have been pretty strong when she was wielding a knife at my daughter.'

She felt a shot of pleasure seeing Julia wince. 'I don't think that's quite what happened.'

'Really? You know what happened? If that's true, why are you the one afraid to speak to the police?'

'Because they will look at the bare facts. Not at what has really been going on here. That your daughter has been part of a group making my daughter's life an absolute misery.'

'If that's what you think, why have you never mentioned it before? How come you have had no idea what has been going on?'

Fire flashed in Julia's eyes. 'Hang on a minute. Your daughter is the one who is out of the house every day and night. You don't seem to know where she is half the time.'

'My daughter is out of the house because she has *friends*. She's not a weird recluse!'

That was nasty and Samantha knew it. And, although she was not about to admit it to Julia, it was also not true.

Once Keira had started talking to her, it had all come tumbling out. Sometimes she looked at Samantha, other times she stared at the tissue she was shredding onto the blanket.

'They aren't my friends, Mum. Not really. I haven't really felt part of it all for a while.'

This was a total shock. 'What do you mean? You've practically grown up together. Cleo, Phoebe, Katie, Mia, Tilly, all you girls. You've spent so much time together.'

'I know. We were friends. Maybe. But everything changed. This year, it's all been different. I've seen them be different. To me. And to Grace.'

Grace again. A few days ago, Samantha had felt guilty that Keira had left Grace behind. Sorry for the quiet girl with no friends. Now she seemed to be at the centre of everything. 'What did Grace do?'

Keira shook her head. 'She didn't do anything. She's just... well, she's just Grace, you know?'

Samantha did know. She'd always been a quirky kid. But what difference did that make to Keira? 'I'm not understanding, Keira.'

Keira sighed, looked at her. 'When Grace started, they knew that I knew her. They've been horrible to her. Really horrible and' – she paused – 'I was, too.'

An unpleasant feeling prickled in Samantha's stomach. Maybe Julia's bullying accusation was true? 'Oh, Keira.'

'I know. I'm not proud of myself. But it's not like anyone in the group listens to me, anyway. I'm not like Cleo and Phoebe. People just do what they say and follow them around. People like me. I'm just a follower, I suppose.'

It was breaking Samantha's heart to hear all of this. Her beautiful, confident, popular – or so she had thought – daughter, saw herself as such an unimportant person. 'Why did you stay friends with them, then? Why not stay with Grace?'

A flash of the Keira she knew: exasperated, frustrated by her naïve parents. 'Oh, Mum. You don't understand what it's like! If I stopped hanging around with them, I'd be nobody.'

Samantha felt a chill down her spine. *Nobody*. Of course she understood. Because hadn't she done the exact same thing?

She hadn't wanted the drink that Julia had made her, and now she pushed it away. 'This isn't getting us anywhere; I need to speak to Grace. Or I swear I will go straight out that door and call the police.'

Julia stood up. 'Grace is in her room. I'll ask her if she wants to speak to you.' She didn't look at Samantha as she left.

Samantha sat, tapping her fingernails on the table. She didn't even know what she was going to say to Grace. Keira had asked what Grace had said and Samantha had foolishly told her. Then Keira had corroborated the story. 'It just happened fast, Mum. It's not her fault.'

There was a piece of this puzzle that was missing, though. Keira was in hospital, so she couldn't push her too hard. But she wouldn't make the mistake of telling Grace what Keira had said. This time, she was going to get the truth.

But when Julia reappeared in the kitchen, she was alone. Her eyes were wild. 'She's not there. She's gone. And she's not answering her phone. Samantha, I'm scared. You didn't see her. I'm scared she's going to do something terrible.'

Without thinking, Samantha jumped up and grabbed her phone and keys. 'We'll find her. Come on, let's make a list of where she might be.'

THIRTY-FIVE

JULIA

Samantha's car was almost silent. The leather interior and walnut dashboard muted the minimal sounds from the engine. She drove too slowly.

Julia's head twisted back and forth, searching out of every window, praying for a glimpse of Grace. When Grace was small, and they were going to a play centre or somewhere else busy, she'd dress her daughter in bright reds or yellows to make her easy to spot. Now her wardrobe of black clothes rendered her invisible. How had Julia never realised that might be the reason she wore them? Social camouflage. 'Maybe I should have taken the van. We should have split up. We would be looking in twice as many places.'

Samantha's calm voice was in contrast to her white, pinched face. 'You're in no position to drive right now. I don't want to be visiting you in hospital, too.'

So, she'd visit her? Was that an olive branch, or just a habit? 'I can't even think where to look. How bad is that? My child leaves the house and, not only do I not notice, I have no idea where she might have gone.'

'When are you going to stop blaming yourself?'

'What?' For a second, Julia took her attention from the road and glanced at Samantha.

'Blaming yourself. For everything that happens. Grace's lack of friends. The fact she doesn't go out much. Her shyness. For as long as I've known you, you've made it your fault – you didn't take her out enough, or she's too much like you. As if that's a bad thing.'

Julia's eyes blurred and she pushed the tears away with the heel of her hand so that she could see the wet grey street more clearly. 'Maybe it is a bad thing. Being like me.'

'That's ridiculous.'

'Is it? Failed marriage. Daughter who is' – she couldn't bring herself to tell Samantha about the self-harm – 'miserable. Living in a flat the size of a shoebox at nearly fifty. Not exactly the success story of the year, is it?'

Samantha took a hand from the steering wheel and counted out her reply on her fingers. 'Bringing up a child virtually on your own, having the courage to start over once your marriage ended, building your own business from scratch, being a flipping nice person to everyone she knows.'

This wasn't about her, it was about Grace, but Julia couldn't let that one go. 'Not nice enough to claim as a friend, though, eh?'

Samantha frowned. 'What do you mean?'

She had no idea why she was bringing this up now. 'I heard you. At the garden party. Talking to that woman with the uber-posh accent. Denying that we were even friends.'

When Samantha didn't reply, Julia took her gaze from the road for a second to look at her again. She could almost read the confusion crossing her eyes.

'At what garden party? The one at my house three years ago?'

'Yes. I was in the toilet. I heard that woman's opinion of me and Grace. She was talking to you outside, and you just let her talk about us as if we were nothing. You made it sound as if we barely knew each other.'

Samantha shook her head like she was trying to retrieve the memory from the recesses of her brain. 'I don't even remember that, Julia. That's crazy. Have you been thinking about that for three years?'

To say she'd been thinking about it for that long would be an exaggeration, but it had definitely changed things. Up until that point, they had been friends; after it, she hadn't really been able to see Samantha as someone she could trust. 'I just think that friends should be loyal. Should stick up for one another.'

Samantha sighed. 'I know you do. But it's different for me.'

What did that even mean? 'Different, how?'

Samantha looked uncharacteristically flustered. 'It's just… look, we can talk about this another time. What about Grace's friends? Have you tried calling any of them? Or their mothers?'

Julia barely knew Grace's friends from St Anne's. Or their mothers. This wouldn't have happened to Samantha. She knew all of Keira's friends' parents. Drank coffee with them. Had dinner with them. Was that why Grace found it so difficult to make friends? Because she'd had no blueprint of how to do it?

Fear, guilt, love all battled in her chest so that she could hardly breathe. 'I don't have their numbers. I don't know where they live.'

Samantha glanced at her. Was there judgement there? 'What about the friends from her old school? Could she have gone to one of them?'

That was more possible. She did at least know where one of them lived. 'Bridge Street. We can try Beth.'

When they got to Bridge Street, Julia wasn't 100 per cent sure that they were at the right house. But this was no time for timidity. She knocked hard on the grey front door. When it opened, she almost wept at the sight of her daughter's old friend.

Beth was more shocked than emotional. 'Julia? Oh, hi.'

'Hi, Beth. I'm looking for Grace. Is she with you? Have you heard from her? Do you know where she might be?'

Was Beth more confused by the barrage of questions or the thought that she might know any of the answers? Either way, her face reddened before she spoke. 'No. I haven't heard from Grace in months. She didn't reply to my messages after she... after she left, and so I just kind of... left it.'

Beth was one of the friends who hadn't stood by her. Of course Grace wouldn't have been to see her. What had Julia been thinking? Still, she had nothing else to go on. 'Do you know anyone she might have gone to? Or where she might be?'

Beth's hand flew to her mouth. 'Has she run away?'

The last thing Grace would want was her old 'friends' gossiping about her. 'No, it's just that I need to tell her something important and she went out without her phone.'

Did Beth look disappointed? 'Oh, well, maybe she went to Recreation Park? She used to go there a lot on her own. We used to tell her not to, but she didn't care.'

The park? So, she went there frequently? That explained why she'd happened to be there that night. 'Okay. Thanks.' She turned to go and then couldn't help herself from turning back. 'Friends are supposed to look out for each other, you know. Whatever happens.'

Beth blushed again and shut the door.

When she slipped back into the car, Samantha was on her phone. 'Yes... I'll be there in half an hour... Love you, too.'

Julia clicked her seatbelt into place. 'Nick?'

'Yes. He just wanted to know when I'm coming back. He needs to make a phone call and it might take a while. Adam's there, but Nick doesn't want to leave Keira in case he misses the doctor doing his rounds.'

'Just drop me back to the van; you go.'

Samantha was leaning forward to look in her left-hand wing mirror. The parked cars lining the one-way road made it difficult to see what was coming. 'I've told him I'll be there in thirty minutes. Let's find Grace first.' Without looking at her, Samantha reached over and squeezed her hand.

That was what made Julia start to cry. 'I'm so sorry, Samantha. I just didn't know what to do.'

Samantha pulled out behind a silver people carrier. She repeated herself: 'Let's find Grace first.'

She was right. This wasn't the time for reconciliation or retribution. Julia moved so that she could fit her hand into the pocket of her jeans for a balled-up tissue. She blew her nose. 'Shall I call the police?'

Samantha clicked her indicator to turn left towards the park. 'It's daytime and she's fifteen. I don't think the police will be interested in helping just yet.'

Julia had to say it. 'But in the circumstances. If they know what's going on.'

Samantha didn't answer immediately. 'I don't think we should call them yet.'

That was a small relief.

For the next couple of minutes, there was silence. Then Samantha spoke. 'Nick's phone call. It's actually a phone interview. For a new job.'

Was she just trying to give Julia something else to think about? Because Nick's professional development wasn't really up there right then. 'I see.'

'It's in Scotland.'

That did grab her attention. 'Wow. Would you all have to move up there?'

Samantha nodded, but her face was devoid of any clue as to how she felt about such a big change. 'Yes.'

Julia realised that she would miss Samantha a great deal if

they moved, but, right then, she had no spare emotion to offer. 'I see.'

Samantha pulled over into the car park and the two of them jumped out and started to scan the park. Julia wasn't sure what to do. Should she start calling Grace's name like a stray dog?

She walked a few more steps before realising that Samantha wasn't beside her. She turned to see her standing still and looking to her left. 'This must be where it happened.'

Julia froze. She'd been so focused on finding Grace that – amazingly – she hadn't actually thought about that. She saw what Samantha saw: a patch of grass, a bench and a stray piece of jarring yellow and black 'police line' tape caught in a bush. 'How did this happen to them?'

Samantha was deathly pale and her breath came in short gasps. Wrapping her arms around herself, she shook her head slowly, her eyes filling with tears. 'I can't... I'm sorry, I can't do this. I need to be with Keira.'

Julia stepped back towards Samantha, reached out her hand to her shoulder. 'Of course, you go to her. Thank you for—'

But Samantha had already turned on her heel and walked away.

Julia couldn't worry about Samantha right now. She couldn't even worry about Keira, or the police, or anything except finding Grace. Yes, Grace was fifteen and more than capable of looking after herself, but her words rang in Julia's ear like a knell. *I don't want to be here.*

She shivered. The sun was low in the sky and a cold breeze was turning into a wind across the park. She shoved her hands into her pockets to find her gloves, but there was something else in there with them.

A note. In Grace's careful handwriting. Julia had worn the jacket earlier, so Grace must have put it in there before she left the house that afternoon.

Dear Mum

I'm sorry. I know you think this is your fault, but it's not. You are the best mum I could have ever had. I hate that I keep hurting you and give you so much trouble. I just wanted to tell you that I love you and I'm sorry.

Love Grace x

With every word, Julia's chest got tighter and tighter until she felt she couldn't breathe. 'Oh, Grace. What have you done?'

THIRTY-SIX

SAMANTHA

Samantha was halfway back to the hospital when she realised that she'd left Julia at the park with no car.

'Dammit.' She hit the steering wheel with the heel of her hand.

She almost turned around and went back for her, but the thought of being in that park, back where it had happened, just turned her stomach. Julia would be okay.

Even as she thought that, she felt unsettled. Was it true that she was a bad friend?

She could just remember the garden party Julia had referred to. She'd been so anxious about it beforehand. It had been the first time she had hosted such a large group of the St Anne's mothers and their husbands. She had spent weeks researching the right wine and finding a caterer who she could rely on. Nick hadn't helped much. 'I thought they were coming to see the garden? Anyway, if these people are your friends, surely they won't care what shape the wine glasses are?'

It had felt like the right thing to do; Julia needed to grow the business after her divorce and Samantha had lots of friends with large gardens and pots of money to spend on them. Still, when it came to it, she'd regretted ever having the idea. She'd been like a cat on a hot tin roof the whole time, trying to make sure that everything went perfectly. If she hadn't made much of her friendship with Julia, it hadn't been on purpose. Surely Julia could see that Samantha had been doing her a favour by offering up her many friends as potential clients?

Friends. She thought of Julia's definition of friendship. *Friends should be loyal.* Then she remembered that other WhatsApp group.

She hit the steering wheel again. Three times. 'Dammit. Dammit. Dammit.'

It felt so different walking into the hospital this time, knowing that Keira was okay. For the first time, she actually noticed the other people around her, smiling as she passed them. Still, she couldn't wait to see Keira again, kiss her, hold her hand. But she hadn't even made it halfway up the corridor when Adam stood up from the seats outside and came loping towards her. 'Hi, Mum.'

Despite her relief that Keira was safe, fear was never far from the surface. 'What are you doing sitting outside here? Is everything okay?'

He smiled. 'Everything is fine. She's just having a sleep. Why don't we go and get a coffee?'

Somehow, he had guided her past the entrance to the ward and in the direction of the hospital canteen. 'I don't need a coffee. I'll just go and sit with her for a bit.'

'Well, I need a sandwich or something. Will you come with me? I haven't seen you for the last couple of months and I owe you a slice of cake after all those food parcels.'

The last part, emphasised as it was by a disarming smile, won Samantha over. She had missed Adam since he'd returned to university in September. After having him home all summer, it had been a wrench when he'd left for the train station again.

'Okay. It would be nice to have you to myself for a little while. Where's your dad?'

'He had a phone call to make. About the job.'

She was surprised Adam knew about it. 'He told you?'

'Yes. Earlier on. He sounds pretty excited about it.'

'Does he?'

'Yeah. One of his old workmates who lives there has sent him some emails with houses he's found and he's been filling him in on what it's like up there.' He shrugged. 'It does sound pretty great.'

Obviously Nick's old colleagues would know nothing about what was going on down here, but Samantha still felt irritated at the thought of them tempting him with promises of great restaurants and – she knew for sure – golf courses.

They'd reached the entrance to the canteen and Adam stepped forward to hold the door open for her. When did he get so grown up? So thoughtful?

They must have just missed a huge rush because, though the queue for hot drinks was short, there wasn't a spare table anywhere. At least she'd be able to return to Keira sooner. 'Shall we just take them back with us?'

'No, let's go for a walk outside. Apparently, there's a nice garden with benches.'

Adam seemed pretty determined to have her to himself. If she didn't know him better, she'd think he was feeling neglected. But that wasn't Adam's style. 'Okay. But I don't know how long I'll last. It's getting cold out there.'

As she said that, she thought of Grace, out there somewhere, and Julia searching for her. Would Julia let her know when she was found? Should Samantha be the one to call?

Adam was right about the garden. Although it wasn't huge – you could walk the square perimeter in less than a minute – it was bright with winter blooms, and leafy. They sat themselves down on a bench and shuffled in close together for warmth. 'Julia would love it here.'

She couldn't stop thinking about her. Couldn't stop thinking about what she'd said about friends being loyal. And Grace, too. Keira had made her promise not to tell anyone what Grace had done, but she couldn't do that forever. At some point, she was going to have to tell Nick. And the police.

She focused back on Nick's news. 'So, your dad has persuaded you that Glasgow is a good idea?'

Adam laughed and wagged his finger. 'Nope. You're not going to pull me into it. It's not as if I'm going to be living there, is it?'

They had never talked about whether Adam would come home permanently after graduation and she wasn't about to ask. There was only so much her heart could take right now. 'Still, you must have an opinion.'

Adam took the lid from his hot chocolate and blew on it. The steam floated on the cold air. 'I've only been to Glasgow once, but it seemed like a great place.' He frowned. 'You're not keen on Scotland, I assume.'

She sipped at her peppermint tea: it was still scalding. 'It's not that. I actually love Scotland. It's just that I don't like the idea of your father making all these plans behind my back. He didn't even tell me that he'd been made redundant.' Her voice wobbled as she spoke.

It wasn't fair to be talking to Adam like this. She hadn't known she was going to say any of it until the words came out of her mouth. Since Adam had gone to university, something had shifted in their relationship. There were times when he was the one being the grown-up.

'I don't think it was like that, Mum.'

It was exactly like that. Now she had started to talk about it, it all came out. 'And it's not just your dad. Keira has this whole other life and maybe even a boyfriend I knew nothing about. What are *you* going to tell me? You haven't actually been studying at university for the last two years at all?'

Adam laughed. 'I can confirm that I've definitely been there. How much studying I've done might be more up for debate.'

He raised an eyebrow to make her laugh, but she wasn't feeling very jovial. Now that Keira was out of danger, the reality of everything was coming crashing down around her: Julia's judgement on her friendship, Nick's secrecy about his job and – worst of all – Keira seeming to have a whole other life that she knew nothing about. 'I don't understand why they've been lying to me.'

Seemingly wrestling with his next words, Adam drank his hot chocolate in silence for a while. She knew the expression on his face. He was about to tell her something he didn't want to say. She'd seen it before when he had completely changed his A levels without telling her.

'It's not entirely their fault, Mum. The way you are sometimes are is, well, it's a bit difficult.'

She hadn't been expecting that. 'What do you mean?'

He sighed. 'Nothing. This isn't the time to be talking about it.'

Her throat was tight with emotion. He made it sound as if this was a conversation that he'd been waiting to have with her for a long time. 'Yes, it is. Tell me, what is the way I am sometimes?'

He sighed. 'It's just that you have these... I don't know, these... ideas about how our life should be. Where we go on holiday. Who our friends are. It's all really important to you, but sometimes it can be tiring to live up to it.'

There was a hard knot in her throat which was threatening to choke her. 'Live up to it? All I've ever wanted is for you to have a good start. I want the best for you both.'

'We know that, of course we do. Oh, Mum, I don't want to upset you.' He put an arm around her and, much as she didn't want to cry, she couldn't stop tears from dripping from the end of her nose.

She shook her head. 'Maybe I need upsetting. Julia just told me that I haven't been a very good friend. Maybe I haven't been a good mother, either.'

'Hey. I didn't say that. You've been a brilliant mum. The best. It's just that it feels like you want our lives to be perfect and they can't be. We're not perfect. And that's okay, isn't it?'

She looked at her handsome, clever, generous boy. He – and Keira – were both perfect to her. She had tried so hard to make their lives, their home, their friendships as good as they could be. How had she got it so wrong? 'Does your dad think this, too?'

'Oh, yeah. We've got a family group chat where we all complain about you.' He nudged her to show he was joking. 'Don't be ridiculous. Dad wouldn't let either of us say a word against you. But I do think he was worried about telling you about the job. He knows how much you love our house and being able to do all those dinners and events with your friends.'

That stung more than Adam would have intended it to. Was that what Nick thought was important to her? A big house and posh restaurants? Maybe Julia wasn't the only one who had misunderstood her. Although, if everyone in her life had misunderstood what was important to her, maybe she was the one in the wrong.

Tiredness washed over her. She wanted to speak to Nick and to Julia. But first, she wanted to check in on Keira. She reached over to kiss Adam on the cheek. 'Thank you. For being honest with me. Am I allowed to go and see your sister now?'

Adam glanced at his watch. 'Yeah. It should be okay now.'

That was a weird thing to say. 'What do you mean, "okay now"? What's going on?'

'Nothing bad. It's just that Keira has a visitor and they wanted some time alone.'

Anxiety crept up Samantha's spine. 'Who is it? One of her so-called friends from St Anne's?'

He tipped up his cup to drain the last of his hot chocolate, then stood up and held out his hand for hers. 'Kind of.'

She felt sick at having something else kept from her. This entire trip to the canteen and garden had been designed purely to keep her away. 'Who is it, Adam? Who is with her?'

Adam took a deep breath and looked at her. 'Right. Don't be cross.'

THIRTY-SEVEN

JULIA

Recreation Park wasn't vast, but it was large enough for it to take one woman quite a while to find a daughter who might not want to be found. Aside from the pond, and clumps of trees which could easily hide a slight fifteen-year-old, there were two different playground areas and various benches where Grace might be. Julia passed several young families as she criss-crossed her way over every inch of it. A dad running after a toddler whose pudgy, uncertain legs were surprisingly fast; a grey-faced mother pushing a crying baby in a pram as if she were sleep-walking. Julia could remember those days as if it were yesterday. How exhausting, overwhelming and yet wonderful they had been. She wanted to warn each of the parents she saw: *It goes so fast. It goes so fast.*

She hadn't found the first years of motherhood easy. Grace hadn't been a particularly difficult baby, but the sheer relentlessness of every day had sometimes felt like a slog. Julia's mother – on the phone from her home in Spain – had urged her to meet some other mums. *Go to a baby group.* She'd tried. But making new friends was a lot harder than it sounded. What were you supposed to do? Just sit next to someone and strike up a conversation about weaning or nappies or how bloody hard it was to have a husband who worked every hour God sent and left her feeling like a one-parent family?

Which was why, when Grace and Keira's friendship had brought her Samantha, Julia had been hopeful that, finally, this might be a friend she could arrange play dates with and talk about all the tiny worries and successes of bringing up a child.

She checked her phone again. John hadn't responded.

She had left John a voicemail pretty soon after Samantha had left. 'Hi, John. I need your help. Grace left home without telling me and I have no idea where she is. I'm worried about her. Really worried. She's not in a good way. Can you call me? Or come? I'm in Recreation Park. Sorry to bother you when you're probably catching up on your sleep after your long shift, but... yeah, I just need your help. Call me. Thanks.'

Why had she apologised? She was calling him because their daughter might be in danger of doing something awful and she had apologised for bothering him. What was wrong with her? Samantha had asked why she always took the blame for everything. Was that why she was apologising now?

Meanwhile, the park looked bigger every time she scanned it. She needed another pair of legs, another pair of eyes. What about Nina? Maybe she could help?

The phone rang several times before Nina picked up. She sounded out of breath.

'Hey, Julia. Ask me where I am.'

That threw her. 'Er, hi. Where are you?'

'Up a flipping mountain in North Wales. Rob keeps telling me it's just a hill, but...' She broke off and started laughing. Julia could hear her husband shouting, 'It *is* a hill!' in the background.

Nina came back on. 'Sorry, Rob surprised me with a midweek break and we're doing some kind of walking tour with the promise of pubs. Rob has wanted to do it for years so now we haven't got the boys at home we thought, why not? We'll be back on Friday, though, if you want to take me up on that offer of a night out? Anyway, what can I do for you?'

All the way away in North Wales, Nina wouldn't be able to do anything and there was no point dampening her mood by offloading about Grace. Julia tried to keep her voice light. 'Nothing important. I was just going to see if you were free to meet up, but we'll sort it when you're back. I'll let you get back to your mountain.'

'Okay, love. Take care. I'll call you when I'm home.'

Julia had reached a bench and she sank down onto it. Her mother was in Spain and she didn't want to talk to her until this was all over. What was the point in worrying her when she couldn't do anything from there? Nina was in North Wales and John was probably fast asleep after his early shift. Meanwhile, Grace clearly wasn't here, but she had no idea where to go next or who to ask for help. For a few moments, she leaned forwards, holding onto her waist, and let the tears come.

'Are you okay?' An older man with a small white terrier was standing in front of her, looking very concerned.

She shook her head. 'No. I'm looking for my daughter. I can't find her.'

'Oh, dear. How long has she been gone?'

She looked at her watch; time seemed to have lost all meaning. 'Almost two hours.'

His eyes widened. 'Oh, no. Have you called the police? How old is she? What does she look like?'

Julia took a tissue from her pocket and blew her nose. 'She's fifteen. She's got long, dark hair.'

'Fifteen?' He laughed. 'Sorry, I thought you meant a little kid! Teenager, eh? She'll come home when she's hungry.'

He walked away, shaking his head and chuckling to himself. Of course, she could understand his reaction. To anyone, a fifteen-year-old sounded a lot less vulnerable than a five-year-old. But Grace *was* vulnerable. *I don't want to be here anymore.* Julia heard her saying that over and over again.

When she was five, Grace had had Keira to protect her. And now she was on her own. 'Oh, Grace. Where are you? Please be okay.'

Again, she checked her phone, and again tried to call her daughter. It rang and rang, then connected to voicemail. 'I'm not answering. Don't bother leaving a message. Just text me, you weirdo.'

Despite the teenage negativity of the recording, Grace sounded so upbeat, so cheery. How long had it been since she had used that tone of voice? It was so hard not to cry again. Julia ignored her daughter's instruction. 'Where are you? Where are you? Please, Grace. Call me. Let me know that you're okay. We can work everything out, I promise.'

Should she promise? From when she was very small, Julia had brought Grace up to know the strength of a promise. That it should never be used unless you really, really weren't going to break it. Could she promise that this was going to be okay? That Samantha or Keira wouldn't tell the police? That their whole world wasn't about to implode?

The longer Grace was missing, not answering her phone, the more scared Julia was getting. At some point, she was going to have to call the police. Samantha was right. They were not going to be concerned about a fifteen-year-old not answering her phone for two hours; to get them to take her seriously, she would need to tell them everything she knew about Saturday night.

She stared at the screen of the phone. Should she just call them now and get it over with?

Her phone rang in her hand and she almost dropped it. Samantha's name moved across the screen and she took a deep breath before accepting it. 'Hello. Samantha?'

Samantha also sounded breathless. 'She's here, Julia. Grace is here with Keira. And they want to talk to us together.'

THIRTY-EIGHT

SAMANTHA

Samantha had paced the corridor so many times that she was getting annoyed with the squeak of the soles of her shoes on the hard floor.

When Adam had finally allowed her into the ward, she'd marched straight to Keira's bed, where the two girls' faces had turned to look at her. Though Grace blushed, they were both difficult to read. Guilt? Defiance? Secrecy? Had she been so inscrutable as a teenager? Maybe that was why she'd caused so much impatience in both her part-time families.

'Grace. I'm surprised to see you here.'

Grace fidgeted in her chair, looking uncomfortable in her own skin. 'I just came to see Keira.' She looked towards her friend. It was a familiar gesture.

Keira was looking much more like her normal self. And sounding like it, too. 'Mum, can you give us a bit longer? We really need to talk.'

Anger bubbled in Samantha. 'Do you not realise how terrified your mother is right now, Grace? She's out looking for you.'

Again, Grace looked at Keira, who took control. 'Can you call her, Mum? We really need to talk right now.'

Samantha had to bite down on her lip not to lose her temper. It took a few moments to compose herself. 'We need to know what's going on, Keira. This is unacceptable.'

Unacceptable was no way strong enough for what Samantha wanted to say, but Keira nodded. 'When Julia gets here, we'll talk to you both. I promise. But please can we just have ten more minutes?'

Ten more minutes. If she'd had a penny for every time they'd said that when it was time to go home from a play date. Lost below a pile of Lego or Barbie dolls. *Please, Mummy. Ten more minutes.* They weren't eight years old anymore, though. And this wasn't a game. 'I'm calling Julia now. As soon as she gets here, we want the truth from you both. I'll go and get Dad from the canteen, too.'

'Can it just be you and Julia first? Then you can tell Dad.' Keira's voice was uncharacteristically uncertain. It wasn't as if Nick was a strict authoritarian. What did she not want to say in front of him?

'Okay. You can tell me first and then I'll speak to Dad.'

As soon as she'd left the girls, she'd called Julia, to put her out of her misery and to offer to collect her. But Julia declined. 'I'll call a cab. It'll be quicker.'

Samantha recommenced walking up and down the corridor, unable to sit down and stay still. It was tempting to go and find Nick and Adam in the canteen, but she didn't want to miss Julia's arrival. What were the girls going to tell them?

Nick might be having his phone interview by now, anyway. She realised that she hadn't wished him luck. Or said anything encouraging at all. It was just too much to think about that on top of everything else. Why did he have to do this now? Yes, Keira was awake, but there was still so much uncertainty – she was still in hospital, for goodness' sake. How could he have a job interview like nothing was going on?

Because he had to. She knew that. His job was what paid

their mortgage and bills. Of course he was going to worry about losing it and not having another to go to.

But Glasgow? It was hundreds of miles away. Away from their families, their friends. Surely there were other jobs, other companies? And if there weren't, there had to be other options that didn't mean they had to leave their home.

She was still pacing twenty minutes later, when she heard the door at the end of the corridor open at the same time as she heard her name. She turned to see Julia running towards her. 'Samantha. Is she okay? Is Grace okay?'

She waited for Julia to reach her. Her breathlessness gave away that she had probably run all the way from the taxi rank near the emergency department. 'Slow down. She's fine. They're in there now. They wanted ten minutes to talk, and they've had double that. It's time they told us everything, don't you think?'

Julia nodded, the relief practically dripping off her. 'Let's go.'

THIRTY-NINE

JULIA

Julia practically fell onto Grace. 'I was worried sick.'

Grace squeezed her once and then let go. 'I am fifteen, Mum. I normally leave the house on my own.'

Swallowing down the litany of fears she'd had over the last couple of hours wasn't easy, but Julia managed it. 'You don't normally leave notes in my coat pocket that terrify the life out of me.'

Grace's eyes rounded and her hand went to her mouth. 'I'm so sorry. I put that there yesterday. I didn't think you'd have seen it yet.'

Julia couldn't remember if she'd even worn that coat yesterday. 'It's okay. Telling me you were going out would have been nice, though.'

Grace wrinkled her nose. 'Yeah. Sorry. I just didn't want to get into it with you and Samantha. I needed to see Keira.'

Seeing Keira sitting up in bed, it was difficult to remind herself that they had all been worrying about whether she would make it. She looked pale and a little tired, but other than that, she was her normal self. 'Hi, Julia.'

'Hi. How are you feeling?'

'I'm okay. There're some spare chairs over there.'

Samantha was already sitting near the top of the bed. Julia fetched a chair from the far wall that Keira had pointed at and sat at the bottom of the bed, next to Grace. It felt as if there were battle lines drawn, but she was unsure who was on which side.

'So, what's going on?' Samantha looked at each girl in turn.

Grace was picking at the skin around her thumb nail and Julia reached out to make her stop.

Keira took a deep breath. 'Okay. We're going to tell you everything, but you need to listen and not start doing things.'

'What do you mean?'

Grace was nodding in agreement. 'Like calling the police. Making a big deal. Telling everyone.'

Samantha looked like a volcano on the brink of eruption, but her voice was icily calm. 'Forgive me if I think my daughter being stabbed is a reason to make a big deal.'

Grace flinched at her sarcastic tone. Julia didn't want Samantha speaking to her like that. 'I think we need to listen to them.'

For the first time, Keira looked nervous. 'I'm not really sure where to start. Okay, I do. I did have a boyfriend.'

'The one in the Instagram pictures?'

'Yes.' Keira glanced at Grace. What did that look mean? What did they both know about this boy?

'Okay. Was he from school?'

Keira shook her head. 'I met him at Adventure City. There was a group of boys and they all started talking to us. They followed us onto the Galacticar and, somehow, I ended up sitting next to him. All the girls were so impressed, I just kind of went with it. Nothing really happened. But we were up there again the following Friday and they were there, so we hung out with them again and we kind of...' She trailed off, clearly embarrassed about talking to her mum about this.

Samantha took her hand. 'It's okay, you can say anything.'

'Well, we kind of got together and it was really good. He was really nice to me, kept telling me how beautiful I was. All the other girls were really jealous.' Keira bit her lip.

Julia understood. She really did. Having an out-of-school boyfriend was a status symbol. Social currency.

Surprisingly, Grace took over the story. 'The thing is. I know... knew him, too. He used to go to my old school.' Her face blushed a dark red. 'He wasn't very nice to me.' She turned and looked at Julia, her eyes saying everything she couldn't.

'Oh, sweetheart. Was he the boy who—?'

Grace's nod cut her off. She didn't want her to finish and Julia was happy not to say the words aloud.

Samantha was, of course, confused. 'How was he not nice? Was he involved in the bullying?'

Julia opened her mouth to speak for her daughter, but Grace got there first. 'At a party, I was drunk and he... he took advantage of that.'

Samantha didn't need the details explained. 'Oh, Grace, I'm so sorry.'

Grace pushed away furious tears with the back of her hand. 'When I saw Keira with him, I had to warn her. Tell her what he was like.'

'And I was a total idiot.' Keira was frowning. 'I was enjoying all the attention. I know that now. Not from him, so much. From my friends. I was someone for a while. They were all really impressed when I told them I'd been to parties with him and his friends. When I told them...'

She trailed off again and looked at Grace. Grace smiled at her, then spoke to Samantha. 'He's in some sort of gang. I don't know the details because I don't have anything to do with anyone from my old school anymore. But he is really bad news.'

Samantha's anger had evaporated to be replaced by a look of

shock and fear. 'Oh, Keira. Why were you with someone like that?'

'I don't know, Mum. I feel so stupid. And Grace tried to warn me what he was like, but I didn't want to hear it. I just thought she was being jealous or something.'

'So, how does this fit in with what happened to you?'

'I was at the park with him. He was – well, he wanted more than I wanted and it was getting a bit too much. Then Grace walked past.'

'It was just a coincidence. I like walking in the park when I'm feeling down and I just saw them together. He – Lee – he was pulling her about a lot.'

Keira looked as if she might be sick. 'We'd been sitting on the bench and he wanted... he wanted to sit on the ground, in the bushes. He said it would be private. But I knew what that meant and I wasn't ready for that.' Her bottom lip began to tremble. She looked like a young child.

They *were* still children. That was the problem. They were children trying to deal with adult issues.

Samantha stood and took Keira in her arms for a moment. 'Oh, baby. My poor baby.'

Grace turned to Julia. 'When I got there, I realised who it was and all I could see was him pulling on her arm. Trying to get her off the bench.'

'He was saying that I was being a child. That if I was serious about him, I had to show it or it wasn't worth him sticking around. All his mates had been telling him that I was leading him on.'

'I called out and asked if she was okay.'

'And I wasn't, but I didn't know what to say. Lee told her to leave us alone.'

'But I could tell she didn't want it. I know what he's like, so I came closer. Told him to get off her.'

'He did let go of me, but then he started on Grace.'

'He was right up in my face. I could feel his spit on me. He was calling me loads of names. It was awful, but I wasn't going to let him scare me. Not again.'

'I was worried he was going to hit her. So, I got up and told him we should go.'

'I was just so angry by then that I started yelling. I don't know where it came from. I was shouting and telling him how vile he was.'

'And that's when he pulled the knife out.'

Samantha must have known as well as Julia did that this was coming, but they both took a sharp intake of breath.

'He was waving it in my face. Telling me he was going to use it if I didn't go.'

'And then she said that there was no way she was leaving without me.'

The two girls looked at one another and smiled. In any other circumstances, it would have made Julia's heart sing. 'What happened?'

Keira frowned. 'We're not really sure. I remember him lunging towards Grace and I tried to grab his arm. Maybe I did grab his arm.'

'I tried to move out of the way, I think. But I remember seeing his face. It was so red. So angry. And then he kind of twisted around. And then... then... Keira just fell on the ground.' Grace put her hands up to her face; the memory must have been painful.

Julia rubbed her back. 'Oh, sweetheart.'

'I called the ambulance straight away,' Grace directed this at Samantha. 'I called them and I held Keira and I kept talking to her, like the woman on the phone told me to. I told her to stay awake, not to fall asleep, not to...' Her face crumpled into tears and Julia pulled her close, rocking her in her arms.

Over the top of Grace's head, she saw Samantha do the

same with Keira. Samantha spoke into Keira's hair. 'It's okay now, girls. We'll help you to tell the police all of this.'

Both girls answered together. 'No.'

Julia could see that Samantha was as confused as she was. This wasn't their fault; it wasn't their knife. Why did they not want to make sure this nasty boy was arrested for what he'd done?

FORTY

SAMANTHA

Samantha's phone rang; it was Nick. 'Hang on a minute, I need to talk to your dad.'

'Please don't say anything yet. Please, Mum.'

Keira looked so desperate that Samantha nodded agreement. What exactly did she think her dad was going to do?

She pressed to accept his call, stepping outside the room before she spoke. 'Hi, Nick.'

'Hi. Are you in with Keira? I'm outside the ward and they've told me you've already got three people around the bed.'

'Yes. I'm here with Julia and Grace. The girls are just in the middle of talking about something. Do you mind waiting just a little while?'

'No, that's fine. It's nice that she has a friend with her. The interview went well.'

It wasn't Nick's fault that he had no idea what she was in the middle of. 'Oh, good.'

'Yeah. I mean... I got it. They told me it had only really been a formality. They've offered me the job.'

Her heart sank like a stone. 'In Glasgow?'

'Yes. I know we need to sit down and talk about this, but it's a great city. I think you'd love it, and I know that Keira is halfway through her GCSEs, but—'

'Nick, stop. I can't talk about this right now.' There was so much buzzing around her head that it might explode. 'Can we wait until later and talk then?'

He was so apologetic she felt bad about snapping. 'Oh, yes. Of course. Sorry. It's just that it went well. I'm getting ahead of myself.'

That didn't make her feel any better. 'Why don't you drop Adam home and then come back? We'll be done by then.'

'Oh. Okay.' He sounded hurt, but she couldn't deal with his emotions on top of her own right then. Partly it was guilt. It felt wrong, not telling him what the girls had said. That's why she was talking to him on the phone rather than going outside into the corridor where he and Adam were waiting. If she saw his kind, supportive face, she wouldn't be able to stop the tears from coming, wouldn't be able to stop herself from telling him everything. And she wanted to get the full story out of Keira before she ran the risk of her refusing to talk about it again. By the time Nick came back, she would be able to tell him, and Adam needed a rest from being here, anyway. Now Keira was through the worst, he would need to catch up on the studying he'd missed, too.

Before she walked back into Keira's room, she leaned against the wall and closed her eyes for a moment. Shock and fear had kept her upright for the last few days; now she just wanted to sleep until everything was back to normal again.

Their three faces turned towards her as she pulled her chair out from the bedside and sat down. 'What have I missed?'

Julia shook her head. 'Not much. The girls are adamant that they won't speak to the police about this boy. They are frightened of what he might do.'

Samantha frowned. 'That's ridiculous. If we tell the police, he'll be arrested. He won't be able to do anything.'

Keira's face was screwed up in frustration. 'Mum, you're so naïve. What happens if there's not enough evidence? There was no one else there. And even if there is...'

This time, it was Keira who looked to Grace for support. Samantha had been surprised to hear about this other side to Grace. Standing up to this boy, staying with Keira until the ambulance came, even keeping this whole thing a secret for the last few days. Now she was taking on the role of spokesperson for the two of them. 'Before he left, Lee threatened us. Well, me. He said that he'd come after me if I told anyone. And after my family.'

'That was just a threat, though. Once the police arrest him—'

'My dad is a policeman. He tells us all the time how much work he does and then the kid gets a short sentence, and only serves half their time, anyway.'

Julia closed her eyes behind her daughter, which confirmed that this was exactly what Grace's father had said. 'Oh, Grace. He won't be able to get to you. We'll make sure of that.'

'You can't make sure of that, Mum. You can't keep me safe. And it's not just me. He threatened you, too.'

It was painful to see the fear in her. If she had been Julia, Samantha knew that she might well have kept silent, too.

Julia was struggling to keep her face from collapsing into tears. 'You don't need to worry about me, love.'

Keira looked emotional, too. 'And even if he does get put in prison, he has so many friends, Mum. If he doesn't come for us, they will.'

What had happened to her life that she was suddenly in a scene from a soap opera? It was awful to see how scared Keira looked. Her confident, sassy daughter, reduced to this by some horrible, horrible boy.

Was Keira right? Was she naïve? She had certainly never – not in a million years – expected to be in this situation. This was Southcliff, not some inner city. When did things like this happen here?

But she knew things like this *did* happen here. Weren't there headlines in the local news? She hadn't always lived in this ivory tower. This wasn't the way she'd been brought up. After her parents had divorced, there had been no spare money for all the clothes and holidays of the type that Keira and Adam had enjoyed. And her home had not been a large five-bedroomed, three-bathroomed house on Anchorage Road. It was the box room at her mum's and a mattress in her half sister's room at her dad's. She didn't take what she had now for granted, but maybe she *had* forgotten what the life outside her Farrow & Ball painted walls was really like.

Keira was twisting the bedsheets in her hands. She didn't want her getting agitated. 'It's okay. We're not going to make you do something you don't want to. Is there anything else we need to know?'

The girls looked at each other and then shook their heads. Despite the awfulness of the situation, it was lovely to see them together, sharing confidences, looking for support. Julia was watching them, too: was she thinking the same?

The two of them needed to talk. 'Julia, shall we go and get a coffee?'

When you've known each other for a long time, you don't need the subtext. Julia nodded, gave Grace a squeeze and a kiss on the top of the head and then stood. 'Yes, let's.'

As soon as they reached the corridor, Samantha turned. 'This is unbelievable. We do have to tell the police, don't we?

'Yes. We do. But I don't want to cause any more upset for the two of them. We need to think of a way to do it that won't make things worse for them.'

'Can John help?' He was a police officer, after all. And it wasn't as if the two of them were on bad terms.

But Julia looked uncertain. 'Yes, I'm sure he could. But you know what he's like. As soon as we tell him, he'll just report it and the girls will be interviewed and it'll be another thing that happens to them, rather than something they have decided to do themselves.'

It made sense. That was the thing about Julia, she always made sense. She was a good friend. 'I'm sorry, for the way I've been. Towards Grace. And you.'

Julia shook her head. 'Don't apologise. You were protecting your baby. It's what we do, isn't it?'

Samantha couldn't stop her eyes from filling. 'Yes. It is.' There was more that needed to be said between them, she knew it. But now wasn't the time. Instead, she found a tissue in her bag and blew her nose.

Julia did the same. 'I don't even know what this boy looks like.'

Samantha did. She thumbed through Keira's secret Instagram account until she found the picture of her with him at a party. If she'd found it unpleasant before, now she found it repulsive. If she could have reached through the screen and hit him, she would have.

Julia had a similar reaction when she passed it over to her. 'Well, he's a right little charmer, isn't he? I wonder what he's up to now?'

Samantha pressed his name on the screen where Keira had tagged him and it connected to his profile, where she saw more recent pictures: him on a bike, with friends, with a girl. How dare he be smiling, enjoying life? One of the photos had been taken only that morning. A strange pose, with his right fist towards the camera. His left arm draped around a girl. A girl Samantha recognised. 'Hold on. I might have an idea.'

FORTY-ONE

JULIA

You can't make sure of that, Mum. You can't keep me safe.

Those words had been swirling in Julia's mind like a malicious storm. Fear and pain, turned to anger. And vengeance. Right then, if she could have killed that boy, she would.

Samantha's idea didn't seem terribly strong to her, but what choice did they have? Already the girls might be in a great deal of trouble for concealing information from the investigation. She could only hope that the police would take pity on them, for their fear and youth. Even if this was the case, though, they wouldn't extend that same acceptance to her and Samantha. They were adults. They should do the right thing.

But what was the right thing?

They'd agreed to wait a while longer before speaking to the girls again. They both had enough experience with teenage girls to know that you needed to let the emotional embers completely cool, or else you ran the risk of re-igniting their fire.

The corridor had been quiet enough for their whispered conversation to be unheard. When the doors at one end squeaked open, they both looked up. Nick – solid, dependable Nick – strode towards them with a coffee cup in each hand. 'I stopped off at the Costa before coming back. I know the two of you need your regular top-ups.'

He was so thoughtful. It had been difficult for Samantha over the years because he worked so hard, often away on trips for several days at a time. Samantha had joked many times that Julia would make a better wife than Nick was a husband. At times like this, though, Julia envied their relationship. Even if Nick was in another time zone, Samantha only had to pick up the phone to run something past him, to get support. If she fell, he would catch her. Always.

After releasing his wife, Nick leaned forwards and kissed Julia on the cheek. 'It's good to see you. How's Grace?'

She glanced at Samantha. The irony that this was an echo of their daughters' behaviour not fifteen minutes ago wasn't lost on either of them. Friends were friends, whether you were fifteen or nearly fifty. 'She's okay. We've left them to catch up.'

Nick had always been welcoming of both Julia and Grace. There were times when he had joked that they should set up a spare room for the two of them. Some husbands were possessive of their wives' attention, but he was like a friendly bear, welcoming Julia and Grace into his pack. 'That's great. It'll do Keira the world of good to see her BFF.'

He said the last part in a funny voice, mocking his own use of the girls' teenage jargon. They probably didn't even use that word any longer.

Even though she had a teenager, moments like this struck Julia that they were the older generation now. They were the ones out of touch. Social media, secret Instagram accounts – that was just the start of it. Their girls were stepping out into a world that they didn't understand.

And Nick was clearly out of touch with who his daughter's friends were. It had been months and months since Grace and Keira could have been described as best friends. From conversations with John over the years, there seemed to Julia to be a canyon of difference between male and female friendships. They were less intense, less deep. For Nick, the fact that he hadn't seen Grace at his house in months wouldn't have crossed his mind, especially as he was away so much.

Samantha took her husband by the arm. 'Can we go and get some fresh air for a minute? There's some stuff I need to tell you.'

He looked surprised. 'Okay. Sure.'

Once they were gone, Julia toyed with her phone. For the first time in a long while, she felt utterly and completely alone. She had never been the kind of woman who needed a man. She and John hadn't met until their very early thirties so, even though they had quickly married and had Grace, she had spent most of her twenties as a single woman, and happy to be so. When they'd divorced, it had been painful to deal with the rejection and the sense of failure, but – in many ways – it had been a relief. There was one less person in her life she had to please. She and Grace had regrouped into a family of two and life had been good. Until the events of last year had started to unravel everything.

Right now, she wanted someone there to put their arms around her, like Nick had done for Samantha. To share the burden, take the strain. With her dad's health as it was, she hadn't even felt able to call her parents and let them know what was going on. No, she had to be the one who sorted this out. There was no one else.

The door to the ward opened and Grace appeared, still pale, but lighter somehow; the curve of her shoulders had lifted, as if she'd dropped a heavy burden. 'Keira is tired. I've come away so that she can have a nap.'

Julia held out an arm. It was so good to have her daughter nestled in to her side. To feel her warm and solid and alive. Her large yawn made Julia smile. 'I'm not surprised you're tired. You've had quite a few days of it.'

Grace didn't move her head from where it rested on the dip in Julia's collarbone. 'I'm sorry, Mum.'

Her cheek resting on the top of Grace's head, Julia closed her eyes. If she could stay like this forever, she would. 'You don't need to apologise to me, love.'

'I do. For not talking to you. Not telling you the truth. I know we don't do that.'

Julia squeezed her a little tighter. 'I know you were scared. I understand. And you've told me now.'

They were quiet for a few moments. Grace's voice, when she spoke, was small and hesitant. 'I don't just mean about this. I mean the other stuff. What happened last year.'

When the issues at Grace's last school had blown up, Julia had never really understood why the bullying had got to the point it had. It had been hard to think that this boy had targeted Grace with these lies almost arbitrarily, or because she was different to the other girls in her year. It was even harder to learn what had actually gone on. It twisted her insides to think that that despicable boy had touched even a hair on her daughter's head. 'It's okay, sweetheart. It's okay.'

Grace sniffed. Again, they sat in silence for a while. 'I was just so ashamed.'

Julia wanted to press her heart to stop it from hurting, to turn Grace to face her so that she could tell her again and again that she had no need to be ashamed. But she didn't want to move away from the circle of her arms. 'This is not your fault, Grace. None of this is your fault. What he did to you – and to Keira – this is on him.'

Grace wiped at her face, but didn't move from her position on Julia. 'I don't know if it was my fault. I don't know if I told him that I didn't want to do those things. At the party, I'm not sure I said no. I can't remember, Mum. I've tried, but I can't remember. Maybe I did let him do it.'

The thought of her precious girl reliving that awful experience over and over, trying to make sense of it, made Julia want to howl in agonised rage. 'You were drunk, Grace. He took advantage of you. It's assault. It doesn't matter whether you said the word "no". It's not okay, it's not right. You are not to blame. Oh, my darling girl, you are not to blame for *any* of this.'

Grace turned her head so that her face was pressed into Julia's chest; her slight frame convulsed with sobs that just kept coming.

Julia rocked her gently and stroked the back of her head. 'It's okay, baby. Mum's here. It's all going to be okay.'

The choice of food in the hospital canteen was limited, but they managed to share a cheese sandwich and some crisps. Grace also picked out a lemon muffin to take back to Keira, and they got back to the ward at about the same time as Samantha and Nick returned from their walk. Julia tried to read Nick's reaction, but his face was stone-like.

When he looked at Grace, though, his expression was kind. 'I understand it was you who called the ambulance? You saved Keira's life, Grace. Thank you.'

Grace blushed. 'I'm sorry we didn't tell you.'

Nick nodded, clearly not about to pretend that he wasn't angry about being kept in the dark. 'Samantha has spent the last twenty minutes talking me around to understanding that. I can't honestly say that I do understand, but I'm not blaming you, if that means anything.'

The way Grace's shoulders dropped from where they'd risen to her ears, suggested the relief she felt at this. 'Thanks. And I'm really sorry.'

She'd done enough apologising for one day. Julia took her hand. 'Shall we go and see if Keira is awake? Samantha and I have something we want to talk to you about.'

Samantha nodded. 'I've told Nick and he's agreed that you

and I should talk to them about this together.'

Nick coughed a dry laugh. 'I think the words "bull in a china shop" were used.'

Samantha had to push herself onto tiptoes to kiss his cheek. 'We won't be long.'

Keira was awake when they came back into her room, and looking a lot calmer than when they'd left. It felt as if they were against the clock in terms of contacting the police with all this information, but they needed to go gently if they weren't going to start the girls off again.

The lemon muffin was a good opener. Keira beamed. 'You remembered that lemon is my favourite.'

Grace blushed. 'Of course I remember.'

Keira looked at Julia. 'Grace and I have talked about all of this, but I am sorry. About the way I treated her. That I didn't stick up for her with the others. I really am sorry.'

There had been so many apologies, but not from the person who really had done so much wrong. It wasn't going to be easy to forgive Keira for compounding Grace's misery. It was far harder to forgive a wrong done to your child than to yourself. But Julia had to give Keira the chance to make up for what she'd done. 'That's all between the two of you. I'm glad that you are friends again.'

As she said the words, Julia realised she meant it. Maybe she couldn't protect Grace from everything in life, but a really good friend could provide the buffer to get her through. Looking at Samantha, she knew the truth of that.

Samantha cleared her throat. 'I'm glad you've found each other again, too. You need your friends to look out for you. Which is what we wanted to talk to you both about.'

She took her mobile phone from her pocket and thumbed through to find the picture they'd both looked at earlier. Julia still wasn't convinced, but she hoped Samantha's faith in the two girls meant that her idea would work.

FORTY-TWO

SAMANTHA

'What the hell are they doing together?'

Keira turned the phone around to show the Instagram picture to Grace, whose eyes nearly popped out of her head. 'Lee and Katie? What are they doing together?' She peered at the caption underneath the photo and read it aloud. '"Cheering up this one, hashtag friends, hashtag together, hashtag morethan".'

Keira turned the phone back to read it herself. She frowned. 'What does "hashtag more than" mean?

Samantha said nothing. She wanted the two of them to work this out for themselves as much as possible before she or Julia had to nudge them into seeing what was the right thing to do.

Grace's hand flew to her mouth. 'You don't think they're getting together? While you are here in hospital? I mean, we know he's an evil scumbag, but isn't she pretty much your best friend? That's just sick.'

Keira's voice was made of steel. 'No. She isn't my best friend.'

When you're fifteen, your best friend is as close as a lover;

the relationship as possessively intense and exclusive and vital as being in love. When you name someone your best friend, it's like making them a gift of your heart and asking them to take care with it. Samantha reached out for Julia's hand and gave it a squeeze. Julia turned to look her in the eye. No explanation needed; she gave her a small nod.

Now Keira was thumbing through the rest of the pictures. 'I can't believe he is just out and about, having a great time. Does he have no shame at all?'

Samantha couldn't help herself. 'He doesn't need to have, does he? He knows he's going to get away with it.'

Keira looked up sharply. 'That's not fair.'

As she often did, Julia stepped in to calm the waters. 'Your mum is just saying that, to him, life hasn't changed, has it? He's carrying on as normal.'

This was *too* gentle; they were never going to get anywhere if they took baby steps. 'And maybe they are going to get together when this is all over.'

Keira threw the mobile onto the blue hospital blanket that was covering her legs. 'She's welcome to him. I don't care what he does.'

'What about her, though? Katie.'

'If she wants to be with him, that's her business.'

'Look again at the picture. They're at a party and her eyes are half-closed. Doesn't she look a little drunk to you?' Samantha knew that Julia was reluctant to push this point too far because of what it would bring up for Grace, but they needed both girls to see how important this was.

Grace picked up the phone and looked again at the picture. She paled. 'She does look as if she could be drunk.' Now she was the one who turned the phone so that Keira could see.

'That's the problem. If boys like this get away with their behaviour – if no one challenges them, or tells people what they've done – they can keep repeating it over and over.'

Samantha could see that this was upsetting Grace, but they had to know how serious this was. 'Or worse.'

Grace's hand was trembling as she passed the phone back to Samantha. 'I don't like Katie, but I wouldn't wish her harm. I wouldn't wish *that* on her.'

No one needed to ask what she meant by 'that'. When all this was over, Samantha was going to do everything she could to make sure that Grace got whatever help she needed to work through all the horrible things that had happened to her.

Keira crossed her arms, winced and uncrossed them again. 'I can't do anything. It's not like I can tell her who to be with.'

'And there's no point me saying anything.' Grace was speaking to the hands in her lap. 'Because, firstly, she hates me and, secondly, people don't believe you if they don't want to.'

She hadn't said it to be accusatory, but Keira flushed. Maybe it was guilt that prompted her to say, 'We can't just let something horrible happen to Katie, though. We can't let him hurt her.'

'What can we do? If she won't believe us, what can we do?'

Again, Samantha kept silent, hoping they would make their way there on their own.

Keira's voice was uncharacteristically soft. 'We could tell the police. About what happened to me. And about what happened to you.'

Grace stiffened and Julia put a hand on her back. 'We'll be with you both. You won't be on your own.'

'But what will they say to us? What will they think about the fact that I called the ambulance and didn't tell them it was me? That I was there and haven't told them?' Grace's lip was trembling, Samantha felt bad that they were putting her through this, but what else could they do? That boy couldn't get away with it.

Keira shrugged in the way she had since she was small,

confident that her way was the obvious way. 'We'll just tell them we couldn't remember.'

'That's ridiculous. That might work for you because you've been unconscious. But I have been here this whole time and I haven't said a word. I'm the one who will be in trouble. I'm the one who is going to have to carry the blame.' Grace looked at her mother for help.

Julia was still rubbing her back. 'I know this is hard, love. But you're fifteen. They will understand you were scared. We can speak to your dad first and he can prepare you for whatever they might ask. And, anyway, it's me that's in the wrong here. I've known you were there almost from when it happened.'

Samantha didn't want to think about that: how angry she'd been that Julia had kept it from her. 'Your mum's right. You're both under sixteen; that's got to count in your favour.'

Panic crossed Grace's face. 'But I don't want you to get into trouble, Mum! I don't want them to say it's your fault. It's my fault. I did it.'

'You didn't do anything. Whatever happens, we can deal with it.'

Keira held out her open hand for Grace to hold. 'I think they're right, Grace. We can do this.'

Samantha smiled at them both. 'We're so proud of you, girls.'

Julia nodded. 'Really proud. I'll call your dad, Grace, and ask if he can come in and speak to you both. Will you be okay for five minutes if I call him now?'

'Yes. I'll be fine.'

Julia gave her daughter another kiss and then left the ward to make the phone call.

Grace's brave face fell a little once her mother had left. She fiddled with the buttons on her top. 'What do you think they'll want to know?'

Samantha assumed it would be pretty straightforward once

they'd got through the awkwardness of explaining why it had taken so long to report it. 'I think they'll just want the facts. They'll want to know what you saw and what you can remember. I'm sure it won't take very long.'

Grace chewed on her lip. 'But what about my part? Do I have to tell them what happened to me?'

It wasn't Samantha's place to tell her what to do, but she was pretty sure she knew what Julia would say. 'It's up to you, love. But what he did to you wasn't right. And it would also help the police to understand why you were scared to come forward.'

Grace nodded. Julia reappeared to take her seat. 'I've left your dad a voicemail. Hopefully, he'll call back soon.'

As soon as she'd said that, the phone rang. Samantha watched Julia pull it out of her pocket before they both realised that it wasn't hers. It was Samantha's, still sitting on the end of Keira's bed. A number she didn't recognise.

'Hello?'

'Hello, this is Detective Inspector Edwards. Is this Samantha Fitzgerald?'

Her stomach fluttered. 'Yes, this is Samantha Fitzgerald.'

'I was hoping to come and see you in person, but I wanted to let you know as soon as possible. We've arrested someone in connection with the attack on your daughter.'

Her stomach practically fizzed with anxious confusion. 'Oh, I see. Who is it? How do you know?'

'I'm afraid I can't tell you too much at this stage, but a new witness came forward. There's more to the case than we first thought, but we'll keep you informed.'

'Thank you.'

When she ended the call, the other three were looking at her expectantly. 'That was the police. They say that they've just arrested someone in connection with Keira's attack.'

FORTY-THREE

JULIA

'Why the hell didn't you tell me about all this?'

John strode up and down Julia's kitchen. As it was so small, in other circumstances, the number of times he had to turn around would have been comical.

The shift he'd worked that day had started at 5 a.m. and he'd been catching up on sleep when she left the message from the park. He'd called her as soon as he'd woken up, and she and Grace had left Samantha and Nick at the hospital and met him back at the flat.

Knowing what he was like, Julia had made him promise not to interrupt Grace until she got to the end of what she wanted to say. Even so, she could see from his face that he'd been bursting to speak the whole time.

He was a good father: always had been. There'd been a parents' evening once when a teacher had actually remarked to them how unusual it was for two separated parents to sit together for one appointment to support their child.

It wasn't feeling so amicable right now, though. 'Why have you kept me out of it? Why do you have to fix everything yourself, Julia? I'm her father. I want to help.'

Once Grace had told him everything, she'd gone to her room and left the two of them to thrash it out. Julia didn't want to tell John that it had been Grace's choice to keep it from him, because that would have hurt him, and it was unnecessary. 'It wasn't like that, John. I was going to tell you about it when we spoke in your car, but I was scared. I don't live in your world. This was all a big shock for me. I didn't know what to do.'

He spun around and threw his arms out. 'But it is *my* world. That's exactly the reason you should have come to me.' He sighed and sank down onto the chair opposite. 'If she'd just told the police what had happened immediately, the little scumbag would have been picked up days ago.'

His exasperation was understandable, but he needed to stop thinking like a police officer and start thinking like a father. 'You know why she didn't. She's just told you. He threatened her. He threatened me. She was scared.'

He ran his fingers through his hair and rubbed the back of his head in a gesture she knew of old. 'I know, I know. But she hasn't got a choice. We are going to speak to the officer in charge right now.'

It was this imperative tone that had always driven her crazy. The 'we' didn't do much for her, either. 'She needs to be the one to make that decision.'

He looked at her as if she was crazy. 'What are you talking about? She was a witness to a serious crime. She has to talk to the police.'

Julia knew he was right, but his tone made her belligerent. 'There is no *has to*. She has had an awful year, John. So much has happened to her. She needs to feel in control.'

'What book did you get that from? This is the *law*, Julia. She doesn't get to control that.'

Everything was so black and white with him. There was no point pushing it further. 'If she chooses to talk to the police, will she be in trouble for keeping this to herself? I mean, it's not as if she actually lied.'

He sighed again. 'I'm pretty sure they'll take into consideration what a shock it was and how scared she was.' He frowned. 'I still can't believe she put herself in that situation. At the party, I mean. She was so vulnerable.'

This was the last straw. 'It's not her fault! He shouldn't have taken advantage of her!'

John held up his hands. 'I know, I know. I'm not saying it was her fault. I just can't bear to think about it. I can't bear to imagine that nasty little weasel even breathing next to her.'

He clenched his fists on the table and Julia's anger dissipated. He was just as upset as she was; he just came at it a different way. 'She just needs you to talk her through what's going to happen. You need to help her to prepare what she's going to say.'

He nodded. 'Of course, I can do that.'

There was something else that she wanted to ask him, but she wasn't sure how to approach it. 'Samantha got a call earlier at the hospital. From the officer in charge of the investigation. Edwards, I think his name was.'

'Jack Edwards? I know him.'

That sounded hopeful. 'Well, when he told Samantha that they'd arrested someone in connection with the attack, he mentioned another witness. Someone who'd identified Keira's attacker.'

John raised an eyebrow. 'Really? I hadn't heard that part.'

Julia turned her coffee mug and wrapped her hands around it. 'And, the thing is, we're a bit confused. Grace doesn't think that there was anyone else around.'

John shrugged. 'The witness might not be for the crime itself. It might be someone who has seen Keira with this lad, going to the park.'

Grace had been turning it round and around in her head,

trying to remember whether there was someone else nearby. She was tying herself in knots with it. 'Can you find out who it is?'

John's eyes widened. 'The witness? No. And even if I did find out, there's no way I can tell you.'

She had suspected as much. Right now, that wasn't the most important information she needed. 'Can you find out for sure that it is this Lee who has been arrested, then? I think it would really help Grace to know that he was in police custody.'

He looked uncertain about that. 'It's not my case, Julia.'

'I know that. But you saw what she was like. She's terrified that this boy is going to turn up here. Apart from going to the hospital to speak to Keira, she hasn't left the house in days.'

John rubbed at his face, clearly weighing it up. 'I'll give Jack a call, but I can't promise anything.' That was something, at least.

One thing Julia did like about John was that he was a man of immediate action: straight away, he leaned back in the kitchen chair, making its legs scrape on the floor, and dialled the number. 'Jack, hi, John Kennedy... Yes, good mate... We must, we must. Listen, this attack in the park... Yes, that's the one... You've got someone for it...? Great work – is it someone we know...? Right, right... Do you have a name...? Cheers, mate... Yep... Will do.'

It was agony waiting for him to get off the phone. When he finished, she looked at him. 'Well. Who have they arrested?'

'Obviously, I can't tell you that.' He paused to look at her intently so that she understood what he was about to say. 'But Grace can stop worrying.'

Julia sank into the chair opposite. 'That's such a relief.'

John nodded, but he wasn't about to let her off the hook. 'Now she needs to speak to the police, Julia. She has to make a statement as soon as possible.'

FORTY-FOUR

SAMANTHA

'You were right, this is a lovely garden.'

Grace had wanted to see Keira before she went to the police station to make a statement, so Samantha had suggested she and Julia leave them alone for a while. The hospital garden seemed the obvious place to go.

'Adam brought me here yesterday. I know it's cold, but I thought you'd like to see it.'

'It's brightening up, though.' Julia pointed at a bench on the far side. 'There's a patch of sunlight over there.'

Now the stress of the last couple of days had reduced a little, there was an awkwardness between them. So much had been said, words that they couldn't take back; everything that had happened had turned a harsh spotlight on their friendship, such as it was.

Despite the sunlight, the seat of the bench was cold and Samantha wriggled to pull her coat underneath her. 'How's Grace feeling about making her statement today?'

Julia grimaced. 'She's not looking forward to it, but John has gone through it all with her. Gently, this time.'

It was a big thing for both of them. 'Keira feels the same. I'm proud of them.'

Julia nodded. 'Me, too.'

The garden was pleasant enough, but sitting on the bench staring out at it wasn't much fun. Samantha had something that might make Julia laugh, though: she leaned into her bag and pulled out a packet of Percy Pigs. 'I got Keira some of these to cheer her up, and I thought we deserved a pack to share as well.'

Julia smiled and took one of the pink pig-shaped sweets. 'I haven't had any of these for ages. The girls used to love them.'

'They did. I remember that Keira used to bite the ears off first and Grace use to squeal that it would hurt them.'

Now Julia laughed. 'They always were complete opposites.'

They were quiet again. Was Julia thinking the same as she was? That the girls weren't the only opposites? 'It was amazing how close they were, despite that.'

'Yes. And it's so nice to see the two of them together again.'

It really was. But it wouldn't be right to just sweep everything that had happened under the carpet. Samantha knew from Keira that the girls had made their peace, but she wanted Julia to know that she was under no illusion about whose fault it had been. 'I know that Keira is really sorry for how things have been at school. That she wasn't kinder to Grace.'

It was difficult to admit that her daughter had behaved badly. It had been so much easier to think of Grace as being different or difficult. That Keira wasn't doing anything wrong. Having to admit that she had been – if not an actual bully – a bystander to Grace's bad treatment by her friends had been really hard.

As usual, Julia was understanding. 'She's only young. It takes time to learn what, and who, is important. She made a mistake, that's all.'

It was magnanimous of her. And of Grace, who seemed overjoyed to be back by the side of her old friend. There was more that Samantha wanted to say. And this was even more difficult.

'I made a mistake, too. And I don't have the excuse of being young.'

Julia didn't meet her eye. She twirled her takeaway coffee cup in her hands. 'What do you mean?'

She knew what she wanted to say, she just wasn't sure how she could say it. 'I guess I didn't know who my real friend was, either.'

Julia stopped twirling the cup and looked up at her. 'You have a lot of friends to choose from.'

Did she? That's what she'd told herself. That those women were her friends. That she was building a network for them all. But it hadn't turned out that way.

She sighed. She was going to have to go back to the beginning. 'Adam had a few words of wisdom for me yesterday. About how I am. Trying to make everything perfect. Keeping up appearances. That kind of thing. Last night, I couldn't get to sleep for thinking about it. And about the garden party.'

Julia frowned. 'I shouldn't have brought that up. It was years ago.'

'You were right to bring it up. I only wish I'd known sooner. Maybe I would have realised how awful I'd been. Not standing up for you and Grace. You're absolutely right. That's what friends should do.'

'If I'm honest, I do understand it. Those women... they are very different from me. And you wanted to impress them. I get it.'

Samantha winced inside. Said like that, she sounded even more shallow. 'I am sorry, Julia. I could explain to you where I think it came from, that need to belong to a group. To be someone. But I'm not a child any longer and I know that I did the wrong thing. Those women are not my friends, not really. They're not like you.'

'Me?' Julia raised an eyebrow.

'Yes, you. I hadn't realised how much I've missed having you around. You and Grace. I'm very sorry about the things I said. About her. About you. I would really like it if we could start again.'

Even though she'd thought this through last night in bed, it wasn't easy admitting this out loud. Putting herself out there, for Julia to accept or reject as she saw fit.

Julia smiled. 'I'm not sure that the nursery accepts fifteen-year-old girls.'

Samantha grinned in return. 'Well, I'm glad of that, because that poster paint was a nightmare to get out of Keira's clothes.'

Julia stood up. 'I need to get Grace. We have to get to the police station.'

'Of course.' Samantha stood, too. 'The hospital might be able to discharge Keira in a few days. How about the two of you come over for dinner on Friday night?'

'Yes.' Julia nodded. 'That would be really great.'

FORTY-FIVE

JULIA

The police station wasn't a particularly impressive building. It looked rather like a large 1960s red-brick house. The car park was at the front and there was parking for twenty-five cars. Parked in the third row, Julia and Grace had been waiting for about fifteen minutes.

'Your dad will be here shortly, and then we'll all go in together.' Julia tried to keep her voice light, but she was just as nervous as Grace. Despite John's job, this was unfamiliar territory for the both of them. When Grace had finally given her statement to the police six weeks ago, they had come to the flat. The last time she had been in this police station, it was to drop off a set of keys that John had left at home.

Grace was pale, her lips a thin, pursed line of anxiety. She nodded, but she didn't look Julia in the eye. After yesterday, chatting with Keira, smiling even, it was heartbreaking to see her slip back into this sadness.

'It's going to be okay, love. The hard part is behind you. Today they just want to go through some details in your original statement.'

Now that the police were preparing evidence for the court,

they had asked Grace to come in and give them some more details about the night of the party. Apparently, some other girls had also come forward and they were hopeful of a conviction.

'I know, Mum. I just don't want to go over it all again. I feel like such an idiot.'

Julia knew how she felt. What must the police think of her as a parent, too? At fifteen, Grace was so vulnerable. And she had failed to protect her. 'You're anything but an idiot. Let's get this over with and then you can show me that place with the hot chocolate that you and Keira keep waxing lyrical about.'

She'd hoped that that might cheer her a little, not make her frown like that. She followed Grace's eyes in the direction of the police station entrance. A slight, blonde girl around Grace's age was coming out with her mother. Grace's voice was so soft she almost missed it. 'Surely not? It can't be.'

With a swift movement, she opened the van door and stepped outside. A gust of cold air swept in in her place, and Julia zipped up her fleece jacket before leaning over to close the door. Then she got out and walked around the back of the van. Leaned against the back door, she held back joining Grace on the steps outside the police station, but stayed close enough to hear.

Her friend's mother seemed to have the same idea. She was making her way to a small white car on the other side of the car park.

Grace was the first to speak. 'What are you doing here?'

The girl had her back to Julia, so she couldn't see her face, but she didn't think she was one of Grace's friends. Not that she'd know, really. Grace hadn't brought anyone home in so long. She'd even begun to suspect that the Jasmine and Safa she'd spoken about didn't actually exist.

The girl's voice was hesitant. 'I had to come in to answer some more questions.'

Grace looked as confused as Julia. 'Questions about what?'

'About Lee. About what he did.'

Julia hadn't thought that Grace could get any paler, but even her lips looked white. 'How did you know? About the attack?'

The girl flicked her hair from the tops of her shoulders. 'I was there. I was the one who told the police.'

So, she was the witness. But who was she? And how did Grace know her?

Grace tilted her head. 'How?'

'I was following him. Lee. I knew that he was seeing someone else and I just wanted to see who it was. I wanted to speak to her.'

'You were stalking him? Even though you weren't seeing him anymore?'

Julia leaned back against the van, wishing she was camouflaged. *Seeing him?* This was another girl this boy had been getting his filthy hands on? Unless she was... Surely she wasn't the girlfriend from the party? What was her name? Evie?

'No, it wasn't like that. I saw them walking up the seafront. He had his arm around her and they were obviously together. To start with, I just thought that she was welcome to him. I even kept walking in the opposite direction. But I couldn't leave it. I came back to speak to her.'

Grace looked disgusted. 'I can't believe you, Evie. How can you be so obsessed with him? Were you really going to have a go at Keira?'

Evie. It was her. What was it about this boy, that he could have so many girls under his spell? His control.

Evie was shaking her head. 'No, you don't understand. I wanted to warn her.'

'You're not making any sense.'

'You know what I'm talking about. You know, because of what happened with you and him.'

Julia took a step forward. Grace had enough to cope with,

without this Evie bringing everything up again. Having a go at her. Why did some girls attack other girls rather than blame the boyfriend, or husband, who had been the one who'd actually cheated on them?

Grace waved a hand at Julia to tell her to stay where she was. She was trembling, but there was something about the way she was standing – tall, shoulders back – which told Julia that she didn't need her help.

'I'm not explaining that all over again, Evie. I was drunk. I know I shouldn't have—'

Something in Evie's face stopped her speaking. Julia still couldn't see the girl's expression, but her shoulders jerked up and down as if she was crying and, this time, the shake of her head was vehement. 'No, Grace. You weren't drunk. Well, you were, but...' She stopped and sighed. 'Your drink was spiked, Grace. He spiked your drink.'

Grace's hand flew to her lips. 'How do you know? What? How do you know that?'

Julia could imagine what was going through Grace's mind, because the same thoughts were flooding through hers. All this time, all the guilt, the bullying, the lies that she had had to live with, and now this girl was telling her that she'd known all along what this boy had done?

'Because I heard him boasting about it to his mates. And because he did it to me.'

For the next few moments, Grace was frozen, statue-like, as if she had to stay very still for the truth to stop swirling around in the air and settle on her.

Evie must have taken her silence as an invitation to confess. 'He was pushing for our relationship to get more serious and I wasn't ready. I didn't exactly tell him that. I was worried that he might finish with me.'

Julia's heart sank. Why was it like this? Why did these girls have to use their bodies to keep a boy interested in them? Why did they even care about boys yet? If only they could have the wisdom of a woman looking back on her life, telling them not to rush to be older.

'We went to a party with some of his friends. I had a couple of drinks because I was nervous but it was not enough to make me pass out. But I did. And then, then…' She tailed off.

Grace, to her credit, reached out a hand and tapped her on the arm. 'You don't have to say it. I know.'

Julia's heart tore with love for her daughter: pride that she would be so forgiving, anger that she had a knowledge Julia would have done anything to save her from.

'But I do have to say it.' Evie looked at Grace. 'You did, didn't you? You had to say it and you had to hear it, too. Everyone was talking about it. Oh, Grace, I'm sorry. I am so, so sorry.'

Grace stuck out her chin. In her place, Julia would have told this girl exactly what she thought of the way she'd treated her. But her daughter was better than that. 'What have you told the police?'

'All of it. All my part of it. I told them that I heard him joking about with his mates the next day. About me. And about you. And what I saw at the park. I saw them go in together. I saw you. And then I left. I didn't want you to see me. I was ashamed.'

'So you didn't see the attack?'

Evie shook her head. 'No. But I told them enough that they went to speak to Lee. When they turned up at school, he ran. That must have made it even worse for him.'

'That's when they arrested him?'

'I assume so. There were so many rumours flying around school. That he'd had drugs on him. A knife.' She shrugged. 'You know what rumours are like.'

Of course Grace knew what they were like. Hadn't rumours

made her life a living hell? Driven her out of her school? Destroyed her friendships?

Across the car park, Evie's mother opened her car door and called over. 'Evie, love, we need to get home. I have to take your brother to football practice.'

'I need to go. I am sorry, Grace. For everything.'

Grace nodded. 'Thank you.' She waited until Evie had run to the car and, waving, driven out of the car park. Then she almost fell onto Julia, her tears streaming down Julia's neck. 'It wasn't my fault, Mum! It wasn't my fault!'

Julia surrounded her with her arms and whispered in her ear: 'No, my darling. It was never your fault.'

FORTY-SIX

SAMANTHA

The day Keira came home from the hospital was almost as wonderful as the day Samantha brought her home as a newborn. They had a honeymoon period of a few days before Keira had told Samantha to 'stop fussing' around her, and normal life began to resume.

However, there was one part of Keira's life which she was not willing to resume. Even weeks later, she was resolute about not going back to St Anne's.

'It's not happening, Mum. There's no way I'm going back there.'

By this time, Nick was already working in the new office in Glasgow and coming home at weekends, and Adam was safely back in Durham, so it was back to it being just the two of them. Samantha still hadn't decided for sure whether they were going to move there, too, or live this kind of split existence.

'You have to go to school, sweetheart.'

'I know that, but not there. I'm not going back.'

Samantha had no idea what to do. Keira was a few months away from her GCSEs. Changing schools at this point might have life-changing repercussions if she fell too far behind. And that was if Samantha could even get her into another school at this point.

Was this what it had been like for Julia all that time when Grace hadn't wanted to go to school? Maybe Samantha could have been more sympathetic. She'd made all the right noises about Grace 'getting there' at some point, but she hadn't really understood. Apart from actually dragging her there – which was physically impossible, now that Keira was as tall as she was – what else could Samantha do? The school weren't putting any pressure on her yet, and they were sending home schoolwork which Keira was diligently completing, but that wouldn't last forever.

Nick hadn't been a great deal of help, either. 'If you all come and live up here, she won't have to go back there, will she? She can start again.'

Start again. Those two words filled Samantha with fear. This house was more than just four walls. She had built this comfortable home for them – all four of them – as a safe and solid place the children would always have to come back to; whether it was after university, when they were saving for a house, when they had children of their own and needed a break. She had always envisioned that this would be the place where she and Nick would grow old together.

He had tried to understand. 'I get it, I do. I know you don't like change.'

This flippant phrase didn't even come close. 'It's not a *change*. We're not talking about a new toothpaste or a haircut. You are asking me to pack up everything we have, leave behind the house we started in, brought our babies back to. That's not a change – it's a reconstruction of our whole lives.'

She knew she sounded dramatic, but it was how she felt. For the last few days she had been walking around the house, trying to work out if she could leave it. There was the doorpost in the kitchen where they had marked the heights of the children every birthday; the small box room that had been the children's first bedroom; the hallway she had walked up and down, up and down, trying to get them to fall asleep as babies. It wasn't just a house, it was a living, breathing reminder of their family history.

'What about all our friends? I won't know anyone up there.'

This had been her second argument and this one had been given even less understanding. 'Aside from Julia and Grace – who will come and visit – you haven't even seen anyone since Keira's been home. And neither has she. What friends are you going to miss?'

He had a fair point. After the debacle of the second WhatsApp group, Samantha had kept her distance from the school mums and there had been no invitations for dinner or lunch, or even for coffee. As Keira wasn't going to the school, she hadn't even bumped into anyone at school events. It was as if that was a life that hadn't happened.

Did she miss it? Miss them? No.

They had seen a lot of Julia and Grace, though. It had been a joy to see the two girls together again. They were still very different – Grace in her dark, baggy clothes and Keira in her tight jeans, off-the-shoulder crop tops and false eyelashes – but they brought out the best in each other. Grace had been practically tutoring Keira in English and Keira had persuaded Grace into starting a new blog for her creative writing, telling her that she was confident that it was only a matter of time before her talent was discovered.

Keira had discovered a talent of her own while she was home. Julia had encouraged her into the garden as soon as she was able, and the two of them had spent hours out there together. For a girl who had called science 'more boring than Dad and Adam discussing a rugby match', she had learned the Latin names of all the plants in the garden and how to look after them. She had even stopped growing her nails long so that she could wield the secateurs more easily. It was so wonderful to look out of the kitchen window and see the two of them laughing together outside, while they clipped and tended and pruned. Samantha had a sneaking suspicion that Keira told Julia things she wouldn't tell her, but that was okay. Because it was Julia. And because Grace did the same with Samantha.

She had stuck to her promise to make sure that Grace got the help she needed. Mental health services being the way they were, it would have taken forever for Grace to see a counsellor on the NHS. Though Julia had argued about it, Samantha had researched to find a great therapist and then had insisted that she paid towards the cost for Grace to see her privately. 'She needs it, Julia. And Nick's new job is paying really well. We can afford it, so take it, you stubborn woman.'

Julia had smiled at that. 'I'm going to pay you back, though.'

As if she was going to let her do that. 'Oh, for goodness' sake. We'll argue that in the months to come. I just want her to get the help she needs now.'

Julia's eyes had filled. 'Me, too. Thank you. You are a good friend.'

As they hugged, Samantha was filled again with relief that she had Julia in her life. 'We're not friends. We're family.'

Sometimes, if Julia had to work, Samantha would be the one to take Grace for her counselling sessions. Often, Grace would want to go home immediately afterwards, but occasionally she would take Samantha up on her offer of a hot chocolate in a cafe before she dropped her back to the flat. Gradually, she was talking more and more. Not about what had happened, but about the future. It was like watching a tightly packed rosebud gradually unfurl. And even more beautiful.

Surprisingly, Grace had returned to school. Julia had spoken to the head teacher and she had been moved to different classes and had the option to go home at lunchtime, so she rarely saw the girls who had made her life so unhappy. She had a renewed focus, too. All she needed to do was get good GCSE grades and she was going to switch to a sixth-form college out of the area to do her A levels. She and Keira had pretty much planned out the next few years of their lives and had even been looking at universities that had courses for both of them so that they could live together in the near future.

'That's after we have a gap year and go travelling in South America, though, obviously,' Keira had told Samantha and Nick over dinner.

Obviously. How could this girl with the same long blonde hair and green eyes as her, this girl she had given birth to, be so much more courageous and adventurous than she had ever been? Especially after all she had been through: not just the attack, but the loss of her friends, the disappointment of being let down and left out?

Samantha had said this to Julia only yesterday, and Julia had just smiled at her. 'Because there's one big difference between the two of you, that's why. Because she has you, Samantha. Because you are her foundation. Wherever she goes, you are her home.'

EPILOGUE

JULIA

'Hurry, up, Mum. We're going to miss the train at this rate.'

Julia was literally three steps behind Grace, but she was having to drag the suitcase too. Grace had been rushing her along since they'd got up that morning. 'I'm coming. Give me a chance.'

Grace turned around and grinned. Moments like this, it took Julia's breath away how beautiful she was. How poised and comfortable in her own skin. She wished she'd been like her at seventeen.

Art college had been the making of Grace. There, her uniform of black clothes and – often unsuccessful – attempts at psychedelic hair dying were at the more conservative end of the spectrum. Some of the friends she'd brought home that term wouldn't have looked out of place standing on a plinth at the Tate Modern.

But she had brought home friends. Weird, but wonderful people who made Grace laugh and accepted her for the quiet and quirky girl she was. There was one boy in particular who seemed very attentive, but Grace had rolled her eyes at Julia's clumsy attempts at finding out whether there was anything more than friendship going on. However, she was sure to have told Keira if there was, so Julia would just have to try and wheedle it out of her that weekend instead.

They were just about to get on the train, Julia pulling the suitcase as Grace pushed it, when she froze. 'Did I remember to pack my sketchpad? Keira wants to see my prep sketches for my coursework.'

'Yes. I saw you put it in last night. Stop panicking.'

This would be the fifth time they'd been to visit Samantha and Keira in Glasgow, and they were both looking forward to it. The girls had big plans to spend the night out in the city centre. Samantha and Julia had equally big plans to sit in front of Samantha's newly installed log burner with a bottle of Rioja.

This visit, Julia had news to tell Samantha. Since Grace had been happily occupied with her new arty friends, Julia had been free to start a life of her own outside the gardens of other people. As well as making Nina overjoyed by actually going to a real-life bar with her – more than once – on a Friday night, Julia had taken the plunge and signed herself up for internet dating. She had her first date planned for the following week and she was terrified. But in a good way.

She and Grace found the seats they'd booked in advance and took a selfie, then sent it to the group WhatsApp they'd started for the four of them with a message.

We're on our way!

A LETTER FROM EMMA

I want to say a huge thank you for choosing to read *Only for My Daughter*. If you did enjoy it and want to keep up to date with all my latest releases, just sign up at the following link. Your email address will never be shared and you can unsubscribe at any time.

www.bookouture.com/emma-robinson

As a teacher of teenagers, I am acutely aware of all the pressures they have to deal with and, while this novel deals with fictional events, the issues for these characters – bullying, violence, sexual assault – are increasingly common. The first idea of writing about knife crime came from my friend, the novelist Kim Nash, after she had seen a mother speaking about the loss of her son on television. Initially, I didn't think this was a topic I could write about, but the more I researched it, the more I learned how much of a problem it has become. I know that I have only touched on it here, but I want to take the opportunity to highlight the fantastic organisations working to take knives off the streets. Charities such as Steel Warriors, Lives Not Knives and Take a Knife, Save a Life all need donations to continue their work.

As always in my novels, I like to explore the power of friendship to help us through life's challenges. In this book, I was able to do so across two generations and several different ages and it made me realise that what we need from our friends doesn't really change whether we are five, fifteen or fifty. We all want to be loved, supported and heard.

I hope you loved *Only for My Daughter* and if you did, I would be very grateful if you could write a review. I'd love to hear what you think, and it makes such a difference helping new readers to discover one of my books for the first time.

I love hearing from my readers – you can get in touch on my Facebook page, through Twitter, Goodreads or my website.

Thanks,

Emma

www.motherhoodforslackers.com

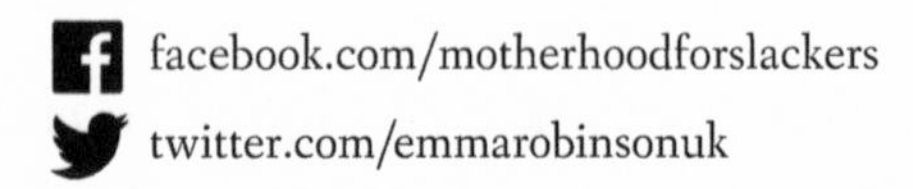

ACKNOWLEDGEMENTS

Grateful thanks are *always* due to my brilliant editor Isobel Akenhead, but this time I needed you more than ever. Thank you for helping me to see where my story was when I had lost it and for your belief that I could do it. Over lunch. Which is always a bonus.

The whole team at Bookouture is fantastic. Another huge thank you to my pal and PR queen Kim Nash for all her support and for giving me the idea to write a story about a knife crime in the first place. (She also writes beautiful romance novels – go look them up!) Thank you to Gabbie Chant for copy editing (I am so sorry about my issues with timelines and character names!), Belinda Jones for proofreading and the cover designer Alice Moore, who does such a fabulous job.

I swore after the last book that I would never write a medical storyline again and yet, here I am. Huge thanks to the Trauma Fiction Facebook page for answering my random medical questions. Any mistakes are mine. Thanks also to the wonderful Carrie Harvey for casting her laser-sharp gaze over the book during final checks. I don't know how you do it.

Father David Rollins, you once joked from the pulpit about me putting you in one of my books; I hope that you enjoy your cameo.

My friends and family deserve to be thanked after every book as I couldn't do it without their faith and encouragement. Apologies to my husband who had to endure a week in a caravan with me stressing about this book, and never complained. Thank you to my mum for putting up with me being a misery when I am overtired with juggling everything and for saying, 'What can I do to help?'

Lastly, to everyone who has bought, read and reviewed one of my books, I am truly grateful. I hope you enjoy this one too.

Milton Keynes UK
Ingram Content Group UK Ltd.
UKHW012008180823
427121UK00004B/263